Valora

by

Matthew Barron

Published by
Submatter Press

ISBN: 0985038829
ISBN13: 978-0-9850388-2-3
eISBN: 978-0-9850388-3-0

For more information, to contact the author, or to order additional books, visit:
submatterpress.com

This book is dedicated to my mother. She bought me comic books when I behaved and encouraged me to pretend when I was bored. She is missed.

Table of Contents

CHAPTER 1

REFUGEES

Gabriel stroked his brown horse, pretending to calm the animal, but really trying to soothe his own nerves. A chilly breeze wound through the maze of crags, and Gabriel folded his arms over his gangly torso, scanning the entrance of the cave for any sign of his master, the Gatekeeper, in the darkness within.

It had been a stressful week, and the young apprentice hadn't shaved or washed. Gabriel was in his early twenties, but his oily brown hair was already receding up his forehead.

Their companion, Tully, one of King Mort's men, wore golden mail. A gold dragon was embossed on his purple tunic. The loose mail did not have the sheen of the real Dragon Armor. Tully tapped his finger against the hilt of his sword.

The rocks were gray. The sky was gray. Ominous shadows circled the summits above them. Wild gryphons stalked these mountains. Gabriel's band had to be out of here before nightfall.

Pop!

Gabriel found another of the five beads on his wrist blackened. "That's two of the decoy armors down." There had been five decoys, all sent on different routes, all linked to the beads on his wrist. He looked to the cave again. "Hister's men are getting closer."

Tully tried to hide his fear. "I don't understand this business of decoys. You should have given me the real armor! Then we would stand a chance!"

Gabriel shook his head. "We can't risk Hister's wizard getting hold of that magic armor. We have to hide it. Let it be forgotten."

"You don't believe that any more than I do. You are just repeating your master!"

Gabriel opened his mouth, but didn't speak. It did seem wasteful to just hide that fantastic weapon away.

Tully had good reason to be afraid. He had seen his king and companions killed. This was his last mission for his dead king. All the kings of Gaul who opposed young Hister were now dead... or worse. Hister had risen from obscurity with the help of his necromancer, and the upstart would soon be in control of all Gaul and possibly beyond.

Gabriel said, "The Dragon Warrior was the first and only person to ever wear that armor. Even he could not live forever."

Pop!

Gabriel winced. Another decoy had been destroyed. "Hister's men must be all over these mountains."

At last a rugged frame emerged from the darkness of the cave. The Gatekeeper had a runner's body. He had traveled the worlds on foot. Curly white hair framed his haggard face, and the three inch long Key hung close to his neck.

Gabriel raised his wrist, showing the blackened beads.

"It is done." The Gatekeeper's voice was clear and light. "It is a much simpler matter to leave a treasure than it is to take one."

The breeze strengthened and Gabriel's horse galloped off in a sudden burst of terrified speed. The horse would be gryphon food if Gabriel didn't get him back.

Before Gabriel could move, a large body of fur pounced lithely between him and his master. For a moment, he thought it was a massive, furry horse, but feathered wings stretched from the creature's back, and where a horse is stiff, this animal was loose and fluid. A second gryphon landed between Gabriel and Tully. Feathered heads strained against leather bridles. There were bits in the monster's hooked beaks. These were not mindless animals looking for a meal. Soldiers in gray mail and black leather rode them. It wasn't natural for those flexible feline backs to be bound in stiff saddles.

Gryphons were independent creatures, and Gabriel had always considered them untrainable. Their feathered heads cocked from side to side. A large, black eye blinked at the young apprentice. Gabriel's heart was a lump of lead in his chest.

Tully drew a silver blade, good steel, but only steel.

"Clever Necromancer," the Gatekeeper said, still calm in the face of these monsters. "We still had two decoys left."

One of the mounted men shouted, "Where is the armor?"

Gabriel looked to the cave behind his master, but the entrance was gone, replaced by a wall of solid rock.

The Gatekeeper sneered and waved his arm. The nearest bridle unbuckled. The gryphon shook his head, further loosening the leather straps. It turned wildly. Its rider uselessly pulled the reins as the animal circled like a cyclone, then reversed. At last the rider fell and found his guts pierced by a giant beak burrowing though his mail.

Hope swelled within Gabriel. These animals weren't trained. The bridles were magic.

The other mounted soldier realized the secret of their control was no longer a secret. He backed his steed away from the Gatekeeper, lifting his mount on its hind legs. Its furry chest hovered above Gabriel. Brandished claws waved up and down as it screeched over the bit in its mouth.

The Gatekeeper was not the only one who could work simple mind magic. Gabriel pointed, letting his concentration flow along his finger. This gryphon's bridle loosened. With a wave of Gabriel's hand, it fell free. The animal folded its wings and fell backwards, crushing the soldier on its back as it rolled in the dust, trying to loosen its burden.

Gabriel smiled at his master with pride. He had learned his lessons well.

Something long and dark suddenly poked through the Gatekeeper's neck. The Key flopped up once and landed back on the wizard's chest. The old man's eyes widened with surprise as he looked down at the arrow. Realization dawned as he slumped to the ground.

Gabriel's heart sank with him. He ran to his master.

Tully went after a black garbed soldier perched on a crag. The assassin discarded his crossbow and drew a short sword.

The Gatekeeper's eyes were losing focus. The clean entry wound had torn when he fell.

"Master!" Gabriel shouted, tapping him gently on the cheek. They had walked the worlds together for over ten years. Gabriel was closer to this man than he was to his own father.

The Gatekeeper mouthed words, but instead of his voice, Gabriel heard his master's thoughts in his head. *Take the Key.*

"No!"

Take the Key. Escape across the Gate.

Gabriel shook his head. His master was still strong. "I can stabilize you. Get you to the other side. Take you to a doctor."

The dying wizard weakly grabbed at the golden key. *No time. This is how it is meant to be. The Key is always passed on.*

Pop!

Tully was dead. A chill from the south followed a black cloud, and the two gryphons fled into the mountains.

Hister's wizard is coming. You must go while you can. The Necromancer can't gain the armor and the Key as well!

"If I run away, he will still find the armor!"

His master's mental voice was barely a whisper now. *With you gone, he will think the secret died with me.* The Gatekeeper put his hand on Gabriel's, and Gabriel found the unbroken chain loosed from his master's neck.

The dark cloud settled in among the rocks.

Go!

Gabriel grabbed the Key and tore himself from his master. He fell amid the rocks, panting. Dark robes solidified from the black smoke. Teleportation was an extremely difficult spell and took much energy. The Necromancer was more powerful than they had realized.

The tall man in the billowing black robe scanned the carnage around him, taking it all in, and Gabriel held his breath. The young Necromancer already had a leathery brown face from hours in the elements. This was a man who had walked the world, learned its secrets.

Once the Necromancer's gaze fell upon Gabriel's master, he lost sight of all else. The Necromancer sneered as he straddled the dead man and jerked his chin back and forth, searching for signs of life. The Necromancer removed a black stone from around his neck, held it between them, and inhaled deeply.

Something indistinct and luminescent, barely perceptible, crept from the dead man's nose and mouth. These ethereal wisps were sucked into the stone like light into a black hole.

Gabriel couldn't believe what he was seeing. What was left of his master's life was being stolen, to be used and perverted by the Necromancer. Gabriel could only hope his master had no sense of what was happening to him. Perhaps Gabriel could have interrupted the ritual. Perhaps he could have saved his master's soul, but he was frozen.

The Necromancer was completely engrossed, but his soldiers were winding through the mountain passes. In minutes they would find Gabriel hiding in the rocks.

Gabriel had no choice but to flee. He crawled over the sharp stones, squinted his eyes, and clutched the Key tight enough to make his palm bleed. Gabriel was not able to stop the Necromancer, but as long as he lived, Gabriel would never stop throwing obstacles in the dark wizard's path.

Gabriel whispered the words that opened the Gate between worlds.

The pantry of Mack's Tavern and Inn was dimly lit by one flickering candle. Magna grabbed one end of a heavy chest.

Buddy bent over the other end, and his thin red hair dangled over his ears. "Lanterns or torches would draw too much attention. We can't get caught." Buddy lowered his voice. "Not even your station could save us from that."

Magna lifted his end of the chest and backed up the rickety stairs. He had complained how dark it was, inadvertently showing his inexperience at this sort of thing. One such as Buddy would normally never question Magna, but this was not a normal occasion.

Old men, women, and children in peasant garb gathered their belongings from amid the shelves and barrels. Buddy squinted his one good eye, struggling to see the wood steps as they carried the chest into the warm summer night.

A short distance up the road, past the darkened blacksmith's and behind the carpenter's shop, a few flickering lights could still be seen in the windows of Castle Valora. The grape vineyards were black, with no illumination but the moon and stars. It was hard for Magna to imagine anything trying to hurt him here. This was his home, his land.

They hefted the load onto one of the waiting coaches. The apparent peasants were led from their shelter under Mack's and onto the two carriages.

"Thank you," an old beggar said to Magna. He had a rim of white hair around his bald head and short wisps of white on his chin. "You are a brave man."

A gold key dangled out of the old man's collar, and Magna's eyes widened with realization. "You're the Gatekeeper!" Magna couldn't imagine this harmless looking person was the most wanted man in Histerland, the arch nemesis to Hister's high necromancer.

The old man winced and glanced over his shoulder to make sure no one had heard. "Call me Gabriel."

Magna couldn't believe he was on a first name basis with the Gatekeeper. "Gabriel."

"If these mages had remained in Histerland, the Necromancer would have treated them as rivals or pawns. Once he had gotten what he could from them alive, he would have stolen their souls to increase his own power." Gabriel looked over the shabby group of men, women, and children. "Perhaps one of these boys will become my apprentice." The old man's features softened. "I won't be around forever."

He turned back to Magna, who suddenly felt naked under the old man's gaze. Gabriel toyed with the black curl of fine hair at Magna's shoulders. "I've never seen a commoner with the latest style of haircut. I suspect you had a great deal to do with this shelter and our supplies."

Magna's face felt warm, and he smiled. "We all have our secrets, *old peasant.*"

Gabriel smiled back at Magna, who helped him step aboard the coach with the refugees. Neither he nor Magna were what they wished to seem.

The carriages sped onto the main road, past the harvested fields, and disappeared behind the apple orchards on its path to the mountainous border where Hister's power waned.

CHAPTER 2

FAMILY POLITICS

Prince Aret of Valora yawned openly. He didn't care that everyone could see. It was Aret's first morning back, and already they had him tending the more monotonous aspects of royal life. To Aret's left, his father, old King Valora slumped in the High Chair. The King spent his mornings hearing the troubles of his people. Aret would never be king and didn't feel his presence should be required. There must have been six villagers waiting for an audience with the King, and probably ten more there just to watch. Aret couldn't imagine why anyone would be here by choice.

Dim light from the heavy chandelier flickered over worry lines on the aging King's face. Aret could tell his father was having a bad day. Normally, no matter how weak he became, his father always sat up straight when taking audience. Today the King slouched in his chair. Aret's father would not be around forever, but everyone knew it was Aret's older brother, Magna, who would be king, not Aret.

Sunlight poured in from the door, past the line of people, and cast long shadows on the stone walls. A blue tapestry with the gold gryphon of Valora hung on one wall. On the opposite wall hung the red flag of Histerland, with a black bird in mid-strike circled by white.

If Aret had not been summoned, he would still be in bed asleep. Or perhaps he would have been pleasantly awakened by the servant girl, Camille. The thought of the dark haired maid caused a slight smile to cross his face.

Sheriff Morto stood before the throne guarding a scrawny peasant. The sheriff wore the blue tunic of the Valoran guard. He was all business. Aret had never seen him crack a smile.

Gruff Woodsman, the peasant's accuser, had a tangle of thinning hair and narrow lips. He bowed to King Valora, reached into his leather coat, and tossed three dead rabbits on the floor. "A poacher, Lord. I found his traps on your lands three days ago. I waited, and this morning caught him emptying the traps."

The woodsman was a creepy character who haunted the forests of Valora. He and his son only came to town on business, and Aret did not recall ever speaking a word to them.

Old Purvis sat on a lower chair next to the King. His wispy gray beard nearly dragged along the parchment as he chronicled the proceedings. Purvis wore the red sash of a Histerland scholar. He was the King's chief advisor and had taught Aret the basics of royal life. No doubt it had been his idea to drag Aret out of bed. Purvis didn't care that it was Aret's first morning back from the fencing competition.

The King eyed the accused. "Is this true?"

The scrawny peasant looked fearfully from the woodsman to Sheriff Morto, then collapsed at the King's feet. There were tears in his eyes. "Mercy! Yes. Mercy, King Valora. Please! I did not know it was your land."

Aret knew, of course, the peasant was lying. All Valorans knew their king's borders.

The peasant could see the incredulity on their faces. "I didn't do it for me, Lord. My family is starving."

The King looked to Sheriff Morto. "Is this man one of ours?"

"I'm afraid so, Lord. He lives out on the southern periphery in a small cottage with his ten children, all under the age of ten. His plot is full of weeds—"

"Of course my plot is weeds," the peasant interrupted. "It was trampled during the Lord's last hunting party."

A hush fell over the room. One did not talk out of turn to his lord. Aret, who had barely been paying attention, smiled to at last have some scandal.

But King Valora only chuckled and turned to Purvis. "Has he been in trouble before?"

Old Purvis looked up from his scrolls. "First offense, Sire."

The King turned back to the gangly peasant at his feet. "If you have a problem, come to me next time before you disobey my laws. You will spend the rest of the afternoon in the stocks. Two of the three rabbits will be sent to your family. If you are caught again, I will not be so lenient."

The peasant kissed King Valora's shoes. "Thank you, Lord. You are wise and merciful."

Sheriff Morto pulled the peasant to his feet and led him to the doorway.

"That's it?" Gruff Woodsman said to the King. "An afternoon in the stocks and he *keeps* the rabbits! How do you expect people to respect the law, to respect *my* authority if—"

A stern look from the King silenced the woodsman. "He knows I won't be lenient next time. All my subjects know what to expect from me."

Aret had not been at all surprised by the King's verdict. His father was known to be merciful for a first offense, and never reacted rashly.

Morto led the peasant past Prince Magna, who was striding in. The peasant smiled up at the prince, saying, "Long live the Valoras."

Aret sat up at the sight of his brother. Now things would finally get interesting. Magna's bright blue tunic matched Sheriff Morto's, including the gold gryphon on the chest. His black, shoulder-length hair bounced with every confident step. Aret thought the curl of Magna's bangs gave him a pompous air. Aret considered his own trim brown hair more practical. It never needed styled and never got in the way.

Magna approached the throne. "You wanted to see me, father?"

"Yes," King Valora said. "I have important matters to discuss with my son," the King announced to the room. "I will give no more audiences today."

Gruff Woodsman stomped away as the guards cleared the villagers out of the room. Then the King thanked his guards and dismissed them as well. He turned to Aret. "I want to talk to your brother alone."

Watching the King yell at Magna would have made the morning's monotony worthwhile. "But Father—"

"Aret." His father was known to be merciful, but when he was firm, he was not to be crossed. Rather than weaken his authority, the King's failing health somehow gave his words more weight.

"Yes, Sire." Aret marched off with lowered head, but stopped in the corridor, just out of view. Under a display of crossed swords, Aret leaned into the cool plaster wall and peeked around the corner.

"We are alone," the King said to Magna. "Tell me where you were last night."

Magna opened his mouth, but nothing came out. At last he said, "I was entertaining Lady Gwendolyn."

"Liar!" the King spat. "I may be old, but I am not stupid. I have had my most loyal guard monitoring your activities with the Underground for weeks. If Hister ever discovered my own son was involved in the defection of mages…"

"What if he does?" Magna said. "At least then we would be able to fight out in the open. Perhaps if you and grandfather had fought him sixty years ago, then I would not need to sneak about like a common thief!"

The King bit his lip. "I am aware of our history, Magna, much more than you. Sometimes, when looking back on things, knowing the consequences of all that happened, it is easy to second guess our decisions, but I was there. A tiny skirmish with his neighbors, that's all it seemed to be. They happen all the time. We could not have known that Hister's reach would one day extend all the way to Valora, and beyond."

"Some of our neighbors sent men to fight," Magna said.

"And our neighbors are no longer in power. Don't forget that. The ruling lines of the nearby fiefs were wiped out and replaced by Hister's allies. We remain in power because we did not oppose him. It is a delicate balance. You must learn to be more tactful when *you* are King Valora."

"Why should I want to be king of a puppet kingdom?"

Aret winced at Magna's comment. That would strike a nerve.

The King closed his eyes, clutched his heart, and waved a wrinkled hand. "To your room! I can't talk about this anymore right now."

Magna marched out, head still held high in defiance.

Aret, not yet twenty, was slightly shorter than his older brother. He met his brother in the hallway. "How dare you insult our father like that!" Aret said. "You know he is ill! He gives you everything, hands it to you on a silver platter, and this is how you repay him?"

"Back from the fencing competition already?" Magna said. "How did you do?"

"Third place," Aret answered. "Prince Brigham of Lyon won first… *again*. I swear the man who got second was using a magic sword."

Magna raised an eyebrow. "If he was cheating, why didn't he get first place instead of Prince Brigham?"

"Quit changing the subject!" Aret demanded. "Why do you torture our father like this?"

"How can you side with him?" Magna asked. "With Hister?"

Aret waved his arms around them. "Look around you, Magna! Our lives are a fairy tale. Histerland asks nothing of us but tax money, the lowest taxes in Histerland, I might add. The people love us as the hereditary rulers of Valora, and Hister has no problems with us. If it were not Hister, then it would be some other power, some other great king of kings lording over us. It makes no difference."

Magna hissed through his teeth. "I can't believe you. Don't you know what Hister does elsewhere in the world?"

"I can't care about the rest of the world, Magna. I can only care about our people and my family. We are safe and happy."

"Our safety is very precarious, and I for one *am not happy*. How could my own brother be such a sheep? Find your next wench and leave politics to the men."

Magna attempted to walk away, but Aret stepped in front of his brother. "I'm not a child anymore. You can't just dismiss what I have to say!"

Magna pushed him hard against the wall. "You have no idea what it's like to have responsibility, and I don't think you ever will. You will always be a child." Magna turned to walk away again, but anger exploded from Aret's chest. Before he even knew what he was doing, Aret had yanked a decorative sword from the wall and pointed it at his brother.

Magna smiled and pulled the other sword from the wall, letting it bounce a few times in his hand to test the weight.

Aret wanted to wipe the smug arrogance off his brother's face. He would show him. Aret was fresh from the fencing competition, while Magna hadn't lifted a sword in weeks. The swords weren't sharp enough to do any real damage, but Aret would make sure to cause some hurt. He charged his brother.

Their swords clanged together. Magna parried, then went on the offensive. They struck and parried. Aret backed down the corridor, knocking over a decorative suit of armor. His anger abated, Aret was ready to throw down his sword and retire to his room, but the armor fell with a clatter. Camille, the svelte maid, jumped out of the way screaming. Then young Enri, hearing the noise, ran in with another young servant. Enri was barely in his teens. He gave no thought to social decorum as he nudged his companion and pointed at his betters.

Feeling the eyes of an audience, Aret went back on the offensive, striking hard and fast. Magna was forced back briefly by the sudden burst of energy, but blocked every attack.

Old Purvis shoved the servant boys aside and grabbed the princes by their ears, just as he had done when they were little. "This is disgraceful! You are supposed to be noblemen! No sparring in the castle. If you want to kill each other, do it on the great lawn." With one last pinch of pressure, Purvis released their ears.

Magna laughed and tossed his sword to the floor. "Don't worry, Purvis. These swords were dull when grandfather was king." He turned to Aret with his nose in the air. "You could never take me, little brother."

Aret scowled. "I almost had you."

"Maybe someday." Magna bowed politely to Purvis and nodded to Camille on his way out.

Camille blushed at Magna's attention, further angering Aret.

Camille was Aret's playmate.

Purvis shook his head as they watched him leave.

"Why is he like that?" Aret asked. "Can't he see what he is doing to our father, the risks he is taking?"

"Your brother is going through a phase," Purvis said. "He will gain wisdom as he gains years."

"Father is sick," Aret said. "We may not have that many years to wait for his wisdom."

"Then perhaps it is time you prepared yourself. It may be *you* who sits on the throne one day."

Aret shook his head adamantly. Magna had been prepared for rule since birth. "No. It has always been Magna."

CHAPTER 3

THE PROMISE

The cold stone walls of the ladies' parlor were softened by curtains of colorful lace and sofas cushioned with hundreds of pillows.

Lady Gwendolyn absently wound a blonde curl of hair on her finger while she read. Her maidens gossiped inanely about which noblemen had taken mistresses, which noblewomen had taken misters, who was pregnant, who was trying to become pregnant, and of course which young princes should be paired with which young princesses. For the most part, Gwendolyn was much more interested in the book she had found in the castle library, a translation of one of the Gatekeeper's Chronicles. The book would probably have been burned if anyone in Hister's court knew it was there.

Nobody quite understood exactly what it meant to be Gatekeeper. It was said that he guarded the Gate between worlds and that he was the only person allowed to walk between them. Gwendolyn wondered what it would feel like to be able to walk between worlds like the Gatekeeper, or even just between kingdoms, travelling anywhere she chose, but never having a real home of her own, a life of constant adventure.

She looked up from her book and giggled alongside her maidens. This was her lot in life. She was a princess.

Gwendolyn had lucked out when she had been promised to Magna. Magna had proven honest, gentle, and he treated Gwendolyn as a confidant, someone he could talk to, someone whose ideas he would listen to. This was more than Gwendolyn could have hoped for.

In addition, Valora was a kingdom like she had never seen. The people were not overtaxed, and the Valoras treated their subjects justly. Because of this, the rulers were truly loved, not just because of their title or station. The people of Valora were loyal to their king because he was loyal to them.

Prince Magna pushed aside a lace curtain. Gwendolyn, always a lady, had to suppress a squeal of joy. Perhaps now she would have something more to listen to than court gossip.

Magna bowed politely to Gwendolyn's servants, and his long, black hair dangled over his neck. Gwendolyn was already planning subtle hints to convince him to cut his hair before the wedding. If she did it right, he would think it was his own idea.

Lady Gwendolyn of Lyon closed her book and dismissed her ladies. The women of court giggled as they left her alone with her handsome prince. She knew what they were thinking, but it was of little consequence. She and Prince Magna would be married soon anyway. The prince kissed her hand and moved pillows aside to make room on the couch beside her.

She could tell Magna was worried and she knew why even before he began telling her his troubles.

The conversation stopped awkwardly when Camille came in with tea. Camille smirked, suspecting something much more common than conspiracy had been interrupted.

Once they were alone again, Magna continued, "How can they act this way?"

"Don't ask me," she said. "I'm just a lady. I don't think of such things." She paused for a moment. "But if you *were* to ask me, I would agree that Hister's rule is unfair. In Lyon, the people are poor and heavily taxed. Any talk of rebellion is quelled quickly. There is always someone ready to betray the plot for a loaf of bread. But, like yours, my family is part of the nobility. We dare not raise a word or a sword. You must see that. You may be in a position to help your people, but not if you get yourself caught and your family disgraced."

Magna furrowed his brow. "So you agree with my father and brother."

"You are both right, in your way," she answered.

Magna's expression lifted. "You are a born politician. You can tell someone you disagree with them and still sound like you are on their side."

"I am always on your side," she said. "I'm just looking at the problem from all perspectives."

Magna smiled and looked into her eyes. "If you were a man, you would be a great king."

She touched the top of his hand with hers. "Stay home tonight. Perhaps you can find ways to strike against Hister without putting your people in danger."

"Perhaps," he said. "You are very wise for a lady, but I have vowed to help sabotage the shipment of tribute tonight."

Lady Gwendolyn's mouth gaped, and she felt her face get warm.

"After tonight," Prince Magna continued, "I will lie low for awhile and think on it. I promise."

"Valora's taxes!" Gwendolyn burst. "You can't! Giving defectors and rebels refuge is one thing, but stealing tribute is another. That's kicking Hister in the moneybags! If you are caught, there is no way you or your father could talk your way out of it! Even if you aren't caught, there will be reprisals!"

"I gave my word, Lady Gwendolyn. You are very wise but you are still just a lady. A nobleman must always keep his word." He stood. "I must go."

Lady Gwendolyn let go of her reserve and clung to his arms.

He smiled. "I'll be fine. It's just one night, one last night." His thin lips gently grasped at hers. Her grip relaxed, and he pulled away, leaving her in the limited world of her chambers. Gwendolyn could only hope that he would come back to her, and that Valora would remain the refuge she had come to love.

CHAPTER 4

SHERIFF'S WARNING

Sheriff Morto smiled down at Morto Junior in his crib. "You should be asleep," he said, as though expecting the baby to understand his words. He dipped his finger in his glass of wine and allowed the child to suck on it, caressing the baby's gums as he did so. The baby looked up at Morto with recognition in his big blue eyes. The baby may not have understood Morto's words, but he knew his father. Morto's oldest son had gone to sleep hours ago, but the baby was still awake.

Morto removed his finger and kissed the baby on the forehead, relishing the faint smell of baby powder.

He then downed the rest of his glass. One perk of working for the Valoras was always having good wine.

His round wife, Reyna, saw him buckling his sword belt back over his blue tunic. "Where are you going?"

"King's business," he answered.

"You aren't babysitting that prince again?"

"If the King wanted you to know his business, he would make a decree."

Reyna shook her head. "You should turn him in. Your blood is as noble as theirs, and you aren't spoiled. Your grandfather was a king."

"Yes, but he fought against Hister. If the Valoras hadn't taken my mother in, I wouldn't be here at all."

"Think with your brain, Morto, and not your sense of loyalty."

"Without loyalty," Morto said, "what else is there?"

"Those kids are going to get what your grandfather got. You don't want to fall when the Valoras fall. You have more right to the throne than those kids. You practically run the fief already."

Morto shook his head, not caring to discuss the matter further. "I'll be back soon."

Sheriff Morto had selected three members of his elite guard, and they were already waiting for him at the entrance to the stables. The men in blue had been talking about girls and jousting competitions. When Morto arrived, their conversation turned to duty rosters and tactics, all business. Even Flynt, fifteen years Morto's senior, stiffened a little when Morto approached. There was no question Morto was in charge.

One of his men appeared startled, and Morto followed his gaze. None of them had seen Prince Magna enter the stables, and there was no way the prince could have gotten past them, yet there he was, brushing his white charger and allowing the horse to nuzzle his chest. Perhaps the prince was sneakier than Morto had given him credit for. The sheriff wanted to ask how he had managed to get past them, but one didn't just interrogate a prince as one did any commoner.

Prince Magna wore ragged clothes and had tied his fine hair back into a short ponytail. It was a better disguise than Morto had previously seen, but Magna's bangs still puffed up in a style only a young royal would wear.

The prince had to have noticed them standing there, but he ignored them. Magna fed an apple to his horse with a glow in his eyes as he watched the animal crunch through the sweet fruit. Despite Prince Magna's arrogance, Morto couldn't dislike a man who showed such affection to his horse.

The sheriff's men looked to Morto, waiting to follow his lead, but they were only here for show. No one was to take action against the prince. Under normal circumstances, it was improper to speak to a royal before he spoke to you. Prince Magna knew this, daring them with his silence, but Sheriff Morto was under special orders from the King himself. Magna would be king one day too, however, and Morto had to choose his words carefully.

Magna was putting a saddle on the horse when Morto finally dared speak. "Awful late to be going for a ride, Lord Magna."

"Did my father order you to stop me?" Magna asked.

"We are not to interfere," Morto said, "but your father begs you to reconsider your actions tonight. If it pleases you, sir, go back to your room and be at peace tonight."

"I must do this," Magna said.

Sheriff Morto took a resigned breath. He knew all along this would be the outcome. "Very well. The King said to give you a special message if you would not heed his advice."

"What's that?"

Morto remained completely deadpan. "Don't get caught."

Magna flashed a cocky smile at the sheriff as he swung his leg over the saddle and rode past the guardsmen.

The prince probably took Morto's words as unofficial sanctioning by the King and by Morto as well. In a way, they were. Sheriff Morto wasn't sure how wise it was to allow Magna to proceed on this course. Every prince was expected to have a certain amount of reckless adventure, and Sheriff Morto understood the old king's logic. Magna was to be king, sooner, Morto feared, than later, and the prince had to make his own mistakes. When Magna became king, there would be no one to correct him.

But Morto worried Magna would go too far and bring the wrath of Hister upon the fief.

The sheriff had a special relationship with old King Valora. They were friends, practically family, and Morto would never have that kind of relationship with Magna.

CHAPTER 5

A LONG NIGHT

Aret finally heard the knock at the door and felt a twitch in his loins. It had taken Camille much longer than normal, and he felt like he was going to explode.

He moved the sheets aside, but the slender silhouette in the door was not the feminine form he had expected.

It was Enri, his young attendant. "Lord," he said. There was a quake to his voice that Aret did not like at all. "You must come to the master's chamber at once."

Aret wasted no time putting a robe over his nightshirt and stepping into his slippers. He could barely keep up with Enri as they rushed down the hall.

A cluster of servants by the King's door averted their eyes when Aret neared, which was the proper thing to do, but there was an unusual somberness to it this night. It was strange for so many servants to be awake so late.

Aret didn't even acknowledge Purvis. He went straight to his father's bedside. Miss Bonnie, a folk woman, sat on the side of the bed, ringing a water-soaked cloth over the King's parched lips. Lines of silver streaked the red hair hanging loose over Miss Bonnie's shoulders. Camille was assisting and gave Aret a brief bow of acknowledgement.

"His fever is worse," Miss Bonnie said. "I fear the end is near."

"Surely you have some potion you can give him," Aret said.

"I have given them all," she said. "Been giving them for days now."

Aret had never seen his father so weak. He remembered when they used to spar with wooden swords, childlike glee in his father's firm face. Now the skin sagged over once-proud cheeks.

No matter how ill his father had gotten, there had always been a quiet dignity, a strength no one could deny. That was gone now. On the bed before him was an old rag of flesh.

At least the worry lines had softened on his father's face. He was at peace. Aret gave his father a kiss on the forehead.

Is this how everyone ended their life? Would Aret die like this one day as well? He turned away from the sight.

Purvis put a hand on Aret's arm, but Aret would not look him in the eye. "There are preparations to be made," Purvis said.

Aret shook his head. "Not yet. He is still alive. He has been ill before and recovered."

Purvis hesitated. "Perhaps, but we must be ready."

Aret let out a long breath. This wasn't his responsibility. "Where is Magna?"

Purvis shrugged.

Aret preferred the anger that swelled in his breast to the grief it had replaced. Magna was the eldest, the future King Valora. He should be here.

Aret rushed down the hall and banged on Magna's door. Hearing no answer, he barged in. The bed was cold. Where was he? He took a deep breath. When he released it, he knocked over Magna's nightstand in a rage. He looked upon the mess he had made and shook his head. His outburst had accomplished nothing.

Not bothering to shut the door behind him, he made for the women's chambers. A matron forced him to wait at the door, and he paced nervously before it.

As soon as Lady Gwendolyn appeared at the door, his rage subsided. Just awakened, Gwendolyn's blonde curls framed her fine skin in a haphazard way that could never have been designed to be so beautiful. It was impossible to be angry around a lady like her.

"Have you seen my brother?" he asked.

Lady Gwendolyn raised her eyebrows. "He is certainly not here at this time of night! What do you think I am?"

Aret shook his head and felt his face get warm. "Of course not! I just thought he may have told you…" Aret paused. "I must find him right away."

Lady Gwendolyn's face softened. "He will return by morning. I'm sure of it."

"But you don't know where he went?"

She shook her head.

Aret stared at her lovely face for a time. She knew more than she was saying, but was loyal to his brother. Aret wondered if his brother realized how lucky he was to have her. Magna would be back by morning and there was nothing Aret could do now to get him back any quicker. Preparations would fall to him.

He forced his gaze away from Lady Gwendolyn and walked away without a word. "What's wrong?" she called after him, but he gave no response.

The mood was even worse when Aret returned to the King's door. He was afraid to look upon his father, afraid of what he would find. The room was crowded with servants.

Purvis met him in the doorway, and Aret asked, "What must I do?"

CHAPTER 6

THE KING IS DEAD

Magna arrived early the next morning. The bells had tolled for the King, and Magna knew before he arrived that his father had passed away. Until he saw the body with his own eyes, he did not truly believe it. No one spoke to Magna, or even looked at him. What could they say? His father seemed so peaceful there, like he was merely sleeping in his bed. But he wasn't breathing, and his strong hands were limp and cold. Magna should have been here when it happened. His father had been sick for a long time. How could Magna have known tonight would be the night his father passed? The last thing Magna said to him was an insult.

Aret gave a wide-eyed look to his brother. Magna expected a jibe or an accusation, but instead, Aret hugged him. A dam burst within Magna, and the brothers shared their tears.

Aret and Purvis were already making preparations. Invitations had been sent and accommodations readied for visitors. The family tomb was being prepared. Magna reviewed the plans, trying to insert himself into the process, but others had taken charge by this point. Things were proceeding without him.

Magna's sister, Mimi, came from Lyon for the funeral. She, Aret, and Purvis stood behind Magna. He forced his way through a short speech, all the time remembering the last angry words he had spoken to his father.

"The weight of kingship is upon me," Magna said. "The words of my father haunt me. I can only try to live and rule like him. I know you all loved him as much as I did. He wasn't just *my* father. We were *all* a part of his family. Together we mourn." Magna swallowed hard and backed away from center stage.

Musicians played a dirge as the body was carried into the family vault. Wailing peasants threw flower petals over the old king in his velvet suit. Magna's father was truly loved. Magna had large shoes to fill.

It didn't seem real. It was as though this were all some disturbing dream. Magna always knew this day would come. He thought he was prepared, but there was no way he could have ever been ready for this moment.

Since he had arrived back at the castle, he had not stopped moving. That night, for the first time, he was alone with his thoughts. Gwendolyn held his face next to her heart. She did not offer any consolatory words. Words were pointless. She was simply there for him.

Kingship was a weight Magna had yet to truly feel. His nighttime exploits would stop forever, of course. It was fine for a prince or a boy to be so reckless, but not for a king. He had a fief to run and people to protect. He would make his father proud.

Enri woke Aret early the next morning. His voice was urgent. "Prince Aret! A black coach has entered Valora with an entourage of soldiers. The High Necromancer is coming!"

Aret jerked up. "Already?" They all knew Hister's wizard would come. He always came when a king was to be crowned, but not until after the mourning period.

Aret dressed in a hurry. He found Magna and Purvis already in the throne room. The High Chair, the king's seat, was empty. It would remain empty until Magna's coronation.

Magna was pacing, mouthing words silently to himself. No doubt he was rehearsing what he would say to Hister's wizard.

Purvis stopped Magna and smoothed his shirt. They had good reason to be nervous. This wizard carried the full authority of Hister.

Aret tried to calm Magna. "Don't be so nervous. This is all just a formality."

Aret and his brother had become closer since their father passed, but the disdainful look Magna gave Aret brought back all the old enmity.

Trumpets blasted, and they all froze in place.

Enri escorted the dark-robed wizard along the red carpet. Leathery skin hung on his tall, thin frame. His body should have collapsed long ago, but iron will kept him upright and strong.

Purvis bowed his head and averted his eyes. Scholars and magicians were direct subjects of the Necromancer. Though old Purvis had lived in Valora all Aret's life, he could be removed from his office with a single word.

Magna kissed the Necromancer lightly on both cheeks, and Aret did the same. The wizard smelled of wet earth and stale incense.

Magna cleared his throat. "I did not expect you so soon, Your Honor."

"You knew that I would come," the Necromancer said in a clear, high voice. "You must be crowned."

"Of course, Your Honor," Magna said. "I just did not realize you would be here so soon. Mourning usually lasts a week before the coronation of the new king. The fief is not ready for a celebration."

"These are dangerous times, Lord Valora." The Necromancer looked beyond Magna, to the empty chair. "We cannot allow a power vacuum, even for so short a time."

"I assure you, Your Honor, the people of this fief are loyal to me and my family. You don't have to worry about us."

"It is not your people that I worry about. Be ready on the morrow. The coronation will take place then."

Aret and Magna exchanged a glance. There was so little time for so many preparations, but they dared not argue.

"Of course," Magna said. "Your things have been carried to your rooms and a banquet is being prepared."

"I will take my meal in my chamber," the Necromancer said. "Alone."

It was disconcerting. A visitor from Hister's court would expect to eat in the great hall, not alone in his chamber, but wizards were always eccentric.

Magna bowed. "As you wish."

The High Necromancer rejoined his entourage at the door, and Magna turned to Purvis. "What did he mean; *It is not your people that I worry about?*"

Aret waved his hand. "You are being silly, Magna. This is all just a formality. He was probably already nearby and wanted to save himself a trip."

Magna took a deep breath. "We have preparations to attend to."

CHAPTER 7

LONG LIVE THE KING

Aret was given the task of informing everyone that the coronation would take place the next day. His father had barely been dead a full day, and already it was all about Magna. Aret wondered if he could ever live comfortably in a kingdom ruled by his brother.

Aret performed his task without complaint. This was not a time to give in to petty jealousies. That is not what their father would have wanted. All the castle staff were busy with preparations, and this was the least Aret could do.

In any event, a home was just a place to sleep between trips and games and quests. Aret almost pitied his brother when he thought of all the fun Magna would miss while busy managing their land. Magna would probably try to pawn some of his responsibilities onto Aret, but Aret could work it to his advantage somehow.

Many who would be invited for the coronation were already in Valora for the funeral. Mimi's husband, Prince Brigham, was absent, but his father and mother, the king and queen of Lyon brought tableware of gold set with precious stones. The king of nearby Vincennes sent word back to his lands, and gifts of food arrived for the celebration. The occasion didn't feel very festive with his father's passing so fresh in their hearts and minds.

The next day, Aret and the royal family sat on a wooden platform waiting for the ceremony to begin. The public had crowded onto the great lawn. The ceremonial crown, never worn except on coronation day, sat on a pillar in the center of the stage.

The verdant leaves had already begun the seasonal transition to yellows, oranges, and dull reds. At times the breeze shifted, and the sweet smell of the bakery mixed with the stench of the stables.

Aret wondered if he could convince Magna, as king, to have the buildings moved further apart. Aret could already hear his brother turning the question back on him, putting Aret in charge of the project. Perhaps it was better not to bring it up.

Aret sat between Lady Mimi and Lady Gwendolyn, but Magna sat alone. Aret almost felt sorry for his brother. Everyone knew the king, but the king always sat apart. The future Queen Gwendolyn seemed to be pouring strength from her eyes into Magna. Aret let his gaze move from her eyes, down her slender neck, to the white breasts under her blouse. Suddenly he did not feel sorry for his brother anymore. Gwendolyn finally looked away from Magna and met Aret's eyes. Aret smiled, blushing slightly. He hoped she did not suspect where he had been looking.

Mimi's eyes were red and puffy. She had fine black hair like Magna's. Aret put his hand on hers.

"I wish Brigham would have come," Mimi said. "My husband is never home. He is always traveling about."

"Beating me in fencing competitions," Aret added.

Mimi smiled faintly. "Yes."

The crowd hushed when the High Necromancer finally arrived on stage accompanied by the Histerland Anthem. The old wizard began the coronation ceremony by praising the former King Valora and thanking the fief for its loyalty to Histerland. The musicians began playing again the moment he picked up the crown. The old wizard leaned near to Magna and whispered in his ear as he placed the crown upon his head.

The color drained from Magna's cheeks, but when the horns played their fanfare, Magna smiled. He waved to his applauding subjects who shouted in unison, "Long live the king!"

Aret was ready for the day to be over. The royal family shuffled over to a large oak table set up on the great lawn. Camille poured rich Valoran wine into Aret's chalice, allowing her blouse to hang open before him. He looked up and met her smile, then followed her with his eyes as she moved along the table pouring wine for the others.

The Necromancer raised his glass in a toast. "To the long and happy rule of the new King Valora."

Magna took a drink, and the people cheered, for they knew when the nobles ate well there would be scraps left for them. The minstrels played enthusiastically when they saw the rich foods that would be theirs when the nobles had their fill. Magna clapped along with the music.

Aret looked around for Camille, wondering how long it would be before he could excuse himself from the table.

There was a commotion by Magna's chair. Magna stood and teetered. He grabbed the table as though trying to steady the world around him.

All the excitement, no food, and just the slightest bit of wine... Aret would never let his brother live this down. He was about to laugh when their eyes met.

Aret had never seen his brother scared before. Magna's eyes lost focus as he fell behind the table.

CHAPTER 8

TRAGEDY AND REVENGE

Lady Gwendolyn stifled a scream with a hand on her mouth. The music stopped at once.

Aret pushed through the crowd of concerned royals. He paused at the sight of his brother, weak and wheezing on the ground. Aret loosened Magna's collar.

The Necromancer crouched beside Aret. He ran a knotted hand along Magna's neck. Magna's eyes were glazing over, and the Necromancer pried open the lids as wide as they would go, staring into them. "He is poisoned." The old wizard looked up. "There is a traitor in our midst. Someone sympathetic to The Golden City, I would guess."

The Golden City, Histerland's most constant rival, lay in the northern sea. Aret clenched his eyes shut. How could this happen now? Their father hadn't even been dead two days, and already new tragedy had befallen them. Nothing could happen to Magna. His brother was to rule Valora for a lifetime, as their father had.

Aret stood before the room, his face red with fury. "Find the traitor!"

Sheriff Morto was already standing at the corner of the table. He nodded with a confidence that comforted Aret.

Before Aret could ask, the Necromancer said, "To make a cure, I must find a sample of the poison. Make King Magna as comfortable as you can." The old wizard rushed to join Sheriff Morto, who was already gathering his men and splitting them into groups.

Four of the royal guard carried Magna into the castle and up the stairs, gently and reverently resting him on his bed. They remained on guard outside the room while the royal family hovered.

Aret sat in a chair next to the bed, his head in his hands. Despite Morto's apparent confidence, the killer would certainly be long gone by now, along with any hope of finding a sample of the poison.

Lady Gwendolyn collapsed on the body. "Who did this?" She abruptly sat up, staring down at Magna.

Mimi put her hand on Gwendolyn's shoulder. "Is he…?"

Aret rose and stared down at his brother, whose blank eyes looked past the girls. Magna's chest expanded, almost imperceptibly. "He is still breathing," Aret said with a sigh, then paced across the room.

"Are you sure?" Mimi asked.

"Yes!" he snapped at her, but immediately regretted it. They were as worried as he was.

He sat again and stared at Magna. There was another slow breath. "He is still alive," he reassured himself and paced the room again.

At last the guards parted, and a servant of the Necromancer called Aret. "The traitor has been caught."

Aret couldn't believe that the criminal could be mad enough to stay after his evil mission was done. He rushed from the chamber and back to the great lawn.

A one-eyed man was hauled before Aret and dropped to the ground. Thinning red hair draped his neck.

"His name is Buddy," Morto announced. "A member of the Underground."

Aret frothed at the mouth. "Why? Why have you done this to my brother? Why have you done this to us?"

Buddy fell forward in supplication. "I'm innocent, Lord! I was Magna's friend."

The Necromancer produced a scroll bearing the broken seal of the Golden City. "This was found in his possession." He sniffed the parchment." It bears traces of the poison used on your brother."

"That's not mine!" Buddy protested.

"Can you help my brother?" Aret implored the wizard. "Can you make a cure?"

Aret could see the doubt on the old wizard's face when he answered, "I'll do what I can." The Necromancer hurried up the steps and into the castle.

Aret's neck knotted like a coiled spring when he looked back to the assassin. "Execute him!"

Immediately Buddy was forced onto the platform, the same platform where Magna's coronation had taken place mere hours before.

Aret looked up to the windows of the castle where his brother was fighting for his life. Lady Gwendolyn looked out upon the scene. Aret's neck and arms ached with tension.

"Please, Lord!" Buddy cried. "I've been framed!"

Where was the executioner? Would Magna be dead before his murderer? Would the last sounds he heard be the voice of the man who killed him?

"I was Magna's friend!" Buddy cried.

Magna's friend, the murderer said. Not *His Highness*, not *Lord*, not *King Magna*, just *Magna*, as though they were equals.

Aret grabbed a sword from his guard's scabbard and charged at the stage. "Give him a sword!" he cried as he ran.

Aret leapt to the stage in a single bound. "Give him a sword!"

Someone threw a sword onto the stage, but Buddy recoiled from it, his one good eye filled with terror.

Aret kicked it towards him.

"I won't!" Buddy cried.

"Then you will die!" Aret said. "You aren't a knight. You aren't a noble. I owe you nothing!" He charged at Buddy's prostrate form, blade held straight at his chest.

Buddy grabbed the sword from the stage and rolled away from Aret's strike. He parried once more before Aret's blade plunged into his heart. Buddy dropped his sword and met Aret's eyes before collapsing with a few spasms.

Aret pulled the bloody sword free and dropped it to the stage. He turned and ran up the castle steps without looking back.

The Necromancer and Purvis were waiting outside Magna's room. Purvis leaned against the wall, and Gwendolyn sobbed inside.

"I'm sorry," the Necromancer said. "*You* are now King of Valora."

Aret was numb. It wasn't possible. He was never to be king. He went into Magna's room. Lady Gwendolyn lifted her head from Magna's chest and came to Aret. She and Mimi embraced him, looking to him for strength, but it was they who supported him as he leaned into them.

Magna was dead. Two King Valoras gone in three days.

The next day there was another funeral and another body carried into the crypt under a rain of flower petals. The tears had been heavy for their father, but he was old and sick. Magna was young. No one had expected this.

Lady Gwendolyn wore a black veil, so Aret could not see what the tragedy had done to her lovely face. Aret supposed she would want to go back to Lyon now. She was technically Aret's ward. He could have her married off to someone. He didn't like the thought of castle life without her or Mimi.

The Necromancer put his hand on Aret's shoulder. "A travesty. A horrible injustice. I will see to it this does not happen again. I have heard that you are a true patriot, loyal to Histerland as your family before you."

"Of course," Aret said. "Especially now. Histerland's enemies have proven themselves Valora's enemies. My father... My brother... They took the best of us."

The Necromancer studied Aret. The wizard's leathery face had sagged under time's pull, but his eyes were unyielding. "Do not fear. You are a worthy successor and will make an excellent king."

Aret shook his head. "I was never meant to be king. It was always my brother who—"

"Nonsense," the Necromancer interrupted. "If there is anything you or your people need to help you in this time of transition, you have but to ask. I have sent a courier to Hister himself. You will have his full support, I promise that. I will leave 25 extra soldiers, loyal to Hister, here to help you keep the peace."

Aret tried to smile. "Thank you, Your Honor. You are a good man. I don't know what we would have done without you."

CHAPTER 9

BODY SNATCHER

More than ever, Gwendolyn tried to escape in her books. Barely three days had passed since Magna's death, and her ladies gossiped as though nothing had happened.

They were avoiding the matter of most importance to them. Without Magna, Lady Gwendolyn's future was a complete question mark. It was unlikely that she would be given to someone who would respect her opinion as Magna had, or that she would be sent to live in a place where the people loved their lords as the Valorans did.

Someone pushed aside the curtains. Gwendolyn's heart leapt at the confident stride and fine black hair. For a moment, it seemed her fiancé had returned from the dead, but it was only his sister, Mimi, who shared so many of Magna's features. It now seemed silly that Gwendolyn had complained so much about the length of Magna's hair, such a shallow thing.

Lady Gwendolyn closed her book, rose, and grabbed Mimi's hands. Camille poured fresh cups of tea.

"I return to Lyon this afternoon," Mimi said. "I'm putting flowers on the tomb before I go. Come with me."

Gwendolyn tried to smile and nodded.

Their pointed shoes crunched over the fallen leaves.

"How are things back in Lyon?" Gwendolyn asked.

"Your family and the castle staff treat me well. Prince Brigham travels ... a lot." Mimi paused for a moment at the mention of her husband. "He has a real spirit of adventure and ambition. He is not the oldest, but I wouldn't be at all surprised if he were a king himself one day."

Gwendolyn nodded. "It sounds as though you are enjoying life in Lyon."

"Yes." Mimi hesitated. "Sometimes, though, it makes me sad to live in such opulence when I see many of our subjects on the verge of starvation."

Gwendolyn nodded. "I felt that way at times," she admitted, "But what are we to do? These are the times in which we live, and we are only ladies."

As they approached the vault, they could see the stone door had been propped open. A man scurried away from the tomb as they approached.

"You!" Mimi shouted to the man. "Who are you?"

Gwendolyn raised her skirts above her knees and raced ahead, giving chase to the intruder. The thought of someone defiling her beloved's body spurred her on. She froze in her tracks when she saw him jump the stone fence in the distance. Her breath caught in her throat. The intruder was wearing Magna's burial clothes.

Mimi was panting when she finally caught up. "Who was it?" she asked. "What did they want in our family tomb?"

Lady Gwendolyn still looked to the fence where she had lost sight of the intruder. "I can't be sure... He was so far away... Of course I know better, but... I could have sworn... For a moment I thought it really was Magna."

Mimi put her hands on Gwendolyn's shoulders. "That's not possible."

"I know. It just looked—"

Mimi saw a passing soldier and waved her hand at him. "Soldier! Summon Sheriff Morto at once."

The young soldier in black bowed and ran to Castle Valora.

Gwendolyn felt her eyes tearing up. She inhaled a shaky breath and tried to hold back her emotions. She didn't want to cry in front of Mimi. She hadn't even cried in front of her own ladies.

Without Magna, she was a leaf to be blown about by forces beyond her control. Her father and Aret would decide her fate. Even her brother, Brigham, had more say in her destiny than she did. If only the figure really had been Magna. If only he were alive.

Mimi drew Gwendolyn's head against her shoulder. Gwendolyn's shoulders shook up and down as she sobbed silently, muffling the sounds in Mimi's blouse.

Soon, the young Histerland soldier returned with Sheriff Morto and one of Morto's men in blue. They found Gwendolyn and Mimi holding one another at the door of the tomb. Gwendolyn stifled her sobs, but she still could not speak. Grief stole the women's voices. All they could do was point at the open crypt.

Morto alone followed the path of the women's fingers, through the wreaths of flowers and into the dark tomb. He was only gone for a minute, yet it seemed like forever to those watching. At last he returned from the darkened archway and said, "Magna's body has been stolen."

"I saw the thief," Gwendolyn said. Princess Mimi squeezed her hand as though trying to restrain her, but Gwendolyn continued. "For a moment I thought it was Magna himself running out of the tomb."

Morto looked sadly at Gwendolyn, and she was shamed by his pity. Gwendolyn was a widow in everything but name.

"It was a thief that you saw, Milady," Sheriff Morto said. "The scoundrel stole Prince ..." he corrected himself, "*King* Magna's ceremonial clothes."

"Who would steal my brother's body?" Mimi cried.

Gwendolyn added, "The entire fief loved him."

"Bodies and possessions of the dead are powerful tools of black magic, but such magic is illegal in Histerland to all but the High Necromancer."

Gwendolyn scrunched her face in disgust at the thought of Magna's body profaned in some dark ritual.

Mimi shook her head in disbelief. "There must be another who sympathizes with Histerland's enemies, probably a magician from the Golden City, right here in Valora. The thief must be caught!"

"Of course, Milady," Morto said, bowing.

A shrill scream shattered the quiet, and Gwendolyn's heart skipped a beat.

Morto was the first to charge in the direction of the scream, and the rest followed. Lady Gwendolyn lifted her skirts to keep up, no longer caring what the others thought of her.

She arrived at Mack's Tavern and Inn just after Morto. The plump innkeeper's wife was hyperventilating and holding her chest. On the ground next to her was a bread roller and a pile of crumbs.

The round woman jumped when she saw the sheriff and two royal women. She bowed. "A bird," she said, catching her breath. "That's all. Took a loaf of bread from the windowsill." She pointed to five loaves of bread, still cooling.

Sheriff Morto narrowed his eyes. "You screamed," he said.

The woman grinned sheepishly. "Startled me," she said. "It was a big old bird. Really big." She retrieved her rolling pin from the ground and waved it in the air. "I came after it, but it was too fast for me."

"You're sure that's all it was?" Morto asked.

"Yes, thank you." She bowed again. "But I sure feel safe knowing how fast you all came to my rescue. I was just telling Mack the other day that this must be the safest fief in all of Histerland and its all on account of Sheriff Morto." She picked up a fresh loaf of bread from the sill and gave it to the sheriff. "I know it's not much, but please take this. Share it with your family."

Lady Gwendolyn now narrowed her eyes.

Sheriff Morto expressed no emotion, but nodded and accepted the gift. "Thank you. Let me know if you have any more trouble."

The sheriff turned, but the innkeeper's wife stepped in front of him. "Speaking of Mack," she said. "Is there any word when he will be released?"

Morto's face was unchanging. "That will be entirely up to the king."

"You know," she said, "we have always been loyal to the Valoras and especially to poor King Magna."

Morto nodded. "I know."

He started back towards the castle, but Lady Gwendolyn lingered. She studied the woman. The innkeeper's wife bowed, and at last Gwendolyn took her leave.

"Don't you think she was acting suspicious?" Gwendolyn asked the sheriff.

"Yes," he said. "Yes I do. But I also know that Mack and Wena were extremely loyal to your," He paused, "to King Magna. They have no ties to black magic. She may be hiding something, but she didn't break into the royal tombs."

"But her husband is in jail?" Gwendolyn said.

"Yes. All of Magna's old cohorts fell under suspicion after he was poisoned, but I have no doubt of Mack's loyalty."

"They are freemen," Gwendolyn said. "They don't owe allegiance to any king."

"They are free," Morto said. "As long as they pay our taxes and obey our laws. Their loyalty to your brother is without question."

There was a short pause before she spoke again. "Aret must be told about the grave robber." She said it with a hint of fear. Aret's emotional state was tenuous to say the least. He didn't have his father or brother's patience or objectivity. She hoped he would learn it in time, but she had her doubts.

Morto sighed. "I know. I'll tell him."

CHAPTER 10

MURDER IN VALORA

The next morning, Morto stood in the entrance to the darkened hall. Bright sunlight framed his back.

King Aret was fulfilling his kingly duty by listening to the people's troubles. There were few in attendance, mostly beggars hoping for a handout from the new king. When Aret's father held audience, even on slow days, one or two subjects would approach the chair with no purpose other than greeting their king. Aret was not his father.

Sheriff Morto waited patiently. Aret hadn't spoken to him since the previous afternoon, when Morto had reported the theft of Magna's body.

At last Aret acknowledged him. Morto nodded to two guardsmen just outside. Morto's men pushed a portly man forward. The prisoner's shabby clothes were speckled with blood.

Aret's eyes widened, and his mouth became a tight line. Morto knew what his king wanted to hear and knew he would be disappointed. His prisoner was a murderer, but had nothing to do with the theft of Magna's body.

Morto cleared his throat. "This man was arrested last night for the brutal murder of a woman that worked at Mack's tavern." He turned to the accused, but spoke for all to hear. "Witnesses say you and the victim left the tavern together just after sundown."

The red-faced man agreed, "Yes. Yes that's right."

Morto continued, calm and matter-of-fact. "She was known to engage in certain business transactions of her own. You argued about the price. When she wouldn't give you what you wanted, you cut her up."

"No!" the accused protested. "A coin, a meal, and a warm place to sleep was all she ever wanted from me. I was her regular. I've been out with her hundreds of times."

Morto nodded his head. "As witnesses agree, but this time something went wrong. What did you use to cut her up like that?" Morto addressed the room. "Tiny rakes tore up and down her young flesh. It was inhuman!"

"No!" the tearful man cried, "It wasn't me. It was the monster."

"The monster of too much ale." Morto looked around the room, but no one seemed to find his little joke amusing.

"The girl was my friend," the accused insisted. "Please believe me! It was horrible. You must catch it! Kill it before it kills again!"

King Aret shook his head and stared the accused down with a burning hatred that chilled Morto. "I've heard enough. You disgust me. You will be executed this afternoon."

The guards dragged the wailing prisoner away. Morto studied Aret a little too long before he remembered his place and bowed his head.

Purvis was still noting the decision in his scrolls when Aret abruptly stood, saying, "I'm done taking audience today," and without another word he returned to his chambers.

Morto lifted his head and gave Purvis one glance before marching out behind his men. The drunkard was the most obvious suspect. Aret had most likely made the right verdict, but he had judged so quickly, so coldly. A man was going to be executed, a murder had been committed on his lands, but King Aret barely seemed to be paying attention.

Sheriff Morto crouched over the dead serf in the straw. There was a witness, the victim's sandy-haired son, but he was wounded. The boy's mother, now a widow, blotted his face. Her blouse was stained with the boy's blood. Deep cuts would not stop bleeding.

Morto wiped the dead man's throat and found thin slices across his neck. Nothing was taken. No blood or flesh was missing.

Miss Bonnie arrived and applied a balm to the stable boy's face. The bleeding instantly stopped.

Morto examined four thin slices on the right side of the boy's face. The wounds were parallel and about an inch apart. It seemed the town drunk had not been lying after all. There really was a monster in Valora, but vindication came too late for the poor drunkard.

"That will leave a good scar," Morto said to the child. "The other boys will be jealous."

The stable boy tried to smile.

"Tell me what happened." the sheriff said.

"I was late," the boy said, "But it wasn't my fault. A sheep had wandered off, and I'd been chasing it. Father was already going to be mad at me, and then the sheep refused to go in the barn. They bayed and pulled away. I had no choice but to huff back to the stable to fetch father." The stable boy looked to the stall where his father still lay. "I was so worried he would be mad at me, but he was in the straw. My father never slept when there was work to be done."

"I tried to wake him," the boy continued, "but he wouldn't move. I shook him. There was blood under him."

Horror contorted the boy's eyes and mouth. His wounds began to seep again. "Something fluttered in the rafters. These two orange eyes came at me!"

"I heard him scream," his mother added.

"I didn't scream," the boy corrected her. "I called for help. It was a demon! Swooped past me with wings like a bat."

"I found him with his face bleeding," the mother said. "And my husband killed!"

Demons and monsters were a rare sight in Valora, but they still haunted the countryside and would wander into towns from time to time. "What kind of demon?" Morto asked.

The boy took a long, quaking breath. "It happened so fast. He was like a skeleton with wings and fire in his eyes. He wore a tunic like yours, with a shiny gold gryphon on the chest."

Morto had never heard of a creature like that. It had to be linked; the attacks, Magna's stolen clothes. "We will get it," Morto said, messing the kid's hair. "Your father will be avenged."

Morto woke his men. He sent them in groups of three throughout the fief. A scream was heard, but the monster was gone when they found the next bloodied victim.

The next day, Sheriff Morto rode through the fief with King Aret and Purvis. They were announcing a curfew. Everyone not on King's business was to be indoors after dark. All able-bodied men would be put into groups under a soldier and sent into the cool night to find the monster.

Aret's white horse galloped far ahead of them. The young king circled his horse around his companions, then slowed to a trot beside them once more, like a bored child might do. Aret patted his sinewy horse affectionately as they trotted along. To no one in particular, he said, "Snow used to be Magna's favorite."

Morto wondered if the young king was taking this situation seriously. This was the first time King Aret had left the castle in days. Morto supposed he couldn't blame the young man for enjoying the open air.

King Aret turned to his companions and spoke in a hushed voice. "Why is this monster attacking our citizens? Where did it come from? Where will it strike next?"

Morto pulled out a map and marked the creature's attacks. "It strikes randomly, unpredictably."

Aret scanned the map. "The cemetery is in the center of all the attacks. It must be another plot by Histerland's enemies. I hate to say it, but my brother's activities appear to have drawn more sympathizers into our midst. I will join the hunting parties tonight."

Morto was surprised and impressed. The new king *was* taking this seriously after all, but Morto could not allow his king to ride into danger. "That is not necessary, Milord."

Purvis added, "You are king now, Aret. It is no longer your place to go on such adventures. Your subjects will carry out your will. They are your arms and your legs. You are their head."

The safety of the king was Morto's first duty. He would not have a third king die on his watch. "With all the women and children safely in their homes, the monster will find no helpless victims tonight, only armed men."

King Aret paused and scanned the horizon. "Very well. I have faith in you." He then spurred his horse, and Snow galloped ahead once more, the king's moment of lucidity seemingly passed.

Again that night, screams were heard. Morto met Gruff Woodsman at a cottage. The monster had burrowed through the thatched roof and killed everyone inside. But this time, the corpse-like monster remained, posturing and hissing at them from the straw roof. It was not so different than a man, a dried-up man. Its tight gray face bore a wide, skeletal grimace. Its leather wings spread one and a half times the creature's height

"Look!" a farmer shouted, "It wears the crest of Valora!"

The monster dove at them.

A farmer plunged his pitchfork into the monster's gut. The monster was unfazed. It swiped its hook-like claws into the farmer's throat, then leapt above their shoulders. The pitchfork still hung from its stomach. Someone grabbed its leg and tried to pull it down. The sharp claws protruding from its boot sliced into the man's arm, and the creature flapped away.

Gruff Woodsman aimed his crossbow and let an arrow fly, but the monster's erratic flight made accuracy impossible. The arrow only hit a leathery wing, and the creature took no notice.

The mob followed the monster to the cemetery. When they arrived, there was no trace of the creature. All they found was the pitchfork lying on the ground without a drop of blood. Gruff Woodsman found his arrow not far away. He turned to Morto and asked, "How can we fight a creature that doesn't bleed?"

Although the days were still mild, nights in the drafty castle were cold. Aret lay in a warm bed of furs, listening to the night sounds outside his window. How could he sleep when his people were outside dying? He was still awake when Enri poked his head in the room with news of the monster's latest escape. Aret kicked the furs off his bed and lit a candle at his writing table.

Only one person could help them, a man who had proven himself Valora's friend and pledged his assistance in difficult times.

Aret dipped his quill in ink and wrote a letter in the dim, flickering light. He waved the paper in the air to hasten the drying, folded it, and sealed it with a drop of hot candle wax. Pushing his ring into the soft wax created the stylized impression of a gryphon, the seal of Valora. Aret gave the letter to Enri and said, "Dispatch a courier. Find the High Necromancer."

CHAPTER 11

THE CURSE OF VALORA

The weight of the crown had already aged Aret. Not sleeping and fretting over the attacks had produced heavy bags under his young eyes. One of his chief duties was to protect his people, and already he was failing. He was never meant to be king.

A little life came back to him when Purvis escorted the Necromancer into the throne room. Aret sat up straight.

The dark-robed wizard bowed. "You summoned me, Lord Valora?"

"Thank you for coming so quickly," Aret said. "You pledged your help to us during our difficult times."

"You want my advice regarding the monster attacks." Like any good wizard, the Necromancer already knew why he had been called.

Aret slumped in the throne and gave a feeble, "Yes."

"I have a hypothesis." The Necromancer raised a wrinkled eyebrow. "But I hesitate to suggest it."

"Please," Aret begged. "You must!"

"I believe this husk is your brother."

It took several seconds for Aret to contemplate what the Necromancer said, but he still could not make sense of it. "That's not possible."

"It would seem so," the Necromancer explained. "It is said that if a man dies with guilt on his conscience, that guilt can come back in his dead husk. But your brother was a man of great honor. I can't think of any reason his spirit should feel guilty."

Aret and Purvis exchanged a look, shame plain on their faces.

Aret looked back to the Necromancer. "If it is my brother, what can I do?"

"Only a family member can kill a husk. If it is your brother, then only you can slay him. Cut off his head, burn the body, and you will release him from his guilt."

Aret nodded. His mind's eye saw a young Magna, face beaming with pride. He remembered play fighting in the woods as children, then fighting for real when they were older. The Valoran crown perched on his brother's head like he was born wearing it. Could this monster really be his brother?

Whatever this thing was, it was Aret's responsibility. It was time to get off the throne and leave the walls of the castle. "Thank you, Necromancer. Again you have proven yourself a great friend to us. A private guest room is ready for you."

The Necromancer smiled as he bowed, apparently quite pleased to have been of assistance. Once the wizard was gone, Aret immediately rang for Enri. Aret instructed the young servant to ready his horse and summon Sheriff Morto to the stables. Then Aret ran up the stairs. He donned a mail shirt and covered it with the traditional blue tunic of a Valoran knight. The mail made his body feel heavy, but also made him feel protected.

In the stables, a freshly scarred stable boy fastened Snow's saddle and brushed his mane. The boy had done this for Aret many times, but Aret never really noticed him until now.

Sheriff Morto waited with his arms crossed. "Your Highness, what are you—?"

Aret left no room for arguments. "I will be joining the hunt tonight."

Morto bowed his head. "As you command, King Aret, but I will be by your side every moment."

Aret eyed Morto. The sheriff would have said the same thing if it was Aret's father or brother going on a monster hunt, but Aret wondered if his tone would have been more respectful for them.

"If it pleases you, Milord," Morto added humbly.

Aret softened. "Of course." He placed his foot in the stirrup and lifted his leg over Snow in a graceful arc. "Try to keep up."

They rode into the light of the sinking red sun. Men congregated in the courtyard with torches and whatever weapons or sharp farm implements they could find. They split into smaller groups and dispersed throughout the fief.

Time passed, and Aret's resolve turned to boredom.

Morto must have noticed Aret's restlessness. "Perhaps the monster left Valora. We gave it quite a fight last night."

A man's scream contradicted Morto. Aret jerked the reins and dug in his spurs, awakening Snow into a burst of speed. They followed the sound back to the center of the fief. Bat wings flapped in front of one of the castle windows. The Husk hovered right outside the ivy covered walls. Just as the reports said, the monster wore the crest of Valora on its chest.

A farmer saw Aret and cried out to him, "My Liege! He didn't wait for us to find him. He attacked us from above."

Aret drew his sword, spurred his horse again, and the mob parted before him. Aret jabbed his blade into the air. The Husk dropped behind Aret's shield. Aret's blade cut into the bloodless monster with no effect.

The creature's skeletal grin mocked Aret. Tiny hooks poked from the monster's fingers and boots. The claws tore into Aret's tunic and found the gaps in Aret's mail. The Husk knocked Aret off the saddle and onto the cold hard dirt.

Morto called out, and the people came to their king's defense. Pitchforks, scythes, and swords jutted at the monster from all sides. The Husk rose into the night with a gust of wind from its flapping wings.

King Aret grabbed Snow's reins and leapt back onto his steed, ordering his people to stay back as he gave chase.

Snow kicked open the gate to the cemetery. Aret paused when he saw the Husk perched on the royal crypt. The monster released a defiant hiss of air.

Aret wondered aloud, "Are you Magna?"

The creature looked at the rosy light on the horizon. It leapt from its perch and flapped through the dawning sky. Aret spurred his horse after him, and Snow leapt the stone wall of the cemetery. Aret chased the monster past harvested fields, past the orchards, down Histerland Road and away from the fief. The Husk could not fly faster than Snow could run. The creature sank below the mist-shrouded horizon, disappearing in the rising sun. Aret slowed his horse and rode cautiously over the arched stone bridge. He grasped his sword firmly in both hands and scanned every direction for some trace of the monster. The tree line was still some distance away, and the monster couldn't have gotten that far from him. Aret lowered his sword in one hand. He turned his horse, dismounted, and gazed at the brightening sky. A soft moaning under the bridge caught his attention, and his grip on the sword tightened.

Aret leapt into the ditch beneath the bridge. Before he could strike, he saw the face of his prey… "Magna?"

CHAPTER 12

MAGNA'S TALE

Magna was pale, and his once blue tunic was gray with filth. He hid his face beneath tangled black hair.

"It *is* you!" Aret said. "Don't be afraid. Your killer is dead. You helped a few mages defect, but in the great scheme of things, it's not that important. Your people love you." Aret touched Magna's shoulder gently with one hand, his sword still firmly in the other. "I release you from your guilt."

Magna squinted tired eyes up at his brother. "What are you talking about?"

"I know how ashamed you must be, but it is of no consequence. You can rest now, Magna." Aret dropped his sword and gave his brother a hug. Magna's hair and tunic smelled of musty earth and unwashed sweat.

Magna slowly put his hands around his brother, returning his embrace. "I may never rest again. I am a monster at night and I hide all day."

"It doesn't have to be that way anymore," Aret said. "I have released you from your guilt. I expected you to vanish, or to fall dead, but since you seem to be alive, you can come back with me." Aret pulled back but kept his hands firmly on his brother's shoulders. "You can even resume your place as king! What a relief that will be! You know I never studied. You were always meant to be king, never me."

"No." Magna shook his head. "I turn into a monster and kill people. What kind of king can I be?"

"But I have released you!" Aret explained.

"You have the power to undo the Necromancer's curse?"

Aret relaxed his grip on his brother and looked into Magna's hollow eyes. "What do you mean *the Necromancer's curse?*"

"You said you killed the Necromancer."

"I did no such thing!" Aret exclaimed. "I'm no traitor."

"You said that you killed my murderer."

"Yes," Aret explained. "A peasant named Buddy."

Magna dropped to the ground and buried his head in his hands. "Buddy was my friend."

"No," Aret said. "He was a Golden City sympathizer."

Magna sighed. "It was the Necromancer who poisoned me and turned me into a husk."

"Either death corrupted your mind or a devil lies through your lips!"

"No," Magna said. "The Necromancer's poison didn't kill me. I couldn't move or speak, but I could see everything around me. I could see the flowers falling over my body and hear the people of Valora crying. I saw you and Lady Gwendolyn. She held me in my room right after it happened. I remember thinking how embarrassed she would be if she knew I could feel her on top of me, shamefully close for a lady before we were properly wed. It's like I didn't quite realize how serious my predicament was. I still thought the spell would pass and I would wake up. I tried to call out, tried to lift my arms to embrace her, to tell her I was okay."

"But I wasn't okay," Magna continued. "Time passed, the sun went down. They lifted the arms of my limp body to redress me for burial. My mind screamed over the sound of my own funeral dirge. No one could hear me! I felt the cold slab of stone under me when they placed me next to father. The torches filed away, and I was left alone in the dark. Still, I tried to force my muscles to move, tried to call for help. Water dripped somewhere in the silence. A fly buzzed around father. At last I resigned myself to my fate. I couldn't tell for sure, but I thought I felt something crawl over me. At that point I didn't even try to react. There was no point."

Aret sat next to his brother. "I can't imagine such a thing!"

"There was a clanging of the gate," Magna said. "The walls and ceiling brightened. The Necromancer set his torch in a holder. I blinked when he looked into my eyes. You can't imagine the joy of being able to blink after so long! I thought I was saved. I thought the old wizard must have figured out I wasn't dead. He told me that the poison he used on me was the same, but less concentrated than what he used to kill our father."

"Ridiculous!" Aret interrupted.

Magna continued, "The Necromancer waved his amulet over my body, a black stone in a gnarled silver setting. I could now move my eyes and follow his movements, but he lowered the stone below my line of sight. It seemed to sink into my chest, a piece of ice inside my soul. Then he returned the talisman to his neck, and I'll never forget what he told me."

"'I could kill you,' he said, 'but that would be too quick. I could easily steal your soul, add it to my collection, but that would be too easy. We trusted you, honored you, gave you everything, and you betrayed us. Oh no. I will give you a half death. As a husk you will bring blight upon your people. They will suffer from your curse as you do. Your own people will hunt you and pray for your destruction. If they fail, I will summon you to do my bidding.' The old bastard smiled. 'You will serve Histerland, like it or not.'"

Magna shook his head and brushed his hands through his tangled black hair. "I wanted to rise up, strike out at him, but I still couldn't move. He laughed as he left me alone in the cold. He left the torch for me to see, but the torchlight barely kept away the gloom. I lapsed in and out of consciousness. Each time I awoke, I could move a little more: a finger at first, an arm later. I finally awoke in a fetal position on the stone slab. There was blood on my hands and tunic. I assumed it was mine, that I had done something to myself as I squirmed around in the dark. I'm afraid I did something much worse."

Magna paused for a moment of dark reflection. "I gazed out the gates of the crypt, trying to figure out where I could go. I was afraid, too ashamed to go back to the castle. I hid and slept, waiting for nightfall to make my escape. But when nightfall came,

I blacked out again. More people died. I awoke famished, hadn't eaten in days—"

"You must have been dreaming," Aret finally interrupted. "Why would the Necromancer poison father?"

"Father knew of my activities but didn't stop me. The Necromancer wanted someone he could trust on the throne, someone easy to control."

Aret shook his head in disbelief. "A *puppet,* you mean, like me."

"Don't be so hard on yourself," Magna said. "None of us had any idea he was capable of such evil. Aret, I'm sorry, but you must kill me... *now,* while I'm a man."

CHAPTER 13

DEAD AGAIN

"No!" Aret shouted. "We will go back to Valora. I will reveal the Necromancer's treachery and force him to remove his curse."

Magna was resigned to his fate. "He is too powerful. He has all of Histerland to back him up."

"Histerland be damned! We will rebel against Histerland. Valora will declare its independence!"

Magna raised his hands as if trying to push down the tide of anger within Aret. "No! You and father were right. It is better to be subtle. The Necromancer doesn't expect any threat from you. Let things settle down. Let him trust you. Then, when the dust has settled, you can find ways to undermine Hister's power without bringing attention to yourself. You are the only thing protecting our people from Hister's tyranny."

"And what about you?"

"I told you," Magna said. "You must kill me."

"I can't!"

"I'm already dead," Magna said. "Bring back my body and your loyalty to Hister will be proven beyond doubt."

"I cannot." The idea of stabbing Magna briefly played itself out in Aret's mind. "I will not!"

"It will be an act of love," Magna explained.

"No!" Aret said. "You can leave, go far away while you are still in control of yourself. You can ride Snow, get far away from Valora, farther than the Husk can fly. Find a place with no people for the Husk to terrorize. I've got a map in my pack."

Aret retrieved his sword and sheathed it. Soft dirt crumbled under his fingers as he climbed out of the ditch. Magna had no choice but to follow his brother up. The simple effort caused Magna to be short of breath. As he approached his old horse, Snow reared up and stomped the ground with his hooves. Magna backed away.

Aret grabbed the reigns and stroked Snow's neck. The horse settled down, but his ears were perked toward Magna and his nostrils flared.

Magna's voice cracked. "He doesn't trust me anymore." There were few things more important to a man than his horse. Magna was silent for a moment. "He's a good horse. He will take good care of you, Aret. One other thing, Lady Gwendolyn was meant to be my queen. She is an excellent woman. I have learned to respect her intelligence as well as her beauty. Take care of her. You can trust her, but be wary of the rest of the court. Someone betrayed me to the Necromancer."

"Someone in our court?"

Magna took a deep breath. "It's time. There is no other way."

"Wait!" Aret said. "We can lock you in the prison at night. You can still rule in the daytime."

"Live with that shame? Locked up in my own castle? I'd rather die again." Magna pulled out the ceremonial dagger he had been buried with. "One of us is going to die this morning."

"You can't be serious."

Magna lunged for Aret, who backed up and shoved his brother away. Magna stumbled and fell back into the ditch.

"You are weak from hunger and exhaustion," Aret yelled. "You can't force me to do anything, let alone kill you."

Magna leapt from the ditch and laughed with a shadow of his old spirit. "You could never take me!" He thrust his knife forward, forcing Aret back.

Aret dodged, yelling, "Brother, you're sick! I can't fight you like this."

"Then you will die! All of Valora will suffer!" Magna's dagger grazed Aret's shoulder, staining his shirt with blood.

"Ow!" Aret drew his sword and batted Magna's much shorter blade away.

Magna suddenly shot forward, tripped, and fell onto Aret's sword. Aret gasped with horror as his brother fell into his arms and slid to the ground.

"You idiot!" Aret screamed. "You did that on purpose! You can't die again."

Magna smiled. "It's alright. It's what I wanted... An act of love... Take my body back... prove your loyalty..."

Aret rocked Magna back and forth. Magna's heart stopped beating, and life left his eyes. Magna's relaxed face was blurred by the moisture building in Aret's eyes.

"I thought I had you back." Aret wiped his eyes with his sleeve. "I will avenge you." He buried his face against Magna's chest. "I will find a way."

Snow was still skittish, but the horse allowed Aret to heft Magna's body over him. Instead of following his brother's instructions, Aret led Snow further down Histerland Road until he came to a crossroads. Aret didn't have a shovel, so he used his sword and his bare hands to break the earth into a shallow grave. It was long, hard work, but it was an act of love.

"The Necromancer has done enough to you. He won't get your body too."

CHAPTER 14

THE GATEKEEPER

It was almost noon when Aret finally arrived back in Valora. He had discarded his outer tunic. He couldn't be seen covered in his brother's blood. Aret dismounted, and the young stable boy grabbed Snow's reins.

Aret held the boy's chin and examined the scars on his face. "What is your name, boy?"

"Rowen," the stable boy answered.

"I will not forget it."

A slight smile crossed the boy's face. "Thank you, Lord." The boy led Snow back to the stables.

Rowen's smile warmed Aret's heart, but it turned cold when he found the Necromancer waiting at the castle door.

"It is almost midday," the old wizard said. "Did you catch him?"

Aret's mouth was dry. He took a deep breath and swallowed. "No. I followed him until sunrise, but then he disappeared. I can only hope I chased him far enough that he doesn't find his way back." To Aret's ear, his story sounded rehearsed. Probably because it was.

The Necromancer nodded. "It is possible, if you chased him far enough. Husks aren't good with direction and they don't read road signs." A wrinkled corner of the wizard's mouth creased with amusement.

Aret was no longer able to look the Necromancer in the face. "We will continue the curfew and patrols tonight, just in case."

Aret climbed the stairs to his rooms, not willing to face anyone.

After three nights with no attacks, the Necromancer bid farewell. Though it galled him, Aret swallowed back his anger and thanked the evil wizard for his mock help.

The atmosphere was lighter when the Necromancer finally left. Aret sat alone in his throne room and stared at the red Histerland flag hanging next to the door. It was a blatant reminder of who really ruled this land.

The Necromancer's black coach had barely left the fief when an old man approached the lonely throne. No one obtained an audience with a king without being announced. The halls outside the throne room were swarming with guards and servants, yet here was this old man leaning some of his weight on a wooden walking stick.

Before Aret could call his guards, he saw the gold key dangling below his visitor's short white beard. "Are you the Gatekeeper?"

"Yes," the old man said in a calm, confident voice. "I knew your brother."

The Gatekeeper was a wanted man in Histerland. If this had been a few days ago, Aret would have called his guards and ordered this man captured or killed. Hister and his wizard would have given Aret medals and accolades. What a difference a few days can make.

"I had no idea my brother knew the Gatekeeper."

"I mourn his loss," the Gatekeeper said. "It isn't natural to lose someone so young and vital. Prince Magna was full of passion and an idealism most lose before reaching his age. Is there anything I can do for you?"

Aret looked down at the old man in silence and closed his eyes in thought. This wizard might have been able to remove Magna's curse. Magna would have told Aret he was still grasping at straws. It was too late to dwell on that now.

Finally, Aret said, "Can you give me something to use against the Necromancer? Something to keep us safe from Histerland?"

The Gatekeeper's brow furrowed. "What do you mean?"

"Hister's high necromancer killed my father and brother. I want revenge!" Aret nearly choked on the words.

The old man hesitated. "Your people would suffer if you were to strike openly against Hister. There is no avoiding that."

"I must work in secret then," Aret said, mad with grief, "to undermine their power. There must be something I can do to strike at them!"

The Gatekeeper nodded his head and closed his eyes. For a moment, Aret thought the wizard considered him irrational. Perhaps he was.

At last, the wizard shifted his weight on his cane and raised his head. "I know of a magic suit of armor, quite potent in the right hands. It's not far from here, but this is not something to take on lightly. It is guarded by traps and a mighty beast."

Aret's eyes glazed over with desire, not just for this weapon, but for a quest away from his grim castle. "I must have it."

"Are you sure?" the old man asked. "It will be a dangerous journey. It would not do for Valora to lose a third king. The Valora line would be gone forever."

Aret wondered what would happen to his lands without his family. Who would Hister place on his throne? Perhaps his people would be better off without him.

So much anger and frustration bubbled under his skin. Aret couldn't continue dying a slow death in these walls. He had to do something. "I am sure."

"Very well," the Gatekeeper said. "You are a new king. Tradition dictates that you must personally pay tribute to Hister and the barons whose fiefs surround Valora. Have you made your travels yet?"

"Not yet," Aret answered. "I was planning to leave in the morning, but I can cancel—"

"No," the Gatekeeper interrupted. "Go as planned. I will meet you on your return trip, and we can make a small excursion."

Aret's face relaxed. "Thank you. A room will be prepared for you. You are a secret but honored guest in Valora."

The Gatekeeper smiled but shook his head. "That is very generous, but I can't stay. I will meet you soon."

"Where and when will we meet?" Aret asked.

"I will find you," the old man said.

Aret nodded his head. The Gatekeeper bowed as much as his old bones would allow before marching out the door.

Aret let out a long breath. The hornets in his gut had settled a bit. Whether this quest accomplished anything or not, at least there was something to be done.

Distant thunder echoed off the stone walls. Aret expected someone to ask about the old man leaving his throne room, but no one seemed to notice his visitor coming or going.

CHAPTER 15

TRIBUTE

The next morning, Aret put Purvis in charge of Valora. The old man already ran most of the day-to-day operations of the fief. Aret was still learning lessons Purvis had attempted to teach him as a child. Aret now wished he hadn't given Purvis such a hard time back then. Aret wished he had paid attention to his lessons.

Aret's escort of twelve soldiers was armed and their horses were waiting. Tribute and baggage had been loaded into two carriages. Two soldiers helped Gwendolyn and her handmaiden into a third. Lady Gwendolyn's dress fit snugly at the waist, but flared out at her shoulders and over her bottom. Aret wondered what lucky king might become her husband. There wasn't a man alive who could resist such beauty and intelligence.

Aret and Enri sat opposite the ladies, facing forward in the coach while the ladies faced back. On Aret's order, he and his entourage rode past his waving citizens, down Histerland Road, and out of Valora.

The carriage jumped and jostled at every bump, but the plush interior made the ride comfortable. No matter how peaceful the ride may have been, Aret could not relax. He stared at the countryside rolling by the window.

In the corner of his eye, Aret noticed Gwendolyn studying him. Even her handmaiden made furtive glances at him. Enri was oblivious. He stared out the opposite window grinning. It was his first time traveling outside Valora.

Aret wasn't sure why the ladies were looking at him as they were. He had hoped they would distract him from his grim thoughts with court gossip. It didn't matter. After this trip, the ladies would no longer be his responsibility.

Aret ignored the women as best he could. The road had wound into the forest now. Leaves and branches blurred by the window as the coach bounced from side to side. Aret's eyes unfocused. He mentally prepared to make pleasantries with people he hated more than he ever imagined he was capable.

King Aret heard Gwendolyn's voice in the fringes of his consciousness. "A Histern for your thoughts, Lord."

She was undoubtedly trying to break his silence. He didn't acknowledge her, hoping she would think he hadn't heard. He knew it was rude, but the time for forced pleasantries had not yet arrived. He was her lord. He owed her nothing and he didn't see the point of getting any more attached to her. This would probably be the last time he would spend with her as his ward.

The coach hit a particularly rough bump, and Lady Gwendolyn bounced out of her seat. Aret caught her in his lap. Her white shoulders were soft and supple beneath her embroidered sleeves. Aret had felt other women before, servant girls and serfs, but never a lady. He noticed her staring at him and wondered how long he had been sitting there with her in his arms. He could feel his face getting warm, and Gwendolyn's handmaiden covered her mouth to hide a devilish smirk. Enri made no attempt to hide his amusement.

Aret was horror-stricken by what Lady Gwendolyn must think of him. "My apologies, Milady."

Gwendolyn backed into her own seat and straightened her dress. "Quite alright. I'm happy to have any reaction at all from you on this trip. You've been so quiet."

Aret turned away, looking out the window again.

She added, "I was surprised and pleased that you invited me along."

"You were my brother's. Now you are my responsibility. He really valued you. He told me to trust you and take care of you."

"Really?" An unabashed smile of perfectly white teeth beamed from her lips. "When was this?"

"Once upon a time," he answered. "There are many noblemen in Hister's court. I'm sure there will be a suitor you approve of."

Lady Gwendolyn's smile disappeared, and lines of worry marred her forehead. "If that is what *you* wish, My Lord."

It wasn't the reaction Aret had expected. "Isn't that what *you* wish? I could send you back to your family in Lyon if you prefer; the betrothal to my brother was never consummated, but I thought—"

"A lady has no wishes, My Lord. With your brother gone, I am yours to do with as you please."

Aret was confused. He assumed, with his brother gone, she would want to find a different king to marry her, someone wealthy and powerful. Isn't that what every lady wanted? "What do you want to do, Lady Gwendolyn?"

Lady Gwendolyn looked at her pale hands folded in her lap. "If I did have a say in it, then I would ask to stay in Valora, at least for awhile. I was raised in Lyon and I have visited Hister's city before. The nobles and Hister's favored live in opulence while the rest live in fear and poverty. Valora is the only place in Histerland I have ever been where it's different. Your people work hard, but they are happy and they love you. I want to make sure that never changes."

Aret's heart suddenly sank into his gut. "What would make that change?"

She shook her head, suddenly unsure. "I don't know. Lots of things. External forces … internal—"

"Internal," he interrupted. "You mean me. You don't think I have what it takes to be a good king."

Gwendolyn narrowed her eyes and straightened herself. "You are the proper king of Valora. You have every capability your brother did."

Aret looked back out the window in silence. No matter what she said, he knew she doubted him because he doubted himself as well. She couldn't know that he was trying to protect her, to get her far away from him before it all came crashing down.

Gwendolyn gave an exasperated sigh and looked out the window as well. Her mouth was clenched tight. The handmaiden offered her a handkerchief to dab her moist eyes, but Gwendolyn waved it away.

Enri looked at the handmaiden, and the two servants silently shared the awkwardness of the ride.

Beneath a bridge, two men dipped their stale bread in the river water to soften it enough for eating.

The wiry man grimaced as he chewed. "We'll make a big score someday, Tiny. Mark my words. When we do, we'll eat like kings."

Tiny was an enormous man with a bald, bulbous head. "This food is not so bad, Brownie."

"You'll eat anything," Brownie said. "Once you get the good stuff, you'll never want to go back to this."

Tiny thought for a moment. "Then maybe it would be better not to try better stuff."

Brownie smiled and shook his head. He heard the clip-clop of distant horses and peeked over the ditch. Three coaches sped towards the bridge, escorted by twelve soldiers on horseback.

Tiny picked up his enormous ax, but Brownie waved him back, and they ducked back under the bridge.

"Not even you can take twelve soldiers," Brownie said. "We'll get the next one."

CHAPTER 16

HISTERLAND CITY

Aret and his entourage put on more layers of clothing as the journey progressed. The country around Histerland City was already cold this time of year. The Black Forest around them was said to be haunted by shadowy ghosts and were-creatures, some under the direct control of the Necromancer, others so wild nothing could control them.

On a hill they saw the long, gray walls of Hister's capital city. The stone wall was indistinct in the distance, with powdery snow falling from the sky. More detail became apparent as they neared. The red flags of Histerland hung from ice-covered parapets, and smoke rose from the city's many chimneys. Ragged skeletons hung in cages along the road. Carrion birds had picked the sun bleached bones clean many years ago. Few people dared to cross Hister these days.

Two young boys with red flags rode up to greet Aret's party. One of the boys rode ahead to announce them. The other boy gave a slight bow and led them under icicled city gates. The road dipped under the wall, forming an arched tunnel 15 feet long. The tunnel opened onto the city square.

Sounds of horns and drums neared them, and their guide raised his hand. They stopped momentarily while a parade of black-garbed soldiers marched through the streets. The citizens of Histerland froze in place and gave a feeble cheer. The soldiers marched around a bronze statue of stout Hister. The bronzed king stood on a pedestal with upraised sword. Finally the soldiers marched back the way they had come, and the people of Histerland returned to their business.

Aret's party proceeded to the castle, and lay citizens cast furtive glances at them as they disembarked. Two of Aret's men took a chest out of the coach. Then the carriages continued to the stables.

Without the music of the parade, the streets were deathly quiet. Aret removed his coat and gloves before entering Hister's hall.

A tall soldier with graying hair and a hint of crow's feet greeted him. "I am Verney, high general of Histerland. I saw you fence in the Nationals last year. You're good with a sword."

Aret tried to smile. "Thank you."

"With a little more discipline, there is no doubt you could have gotten first place. I'm truly sad to hear about your family."

Verney was friendly and seemed genuinely so. This was not what Aret had expected from Hister's high general. Behind Hister and the Necromancer, this was the third most powerful man in Histerland and he was chatting about fencing competitions.

"I could never replace my father or Magna," Aret said.

Verney nodded. "Spoken like a true noble. Are you ready to meet High King Hister?"

Aret nodded. "I brought tribute. I hope it is worthy."

High General Verney motioned to an archway. "I'm sure it is. He is ready for you."

Aret nodded. He gave one last look over his shoulder at Verney before marching alone into a dim circular room. A round opening above the throne let in a thin powder of snow from outside. At this time of day, it lit a path for Aret to follow, but also shown in his eyes, obscuring his vision of the high king.

Aret's heart thundered. He had seen Hister from a distance at competitions, but had never actually met him. Hister was a pale little man with a trim black goatee. He was perfectly motionless on his throne, as though carved from the same gnarled wood. The throne seemed to have grown from the ground beneath him. Pronged branches moved away from his arms, and the high king jerked as though waking from a dream. Light glinted off tiny eyes as they focused on Aret. Hister stuck out his chalk white hand. Aret kneeled and cautiously kissed the high king's clammy knuckles. These hands held the reigns of all Aret knew.

"You may rise," Hister said.

Aret stood slowly, saying, "It would please me if you would accept a small offering." Two of Aret's men entered carrying the chest. They opened it, revealing many glass bottles. "Wine from Valora's vineyards, the sweetest in all Histerland. We have sixty cases like this." Aret had brought twice as much tribute as normal. It was expected that he pay for his brother's promotion as well as his own.

Hister gave a thin smile. "You honor me with your gift. I can see my Necromancer was right to have such faith in you. You will be a fine king."

Aret skipped a breath at the mention of the Necromancer.

Hister continued, "We were saddened to hear of your father and then your brother. Tragic … so tragic. They were our loyal allies."

Aret wondered if perhaps Hister was innocent of the crimes against his family. Perhaps the High Necromancer acted without Hister's knowledge. "Thank you, Lord Hister, king of kings."

"Your father was just a child when your grandfather signed a treaty with me." Hister gazed off into the darkness of the chamber. "It doesn't seem that long ago."

"That was over sixty years ago, Sire." Aret said it as much to remind himself as to remind Hister of the passage of time. He was accustomed to seeing his father as an old man. High King Hister was much older and still physically in his prime.

"Was it …?" Hister looked back to his guest. "We will talk more at the feast tonight." He raised a hand and a boy emerged from the shadows. "The page will escort you to your rooms."

Aret bowed once more, saying "I look forward to dinner, Sire."

Aret followed the boy out of the gloom and into the hall to rejoin his party. Aret paused briefly to let out a long breath of air.

Nobles from all over Histerland loitered in the corridors of Hister's castle. Aret's party followed the boy past old paintings. One was scorched as though plucked from a fire, probably plundered from one of Hister's many conquests. From behind a pillar, a man sprang suddenly from his chess board. The man grabbed Gwendolyn before Aret or his men could act. As she hugged the man, Aret realized who it was. "Prince Brigham of Lyon."

Gwendolyn smiled. "My brother."

Aret nodded his head at Prince Brigham, also his sister's husband, who nodded back and introduced the large, wart-faced man sitting on the other side of the chess board. "This is King Bulba, the troll king."

Bulba scooted his chair loudly away from the table and stood. He had stringy black hair and a scaly sheen to his face. "Pleasure to meet you." He bowed and kissed Lady Gwendolyn's hand. "A great pleasure."

Aret's stomach flipped at the site of Bulba's pointed nose pecking Gwendolyn's delicate hand, but Aret remained gracious. "Pleased to meet you."

King Bulba shook Aret's hand vigorously. "You must visit Troll Keep, little king. It isn't far from Valora, much closer than this place. You can see what troll hospitality is like."

Aret wasn't sure if *little king* referred to his height or the size and importance of the lands he ruled. "Thank you, I'll do that." Aret turned his attention back to Prince Brigham. "Is Mimi here with you?"

Prince Brigham raised the corner of his lip. "No. The woman is at home. Sometimes a nobleman has to get away." He winked. "You know what I mean."

Aret scowled, and Gwendolyn looked away, shamed.

Brigham saw their disdain. "You'll understand when you find a queen of your own. Congratulations on your promotion, by the way." Prince Brigham motioned to the chess board. "Perhaps I could interest you in a game of chess. We have plenty of time before the tournament. King Bulba and I are almost finished."

The burly troll at the opposite end of the board did not agree. "Almost done? I don't think so. It's your move, Brigham. Has been since these nobles so conveniently pulled you away."

Brigham turned back to the board. "Of course." In one move, Prince Brigham wiped his competitor's pieces off the board. He then turned to Aret. "Are you ready?"

Bulba kicked his chair over with a grunt and lumbered away.

"Certainly," Aret said, turning to his entourage. "I will find our rooms after the game."

His people bowed and left the two nobles to their game. Aret caught Lady Gwendolyn looking back over her shoulder as they left. Aret wondered if she thought they were going to discuss her future. It must be so exciting to be such a beautiful lady. She would have her pick of kings and princes to marry her. She hadn't seemed excited in the coach. Perhaps it was still too soon after Magna's death.

Prince Brigham eagerly set up the chess board. "First move is yours."

Aret righted his chair. He skillfully moved his game piece, and Brigham followed.

"How is my sister?" Aret asked as he moved another piece.

"She's fine." Brigham answered dispassionately, studying the board and scooting a game piece.

They continued to play, and Aret made conversation as he knocked over Brigham's pawns. "You congratulated me on my kingship like it was a good thing."

"Isn't it?"

"It comes at too high a price." Aret took more of Brigham's pieces from the board.

Brigham smiled. "Sometimes one has to make sacrifices to advance. You got my pawns, but I've got you. Checkmate."

Aret shook his head in disbelief. There was no place on the board he could move his king. Prince Brigham was always beating him. "Thank you," he said. "It's a lesson I will remember."

They both stood. "I look forward to seeing you at dinner," Brigham said.

Aret bowed and made his way down the corridor. A page helped him find a door with a plaque that read *VALORA PARTY* on it. Aret thanked the page and entered the chambers.

He fell onto the bed and clenched his eyes shut. Enri had already laid out his dress clothes for dinner. Aret only had to fake civility through this one evening. He would leave in the morning and forget etiquette for a long while.

Enri interrupted his thoughts, calling him for the joust. Aret didn't look away from the ceiling. "I think I'll skip the tournament."

Enri furrowed his brow. "One of your guardsmen is participating."

Aret sighed, and Enri helped him with his clothes.

CHAPTER 17

DUEL AT DINNER

A ret had an honored seat at the end of the jousting field. The excitement and the cheering crowds took Aret's mind off things, even though his guardsman lost, knocked brutally from his horse in two charges.

The visiting nobles, all but Aret, seemed to be in pleasant spirits when they gathered in the banquet hall. Aret wondered if any of them were faking as much as he was. Aret's boots shuffled over the sawdust on the floor

Aret and Gwendolyn were seated near the entrance. They sat at long rectangular tables arranged in a square around the room. This arrangement left a central area for musicians and poets to expound Hister's greatness. Brigham, seated at the side of the room, laughed at a particularly humorous verse and tossed a piece of bread. The poet plucked it from the sawdust and gobbled it up.

The great fireplace kept the room pleasantly warm. Hister sat at the head of the table, flanked by his high necromancer and high general. Aret was afraid the Necromancer would sense his discontentment. Aret hoped to avoid talking to the old wizard, but knew he couldn't evade him forever.

Hister had a goblet of wine and a plate of food before him, but he never seemed to touch it. The high king stared past the entertainers like they didn't exist.

Their roasted meat entree had a wonderful smell and a flavor Aret had never tasted before.

"You like it?" Lady Gwendolyn inquired.

Aret nodded. "It's good!"

"They flavor it with spices from Hister's eastern provinces." She took a sip of the wine and said, "This, I'm sure you recognize."

Aret smiled with pride and took a swig. "Part of our tribute, no doubt." Aret tore a piece of bread and inspected the torn half as he chewed. "This is the whitest bread I have ever seen." He looked at Gwendolyn. "Even the whitest bread at Castle Valora has visible wheat in it." He motioned with the torn bread. "I'm going to take this back to our miller."

King Bulba interrupted their conversation. He stumbled as though drunk and waved a turkey leg in one hand. Bulba bowed to Aret and winked at Gwendolyn. His tone was a happy one. "King Aret Valora, I must speak with you alone."

Prince Brigham was looking past Gwendolyn at Aret with a curious smile on his face.

Aret nodded. He dabbed his greasy fingers in a bowl of water and wiped them as he stood. They found some measure of privacy by a supporting archway, and Bulba placed a greasy hand on the shoulder of Aret's dress shirt. "I would like to request the hand of your charge, Lady Gwendolyn."

Aret stood in open-mouthed surprise. Lady Gwendolyn watched the minstrels, oblivious that she was the subject of their conversation.

King Bulba saw Aret's hesitation. "She is the most beautiful woman I have ever seen. My castle is lonely, just me, my son, and our servants. We will revere her as a noble queen should be revered. She will want for nothing."

Aret had hoped to receive an offer like this, but now that he actually had one... The thought of Lady Gwendolyn with King Bulba turned his stomach. "I'm sorry," Aret said. "I can't give her hand to anyone at this time. She is still in mourning. My brother's death hit us all very hard."

King Bulba's smile collapsed. "But I thought... " He scowled at Prince Brigham who quickly pretended not to be watching them. "My apologies, King Aret, I meant no disrespect. I hope you will consider my request when the period of mourning is over. You and your party will be heartily welcomed when you visit Troll Keep."

"Thank you," Aret said. "We will do that. It is important for the lords of our region to be friends. After the period of mourning is over, you and your family should visit Valora as well."

Bulba nodded and retreated to his corner of the table.

Aret made his way around the table and confronted Prince Brigham in a hushed voice. "Did you enjoy that?"

"Enjoy what?" Prince Brigham said.

"Making King Bulba the pawn of your sick joke."

"What joke? My sister needs someone to take care of her. The troll king is rich and powerful. He'll reward us both handsomely for her virginal beauty."

Aret stared at the fireplace. He was disgusted at Brigham's logic, but at the same time, it made sense.

"Unless… " Brigham's eyes grew wide as he studied Aret. "You want her for yourself!"

Aret turned his head and looked directly at Brigham's face. "That's ridiculous!"

"No. No, it makes perfect sense. You took your brother's throne and now you want his fiancée as well."

The blazing fireplace seemed to be putting out more heat. Aret was too angry to speak.

"It's only natural," Brigham said. "Your family has claim on her. It is within your right to marry her instead of your brother, if that is what you really want. I'm just looking out for both our interests. Her value is in her purity. We could turn this into a tidy profit for both of us, but not if you go spoiling her value."

Aret pulled Brigham out of the chair by his collar, trying to hold his emotion back, reminding himself where he was.

Brigham seemed to be implying that Aret would despoil Gwendolyn like some common woman, but he hadn't actually said that. Brigham was just being cold and logical, treating Gwendolyn like one of the pawns on his chess board. Aret released Brigham's collar and smoothed the ruffled fabric.

Prince Brigham laughed. He leapt into the center of the tables and hollered over the crowd. "Excuse me, everyone." The musicians stopped. "The new king of Valora is a fencing champion. Perhaps you would all like a little show."

The nobles applauded as Brigham tossed his glove at Aret. The smile never left Brigham's face. The prince's servant brought out two swords.

Aret was tired and cranky. He didn't need much reason to lash out. He climbed over the tables and took one of the swords, testing the sharpness with his finger. Brigham then took the other. They bowed to one another, and Aret immediately swiped the blade at Brigham. Aret was not just tired and cranky, he was also sloppy. Brigham dodged Aret's two strikes before striking out himself.

The point of Brigham's blade came straight at Aret's eye, but instead stung his right ear. Something fell into the sawdust. Gwendolyn screamed. Aret grabbed the side of his head, and his hand came away sticky with blood.

Brigham laughed and jabbed his sword against Aret's throat. Aret had no choice but to drop his weapon and yield.

Brigham waved his sword through the air, and the assembled nobles cheered.

Brigham had beaten him in competition before, but never so easily. The spectators at the tables around Aret were some of the most influential people in all of Histerland. With warmth still dripping from his throbbing ear, Aret feigned a smile before bowing to his opponent. Brigham returned the gesture. The Necromancer clapped his hands, and both combatants bowed to Hister. High General Verney, who had earlier expressed admiration for Aret's swordsmanship, turned away from Aret's easy defeat.

Someone patted Aret on the back as he left the hall, saying, "Good show!" But Aret never looked up to see who it was. Another called after him, "Brigham's good with a sword. Nothing to be ashamed of."

CHAPTER 18

THE QUEST

The sun was barely up when Aret called his entourage together. He wanted to skip breakfast, but his men needed to eat, so he waited in the coach. He didn't want to face the city nobles again.

Gwendolyn was bundled in a wool dress with a fur cloak and hat. As she climbed into the coach, she handed Aret a pastry from the breakfast table.

He reluctantly accepted it. It was sweet, flaky and filled with jellied fruit. Aret was hungrier than he had realized. He nodded to her, saying, "Thank you," and she nodded back.

His wounded ear stung under his warm hat, but not as much as his pride. He had never felt like such a loser before. To Hister, the Necromancer, and even Brigham, he was merely an insignificant noble from a backward province. He would never be anything to them but an expendable plaything… a joke…a *pawn*. He was a fool to think he could strike out at them.

Halfway home, the coach slowed down, and Aret's guards shouted, "Out of the way."

Aret poked his head out of the cab. In their path was an aged man on a brown horse. He held the reins of a second horse, a white stallion. The old man remained where he was, staring calmly at the oncoming coach.

At last, a quest to steal Aret from his troubles. He slapped the roof next to the coachman. Before the carriage had come to a complete stop, Aret was already out the door. Aret's companions regarded this man as a stranger, but Aret knew him.

The Gatekeeper motioned to the white horse. The animal's warm breath snorted in a mist from his nostrils. "Are you ready?" the old wizard asked.

Aret patted the familiar warhorse's sinewy neck and scratched his ear. "Snow!"

"I obtained horses from your stables for our journey," the Gatekeeper said. "I hope you don't mind."

Aret simply smiled and climbed onto his dead brother's favorite steed. Two guardsmen rode up close. "Your Highness! Who is this? Where are you going?"

Aret waved them away. "Continue on. I will meet up with you back at Valora."

Gwendolyn hung her head out of the carriage and watched King Aret ride away with the stranger. Aret enjoyed the thought of them all wondering what he was up to. It was better to be a mystery than a fool.

Aret and the Gatekeeper rode south, and the weather warmed considerably. It felt good riding free again, out of the carriage and the constant expectations of court. They bounced down the road, and the breeze in their faces brought the scent of roadside flowers. The wind caressed Aret's short brown hair, but stung his bandaged ear.

They stopped to let the horses drink from a stream. The water flowed from the mountains to their south. After the long, sweaty ride, they found relief in the cool water. Aret was free.

Clean and refreshed, the Gatekeeper reached into a pocket and pulled out a flexible, palm-sized tube. The old wizard squeezed out a gel and applied it gently to Aret's wounded ear. "This ointment will prevent infection."

Aret didn't completely understand the purpose of the balm, but it was soothing. The old man covered Aret's ear with a fresh bandage.

"Thank you, Gatekeeper."

"Call me Gabriel."

"Gabriel," Aret repeated. It seemed strange to be so familiar with this legendary wizard.

Tired of riding, they walked the horses down the road. They led them over a bridge. A wiry man in drab peasant garb blocked their path.

"Stand aside," Aret said. He was accustomed to being obeyed.

The wiry man sneered and brandished a dagger. "I don't think so."

A shadow behind them alerted Aret and the Gatekeeper to a stout, seven foot giant with a bulbous head and a colossal ax.

"Drop your valuables!" the wiry man demanded.

"Never!" Aret grabbed the hilt of his sword, but the Gatekeeper, Gabriel, put his hand on Aret's arm before he could draw it.

The old man urged, "Remain calm. They don't want to hurt us. They just want money." Despite his advanced age, Gabriel's knotted hand was surprisingly strong.

The giant's shadow loomed behind them, and the wiry man pointed his dagger at Aret, saying, "Listen to the old man."

The wiry rogue patted Aret's loose clothes and pulled out his money bags. He then groped over the old man and saw the gold key around his neck. The thief backed away in awe. "Alright, Tiny. We got what we need. You guys are free to go."

The ironically named Tiny looked to his companion and said, "What about his sword and their horses?"

"Let them go," the thin man insisted, not taking his eye off the Key. The thief apparently had some idea of its significance, even though the old wizard seemed as powerless as any other victim.

Aret's eyes burned hatred back at the escaping thieves, but Gabriel pulled him to the horses. The old wizard put his foot in his horse's stirrup and groaned as he hefted his leg over the saddle. Aret mounted in one smooth motion, and they continued on their journey.

After a long silence, Aret eyed Gabriel with accusing eyes. He was sick of being humiliated everywhere he went. It was one thing to be debased by kings and nobles, but now even lowly thieves got the better of him! "You are supposed to be a powerful wizard, *Gabriel*!" He emphasized the familiar name. This man didn't deserve a title. "Why didn't you do something back there?"

"They didn't take anything of real value," Gabriel said. "A little money, nothing to a king. You must learn when to act … and what is important enough to fight for. That was not the time."

CHAPTER 19

RIDDLES

Aret and Gabriel trotted their steeds into the maze of mountains. Tumbling stones and rocks from the peaks above startled the horses. A wild gryphon perched on a high cliff with outstretched wings. From this distance, the creature appeared to be a small housecat with an eagle's wings stuck to its back. Aret knew the size of the creature was more comparable to his horse.

Gabriel raised his hand and pulled back the reins. Aret halted Snow on the narrow pass behind the old man, asking, "Why have we stopped?"

Gabriel only smirked and dismounted with a groan. He ran his hand along the almost vertical rock wall as if looking for something. At last he stepped back and quoted an old legend, "*Opensezame.*" The section of rock in front of him faded away. Gabriel then turned to Aret with a proud smile.

Eyes in the darkness reflected the light, and before Aret could warn him, a cat-like paw sprang from the secret chamber and pinned the old man.

Aret drew his sword, but the Sphinx stopped him in his tracks with a look from her hauntingly human eyes. Curly brown hair framed her beautiful maiden's face and hung over her thick lion's neck. A scaly tail slithered playfully behind the colorful feathered wings which adorned her back like a royal cloak.

"You would be wise to stay where you are," she said. "If you startle me, I may accidentally twitch my toes and snap your friend's neck."

Gabriel's head poked out between the Sphinx's toes. "Do as she says. We are safe until we have our riddle."

The Sphinx looked down at the tiny old man between her claws and cocked her head. "Yes. You get a riddle. But if you fail to answer correctly… I will give you one chance to turn back."

"No!" Perhaps Aret should have hesitated, Gabriel looked so vulnerable there under her paw, but they had not come all this way for nothing. "We will not turn back."

The Sphinx smiled. "Very well. I am invisible, liked in summer, hated in winter. I can be gentle or violent. What am I?"

The riddle came so quick, and Aret hadn't been ready. He called back every word in his mind. It was hard to concentrate on games when their lives were at stake.

A gentle breeze picked up speed around the mountains, sending a chill up Aret's back. If it was warmer, such a breeze would be welcome and refreshing. "The wind," it occurred to him. "The wind is invisible. It can blow gentle or hard. It is cool and refreshing in the hot summer months, but steals your warmth in the winter."

The maiden Sphinx scrunched her nose. "You answered the first riddle correctly, but it was the easiest."

"First?" old Gabriel said from beneath the Sphinx's paw. "We answered your riddle, now let us pass."

The Sphinx grimaced. "There are *three* riddles."

"I've never heard this rule before," Gabriel said, still defiant despite his vulnerable position.

"You want by?" the Sphinx said. "You answer three riddles… I always carry you forward. I make you grow, give you wisdom, but kill you all. What am I?"

Aret furrowed his brow and let his sword arm hang limp. A horse carried you forward. He supposed it could kill its rider, but did it give you wisdom? One was taller on a horse; was that the same as growing? He looked down at Gabriel helplessly.

Gabriel frowned. He knew Aret was beaten. "Time," Gabriel said.

The Sphinx gasped.

Aret stared down at the old man, still perplexed.

Gabriel explained, "Time carries us forward, makes us grow, gives us wisdom, but eventually our time is up."

"Cheater!" the Sphinx spat. "You gave him the answer!"

Aret still didn't understand what the time of day had to do with all those things.

Still brave despite the tightening toes around his neck, Gabriel said, "You never said I couldn't answer the riddles. After all, the two of us came here together."

"Well you can't!" the Sphinx hissed. She stared into Aret's soul, and a smile slowly crept across her face. Almost too fast to understand, she chirped, "I serve the dead and hurt the living." she squinted. "Especially the one who wants me most. I am made hot but served cold. What am I?"

"Can you repeat that?" Aret asked.

Gabriel's laughter broke his concentration.

The Sphinx hissed down at the old man under her paw. "What's so funny? Too easy?"

Gabriel tried to compose himself. "What burns in your own heart, Aret?"

The Sphinx gnashed her teeth at the old man. "No hints!"

Aret pondered. What burned in his heart and was, or would be, served cold? "Vengeance! Revenge!"

The Sphinx backed off of Gabriel and circled, thinking intently with her scaly tail undulating behind her. "In the last hundred years, no one has ever answered my riddles correctly. I don't know what to do."

Revenge had been the answer to the riddle. It burns hot and is dished out cold, but Aret wasn't quite sure what to make of the other things the Sphinx had said.

"We answered your riddles," Aret said. "Why don't you just let us pass?"

The Sphinx looked up thoughtfully and took a deep breath. "No. I think I'll kill you anyway." Fire issued from her jaws. Flames washed over Aret, who shielded his eyes with his hands. When the flames passed, he was astonished to find himself unhurt. The grass at his feet remained a pale green, but was scorched black a foot away.

The Sphinx was also surprised to see him unharmed. Aret charged the Sphinx before she fully realized what had happened. Aret thrust his sword into her broad chest. She rolled away, but not before he could stab at her chest again. She swiped Aret head over shoulders into the dust. He knew how to take a fall, but briefly lost hold of his sword. Aret quickly retrieved it from the ground and was back on his feet, panting with exertion and adrenaline.

The Sphinx held her bleeding chest with one paw in an oddly human manner, looking down at the gushing wound with surprise and disbelief. She spread her wings and looked at Aret with a child's betrayal on her face. "Cheaters!" she wailed as she flapped erratically off to die amid the mountain cliffs.

Aret helped Gabriel stand. "The fire. You protected me with a spell?"

"Of course," Gabriel said. "I didn't travel all this way to watch you burn up."

CHAPTER 20

MAGIC ARMOR

A ret followed the old wizard into the cave. The floor was littered with gold and jewels. "Look at all this!"

"We are not here for gold," Gabriel said. "This is what we want." He pointed at a dull set of armor and mail on a mannequin.

"This?" Aret took up the ancient scabbard and pulled at the sword hilt, but it was stuck, seemingly rusted in place.

"Let me help you put it on," Gabriel said.

"You expect me to wear this?"

The old man pulled clunky mail pants up to Aret's waist and slipped the hooded scale shirt over his shoulders. He followed this with a tattered, moth eaten tunic. Within the layers of the tunic, random strips of metal were visible. The mail was stiff and baggy. The scales pinched Aret's skin.

Gabriel lowered a gorget and spaulders over Aret's head, allowing it to rest on his neck and shoulders. This was probably intended to be flexible at the gap between the neck and shoulders, but was corroded into one solid piece of metal. Straps buckled dull metal plates over his elbows and the front of his thighs, and the wizard fastened the scabbard around Aret's waist. Oversized boots and gloves of cracked leather completed the costume.

Aret's arms were frozen at his sides, but he was able to bend his head forward slightly over the gorget and look down at himself. "I can't move."

"One moment." Gabriel groaned and held his back as he bent down to pull a dull triangle of metal out from under the gold and jewels at their feet. He rolled the straps of the shield up Aret's arm, then raised the mail hood over Aret's head.

"I can't be seen in this," Aret said. "I will be a laughing stock!"

Gabriel only smiled, slowly lowering the dingy, dented helmet over Aret's head.

Aret bent his arms with a grinding of metal on metal. His breathing seemed stifled in the helmet, and the cave was only visible through tiny eye slits. "*This* is my powerful weapon?"

The tarnished scales rattled of their own accord, and the suit vibrated around him. Aret felt his heart seize momentarily as metal ribs within the tunic tightened around his chest. Something felt like it was crawling through the fabric, and Aret feared the armor was going to crush him in its embrace.

Rust shook loose from the metal, and the gleaming gold scales tightened snugly around Aret's frame, contouring around his muscles like a second skin. The gold gryphon of Valora flashed on the chest and shield. For a brief moment Aret felt invincible, but was overtaken with dizziness and stumbled to the ground.

Aret opened his eyes and turned his head. He brushed his cheek, and jewels from the floor fell away from his face. Gabriel must have removed the helmet so Aret could breathe. The scale mail now had an organic look, like golden reptile skin, and the tunic had stitched itself together, a brilliant royal purple. Gabriel helped Aret to his feet. The armor weighed Aret down, and he felt weak.

The old man took a sheet of mail and an elaborate saddle off of a wooden rack. He stuffed it into a burlap sack along with a headpiece and brass horseshoes before heading for the exit.

"What about all this treasure?" Aret asked. "We could buy a revolution with all this."

"No," Gabriel said. "Follow me and don't touch anything."

Aret didn't like taking orders, but he followed the old man into the overcast afternoon. He had heard enough stories about cursed and booby trapped treasure. They crossed the threshold, and Aret turned to feel solid rock where the cave entrance had been.

Terrified whinnying startled them. Two gryphons circled the horses. The horses kicked at their assailants, but couldn't defend themselves from all sides at once and were especially unequipped to defend themselves from the sky. While Snow was distracted by one gryphon, another lifted their brown horse into the air and dropped it onto the ground, splintering its bones.

Aret raised his mail hood and pulled a polished ivory sword from his new scabbard. He charged to his horse's defense. One of the gryphons met his charge. Its beak snapped at him, but couldn't get past his new shield. The gryphon flapped into the air, trying to get above Aret's defense, but Aret sliced the creature from neck to gut with one slash. It rolled aside and flopped on the ground.

A winged shadow called Aret's attention to the creature's mate. It was a tiny cat in the sky that grew rapidly with its wings folded back. It dove its steel hard beak straight at Aret, building speed as it whistled towards him. Aret only had time to raise his arm. The creature's beak cracked against the shield as if it had hit a solid wall. Its neck snapped as it flipped over Aret, who felt no impact at all.

King Aret Valora plopped his hind end on the ground next to the dead gryphon, panting heavily.

Snow's nostrils still flared, and his wide eyes scanned for danger. Gabriel whispered in the horse's ear with a soothing voice and caressed Snow's twitching neck. The animal calmed and his breathing slowed.

Without altering the soothing tone of his voice, Gabriel looked to Aret. "I see you have discovered the advantages of the magic armor."

"Yes. Definitely... But I'm so tired."

"It isn't quite ready yet," Gabriel explained. "Bonding with it has put a strain on your life magic."

"Bonding?"

"It won't drain you again," the wizard said. "Each piece of the armor is enchanted. The scale mail was the skin of a dragon.

The shield, as you've seen, disperses any force that hits it. Despite appearances, the sword isn't sharp; it slices by magic. Few things can resist it. It can only be drawn from its scabbard when wearing the leather gauntlets on your hands. If lost, the sword can be called home."

Aret stood. "You've done me a great service. The Necromancer will pay."

Gabriel continued in his quiet calm. "You have a great weapon, but vengeance alone will not free your people. Remember the Sphinx's riddle? *Revenge serves the dead and hurts the living, especially the person who wants it most.*"

"What are you saying? That I shouldn't use the armor now that I've got it?"

"It's yours to do with as you please. I'm only suggesting you use it wisely." Gabriel looked to the dead horse. "We should get out of these mountains before nightfall. May I ride with you?"

"Certainly."

They loaded the canvas bag on Snow, and Aret swung his armored leg over the saddle. He then lifted Gabriel by the arm, helping the old man mount behind him.

CHAPTER 21

RETURN JOURNEY

Fed, brushed, and refreshed, Snow pounded against the dirt road in a sheet of golden scales under an elaborately carved ivory saddle. The horse's headpiece was adorned with brass antlers, making it look like Aret and Gabriel were riding a giant buck deer. The sound of Snow's hooves against the road was drowned out by a hundred more coming towards them: twenty-five Histerland troops on horseback. Aret slowed Snow to a stop.

Gabriel tapped Aret on the shoulder. "I think we should get off the road."

"I am a nobleman," Aret said. "I have nothing to fear." He dismounted and instructed Gabriel to walk Snow into the trees. Aret put on his silver helmet and waited in the middle of the road.

The soldiers slowed and halted a few feet before Aret. Their leader looked down at him. "Get out of the road," he commanded. "We are on urgent business for King Hister."

"What business?" Aret asked.

"We don't have time for this." The commander dismounted and raised his short wide blade. Aret drew the ivory sword from its jeweled scabbard and cleaved the man's blade in two. Aret then impaled the soldier's heart with the magic blade. Two more soldiers dismounted. They came at Aret, followed by four more.

Aret looked into the trees with a smile of pride, but found Gabriel wasn't even watching. The old man was sitting on a tree stump and eating a cracker from their supplies.

Aret shook his head with bewilderment. Ten soldiers fell by his hand, and the rest finally retreated.

Aret wiped the crimson from his ivory blade, and Gabriel emerged from the woods. Aret removed his helmet, beaming proudly. "Did you see me? Twenty-five trained soldiers routed by one man!"

"I saw a completely needless display of violence." Gabriel fished through the dead commander's leather tunic and found a copy of his orders.

"Needless?" Aret said. "All I did was ask them a question. They could have answered me instead of attacking. Where were they off to in such a hurry?"

Gabriel cackled. "Hister's rough tax policies finally went too far. They were reinforcements for Vincennes. Apparently the peasants there rebelled, took over the castle, and locked themselves away."

Aret was horrified. "Peasants took over the castle! Don't they respect their noble lords?"

"Their *noble lords* were living in luxury while they starved. Perhaps they thought they could govern themselves better."

Aret chuckled. "Peasants governing themselves?"

"It's been done successfully in other places, but I'm afraid the time is not yet ripe for it here. You need educated peasants for it to work."

"*Educated peasants?*" Aret had never thought peasants capable of being educated, and the cost of trying to send them all for schooling seemed wasteful. They didn't need schooling to do their jobs.

Gabriel went on, "Peasant rebellions happen somewhere in Gaul every few years or so. The peasants will eat and drink themselves sick while Histerland sends in reinforcements. At least perhaps you've afforded them an extra day of freedom."

Brownie and Tiny sat under their favorite bridge. Brownie sorted coins into three piles. He placed a coin in one pile, saying,

"One for Lyon." Then he said, "One for you," placing a coin in the pile next to Tiny. Tiny smiled a cherubic grin at the sight of his growing pile. Brownie then placed *two* coins in his own pile, saying, "One for me."

Tiny's giant hand grabbed Brownie's thin wrist as the coins fell. "Why is your pile bigger than mine?"

Brownie was worried for a moment, but then smiled confidently. "I don't know what you mean. They're the same size." Tiny looked unconvinced, and Brownie added, "You watched me counting the whole time, right?"

The big man nodded and released Brownie's arm.

"You hear that?" Brownie peeked above the bridge, seeing two cloaked men on a white horse. "Easy pickings. Get your ax ready."

It was their standard tactic. As the travelers trotted over the bridge, Tiny strutted into their path and raised his ax high. The horseman pulled back the reins, halting his steed. Behind the travelers, Brownie brandished his daggers, cutting off their escape. "Hand over your money and you won't be hurt."

The man riding in front put on a silver helmet and tossed his cloak to the ground, revealing gleaming armor over golden scale mail.

Brownie had never seen anything like it. "Leave the armor too." It would be worth a fortune, even if it were only ceremonial. Nothing so compact would be of any use against Tiny's ax.

The knight gracefully slid his foot over the saddle and dropped to the ground. Tiny grinned, showing his four good teeth as he lumbered toward their victim.

The old man remained on the horse and looked back at Brownie, who pointed his dagger at him and said, "Pay attention, Gramps. Pay up or you'll be next."

The corner of the old man's mouth rose into a knowing smile, and Brownie's eyes grew wide with fear and recognition.

Tiny raised his ax high with arms larger than most men and swung down with all his might. The knight casually raised his shield and the ax stopped suddenly against it. Tiny grunted with the impact and began to raise the heavy ax again. Before he could swing it, the knight swiped an ivory sword through the air, and the ax blade fell to the dirt, leaving only a stick in the giant's hands.

Tiny grimaced and ran down the road howling with fear. The knight gave chase, and Brownie charged after them, screaming, "Leave him alone!"

Brownie had forgotten the old man, but the old man had not forgotten him. Their intended victim tossed his cloak and it whipped around Brownie. It squeezed his arms and legs, forcing him to the ground. The more Brownie struggled, the tighter the fabric squeezed.

The knight gave chase to Tiny for a time, but the giant hid in the trees. The big guy was faster than one would expect when properly motivated. The knight returned to the bridge. Brownie was helpless, trapped in the old man's cloak. The old man was out of sight.

"Gatekeeper!" the knight shouted. "Where are you?"

Brownie had been correct. The old man really was the Gatekeeper. No wonder these men had defeated them so easily.

"Not so loud!" the Gatekeeper yelled. He tossed up three bags of coins from under the bridge, all the plunder Brownie and Tiny had worked so hard for. The old wizard then climbed over the ridge with a helping hand from the knight.

Brownie squirmed. His fingers could feel the hilt of his dagger, but he could barely even breath in the constricting fabric, let alone shift his arm.

"I found some interesting things under there." The old man tossed a document to the knight.

"They must have mugged a courier from our brother king," the knight said. "We should kill them and be done with it."

Brownie held his breath. He had always known he would come to a bad end. The life of a thief could not be a long one.

The Gatekeeper shook his head. "Look closer. They didn't steal this. It was given to them. They work for Lyon. A portion of their ill-gotten gains goes back to King Lyon." The Gatekeeper loaded the largest bag of coins onto the white horse. "I assume the larger bag was Lyon's take. We can find much better uses for this."

Brownie winced, knowing the large pile was, unfairly, supposed to be his portion. The two thieves would be lucky to keep anything at all.

The knight whispered to the wizard, and Brownie struggled to hear. "But Lyon and Valora are bonded by marriage. This is one of Valora's supply routes. Valorans would be the primary victims."

The Gatekeeper nodded. "Exactly."

Brownie had assumed these strangers worked for one of the royal families. It seemed they had some connection to Valora.

There was a pause before the knight said, "I should have paid more attention to Purvis's lessons. I should kill them and take all our money back!"

Again, the conversation turned to his death, and Brownie was completely at their mercy. The white-bearded wizard crouched next to him. The Key, symbol of the old man's title and power hung over Brownie. "Lyon's take is now ours," the Gatekeeper said. "You thieves can keep your portion as long as you agree to work for us."

"What do you mean?" the knight asked, and Brownie also wondered what the old man was getting at. Whatever it was, he knew no good could come of it. At least it might be a chance to stay alive.

"They will no longer steal from Valorans, or peasants. They will only steal from Hister's men and Lyon."

Brownie shook his head and yelled in raspy bursts of breath. "Hister's men would kill us. Lyon comes to collect their take every week. They'll kill us too if we don't give it to them. Even if we could stay ahead of Lyon's men, Hister's men are too dangerous to prey upon."

The Gatekeeper smiled. "I'll bet you are crafty enough to think of something. If you honor your agreement, then you will have protection." The old man nudged the money bag. "And much greater rewards. What is it you want more than money?" The Gatekeeper studied him, and Brownie averted his eyes as the old man continued. "A place to call home, perhaps? Respect, perhaps?"

No one spoke. Was the old wizard saying they wouldn't get paid for the extra risk? A home would be nice, Brownie supposed, but it was nothing without money, and respect would never belong to someone like Brownie if he couldn't pay for it. The Gatekeeper and his knight looked down at him and waited. Hearing no answer, the old man ran his finger over Brownie's head and plucked out one of his short brown hairs.

"Ow! Hey!" It hadn't really hurt, but had shocked him. Brownie couldn't even resist this simple defilement. What devilish things could a wizard do with one of his hairs?

The old man studied the invisible filament in his fingers. "Well?"

At last Brownie said, "Do we have any other choice?"

With a single yank, the Gatekeeper pulled his cloak free. Brownie sat up rubbing his arms. His daggers lay free on the ground next to him, but what good were they?

The old man was stern. "Lay low for a time. We will check in on you soon."

"How will you know where to meet us?" Brownie asked.

The old man smiled as the knight helped him back on their white horse. "We will find you."

Brownie shuddered. The old man and the knight rode away without another word, leaving Brownie alone in the dirt. Tiny would not rejoin him until their intended victims passed the horizon line.

They had left Brownie alive, and the Gatekeeper hadn't even cursed him. What was to stop him and Tiny from taking what they had left and finding a new path to haunt? Was an old wizard like the Gatekeeper naive enough to think they would follow his orders with no threat, or at least a more realistic promise of reward? Perhaps Brownie *had* been cursed and didn't even know it. He shivered. Wizards were scary.

Aret removed his silver helmet as they rode, revealing the glittering scale hood. "Why would Lyon steal from her allies… and why did you instruct those men to steal for us… and from Hister?"

"The nobility has never been honorable."

Aret looked at the old man behind him, his mouth open with insult and astonishment.

"There are exceptions," Gabriel added. "What I mean is that it often takes unscrupulous actions to stay in power. Kings are always looking for an advantage, any advantage. Treaties and agreements mean nothing to them unless they are caught breaking them, their hands in the cookie jar, so to speak. Hister is the worst of them."

Aret turned away. "I'm not convinced of that. He's our king. How do I know the High Necromancer didn't act alone against my family?"

"Didn't you notice how strangely Hister acted when you met him? He is under the Necromancer's spell."

Aret pulled hard on the reins and Snow turned around. "We must free him!"

"No," the old man said. "He fell under the Necromancer's spell of his own free will, decades ago. The Necromancer has always been the real ruler of Histerland."

Aret looked to the sky. "Must every piece of my life be a lie?"

Gabriel put his hand on Aret's shoulder. "Think about it. You know it's true."

Aret let out a resigned breath, and some of the tension left his muscles. He steered Snow back to Valora.

The roads of Valora were quiet so late at night. The serfs were sleeping in their beds. Occasionally, a voice was heard from within one of the thatch cottages. Candles still flickered in some of the castle windows. The castle itself was a dark silhouette against a midnight-blue sky and billions of stars.

Aret paused to take in the site of his home.

Gabriel grunted as he swung his leg over the saddle and dropped to the ground. He held himself steady against Snow while retrieving his walking stick. The long ride had not been easy on the old man.

Aret looked down at him. "Where are you going?"

"I have business to attend to."

"Please, Gatekeeper, we have been riding a long time and it's late. Stay with us tonight. We owe you."

The Gatekeeper shook his head. "Thank you, but no. I have obligations, just as you do, and my time, I fear, is short. I have spent my time unwisely, preoccupied with the Necromancer instead of with my family or finding a pupil. Now, it may be too late to make up that lost time. Don't make the same mistakes I have, Aret. Fight for what you believe in, but don't let it consume your life."

Time. That had been the Sphinx's second riddle. The Gatekeeper was not as sickly as Aret's father had been, but he was even older. Did death come to wizards as it did all men? Aret shuddered at the thought of his father on his deathbed.

"You have a friend in Valora, Gabriel."

Gabriel's face lifted, and he gripped Aret's hand. "Perhaps, if we meet again, I will be able to stay longer."

Aret nodded to the wizard, and the old man bowed before hobbling off into the orchards. There was a flickering light behind the trees and a distant rumble of thunder. Gabriel was gone.

Snow trotted quietly into the stable. Aret dismounted and walked his horse to his stall. He was surprised to find Rowen asleep in the straw. Rowen's scarred face was a grim reminder of the Necromancer's crimes against Aret's family.

Rowen opened his eyes sluggishly at the sound of the gate opening. "King Aret?"

Aret bound his cloak tightly around his shiny new armor and spoke in a whisper. "Yes, it's me. I'm glad you are here. You can help me, but we must be quiet."

Together, they removed Snow's new armor and hid it in a locked compartment beneath the horse's stall. The compartment was then covered over with straw, hiding it from view. Rowen brushed Snow while Aret snuck up a hidden passage.

This was the same hidden passage his brother had once taken on his secret adventures. The passageway had been built by the first Valoras to provide a quick escape. Those were troubled times, and after so many generations of peace, the passage had been forgotten by almost everyone.

A dark stairway ended in a chamber hidden behind Aret's bedroom closet. Here he dropped his cloak, unbuckled armor plates, and slid off his gold mail. Aret was happy to let his skin breath. For now, he left the armor in pieces on the stone floor. The next morning he would hang it over a mannequin and store it properly. A wooden panel opened into the closet of the master bedroom.

The room was cold. The servants hadn't lit the fireplace since they didn't know Aret would be back that night. He could call them, but decided not to wake anyone and loaded kindling into the fireplace himself. It only took a few strikes of the flint to spark it to life. The water basin was also empty, but he could wash in the morning. He dropped the rest of his garments on the floor and stepped from the cold stone floor onto the bear-skin rug. He then buried himself in the many layers of quilts and skins on the bed. He shivered once then closed his eyes. The warmth of his body filled the blankets.

Tomorrow, his revenge began.

CHAPTER 22

A PLAN FORMS

A feminine gasp woke Aret. Sunlight poured in his window. Camille bowed in the doorway. "Lord! I had no idea you were back. I'll bring your breakfast." She hesitated and, instead of leaving, shut the door behind her. Camille approached the large bed and leaned her hands on either side of Aret's legs. Gravity tugged at her blouse, revealing the tan, smooth cleavage above her corset. "Or perhaps you need to build an appetite first."

The gesture had no effect on Aret. He shifted his weight and rolled on his side. Larger concerns weighed down his desire. "Breakfast will be fine."

She didn't move away and he could feel her staring at him.

Her voice was hesitant, full of doubt and something like fear. "But I thought… after a long trip, you used to… "

He finally looked at her, and his heart softened. He grabbed her hand. "I know, but things are different now. My father and brother, they… I am king now. We can't."

Her eye's glistened with moisture. She stood and curtseyed. "Of course, Milord, I will bring your breakfast."

Aret rolled back on his side and clutched the pillow. What had she expected? She was a servant and he was king. They had started playing as little more than children, learning the arts of love together. Aret would return from his travels with new games to play. It was harmless fun. She must have known it wouldn't last.

Purvis and Enri interrupted Aret's thoughts. Young Enri immediately went to the closet while Purvis chastised Aret. "You should have told us you were back. We would have prepared a proper reception. The servants are going insane trying to anticipate you."

Aret's bare feet hit the fur rug. He slipped on a robe and ran his hand along his chin. "I need a shave."

Another servant, not Camille, wheeled in a cart of food and filled the water basin.

"I'll fetch the barber," Enri said. He held two shirts. "Which shirt and cape would you like for today? Would you like the crown from the vault?"

"Not right now, thank you," Aret said. "Ceremony will wait for another day, as will my shave. I'll dress myself today."

Enri bowed, covered Aret's chamber pot with a handkerchief, and carried it away.

Purvis looked at the right side of Aret's face and shook his head. "At least you kept your wound clean. I wouldn't be surprised if young men of Valora started snipping the tips of their ears to be like their king. What were you doing, taking off alone with some stranger? Do you know how worried we were? Like it or not, you're not as free as you used to be. You are king, the last of the Valoras."

Purvis finally paused for a breath before continuing. "Speaking of which, we need to discuss potential queens. There are several promising candidates that would strengthen Valora's bonds with neighboring baronies and Histerland. Now that the period of mourning is over, Lady Gwendolyn is on the market again as well, a fine woman."

"Lady Gwendolyn?" Aret said. "She was my brother's!"

"Exactly," Purvis said. "And now she is our responsibility. If we don't find a place for her soon, King Lyon may be insulted. Then again, he might be happy to have her back. A fine lady like that is quite a bargaining chip."

"I don't want to talk about this right now," Aret said. "I didn't get back until very late. Why don't you get one of our Histerland maps out, perhaps an old one too, from before Hister took over. I think it is time we started our lessons again."

"Yes!" Purvis said. His face brightened with new hope for his king. "Yes. A great idea, My Lord."

Aret wondered if Purvis would be so enthusiastic if he knew what motivated his king's newfound studiousness. "But first," Aret added, "Summon Sheriff Morto."

"At once, Lord Aret."

Once Purvis left, Aret pushed his way through his wardrobe, looking for something subdued to wear. He paused for a moment and caressed the back wall, remembering the magical weapon on the other side.

Sheriff Morto entered and bowed. "I'm glad to see you safe, King Aret. I was worried when I heard you left your party."

"You used to follow my brother on his late-night adventures," Aret stated, straight to business.

"Yes," Morto said.

"You know who his friends were, then?"

"Yes." Morto seemed reluctant, unsure what Aret may ask of him. "One of them is still in our jail. They've been keeping a low profile, but I've been watching them. If you like, I can round them up again."

"No. I want to know who they are. Take me to the man in our prison."

"Of course, Sire."

Aret finished dressing and followed Morto downstairs. They passed Lady Gwendolyn and her ladies in the hall. "Lord Aret," she said. "I must speak to you."

Aret paused, unsure what to say. He knew she would want an explanation of his behavior, and, to his surprise, he cared what she thought. "We can't stop now. Perhaps tonight—"

In an unladylike manner, she didn't accept the simple *no* her lord had offered. "It is urgent, a private matter."

Her face was so grave, so vulnerable. Aret's other responsibilities faded to nothing. But then her eyes gradually drifted to the right side of his face, to his wounded ear.

"I have business now," Aret said. "We can talk later."

Aret and Morto continued past the ladies into a seldom-used corridor. The walls were sturdy stone. The only light was from

Morto's lamp and sunlight from narrow window slits in the empty cells.

Aret wondered what Lady Gwendolyn had wanted so urgently. Perhaps his behavior had finally convinced her it was time for her to leave Valora. Perhaps she had met a suitor in Histerland City after all. Perhaps Lyon had sent for her return. Or perhaps, like everyone else, she just wanted an explanation. Aret didn't owe her any. He was king. His hand gently rubbed at his wounded ear.

Mack, owner of Mack's Tavern and Inn, grabbed the bars of his cell when he heard them coming. Prison life had not been too hard on the innkeeper. His stomach still hung over his pants. When he recognized Aret in the dim light, he bowed with his gut almost hitting the ground. "I knew you would come. The Valoras have always been just rulers."

Aret made no expression. "You have been accused of conspiracy. It is said you helped murder my brother."

"No!" Mack said. "I would never hurt Prince Magna."

"Stolen property was found in your cellar, property of Histerland."

"Noble King," Mack said. "Your brother and his allies used our cellar to stash stolen property and to house rebels on the run. We would never hurt him. You must believe me!"

"So you know my brother's allies?"

The stout man shuddered. "They were a secretive bunch. I never knew anyone but Magna."

Aret couldn't help but smile. He could tell the man was lying. "Too bad. As is often the case when a new king comes to power, an amnesty is given to all the prisoners. I am planning such an amnesty, but I could make it conditional in your case. You would keep all your property if… "

"I don't know anything more than I've told you," Mack insisted.

Aret had to respect the man's loyalty. Mack wouldn't be the only one to suffer if he was convicted. His wife would lose any claim on their property and livelihood.

Aret nodded and led Morto back down the corridor in silence. Once Morto had pushed the heavy door shut, Aret instructed, "Release the prisoner and inform him that all his property is restored to him."

Aret returned to his room that night. The servants had relit the fireplace. He sighed as he shut his oak door and let his shoulders slump against it. He had taken a few steps, but still didn't have a clear plan. He had an amazing weapon, but he couldn't use it openly.

He jumped at the soft, feminine voice that interrupted his thoughts. "I apologize for my impertinence, Lord."

"Lady Gwendolyn!" Aret stood tall. "What are you doing in my room?"

"I had to speak to you privately. It won't take long, but you need to be warned—"

"Warned?"

"Your father and brother, it can't be a coincidence. Hister had them both murdered."

Aret closed his eyes and let his shoulders relax again. "I know."

"But Hister couldn't have known about Magna, not unless someone here told him. Someone in Valora betrayed them. It didn't matter before; nothing could be done to bring them back. But when I saw you acting strange... " She looked away. "You may not have much use for me, King Aret, but I don't want anything bad to happen to you, or to Valora."

What did she mean, *no use for her*? She was his responsibility. Hadn't he shown her every kindness? What had caused her to be so annoyed with him?

"People are watching you," she said.

"Who betrayed them?" Aret asked.

She shook her head. "I don't know. There were rumors about Magna's activities, but only people in court knew what he was really up to."

Aret's mind reeled. Of all the court, Sheriff Morto had the most intimate knowledge of Magna's activities. He was a stiff, but a loyal stiff. Could his loyalty to Hister supersede his loyalty to the Valoras?

Gwendolyn pulled at the door, but Aret placed his hand gently on hers. Her smooth hands had never known work or battle. "Don't go," he said. "Not yet."

Her blue eyes gazed into his. "I know your reputation, Lord," she said. "But I'm a lady." She jerked the door, pushing off his hand in the process, and shuffled through the dim corridor.

Aret was surprised to find her words had hurt him. What reputation was she talking about? He called after her. "I only wanted to talk to you."

She turned without slowing and gave a sly smile. "Of course you did, Milord."

The devilish look on her angelic face took Aret's breath away. He continued staring after her swishing dress until she rounded the corner and was gone. At last he shut himself behind his chamber door and tried to force the incident out of his mind.

Was she flirting with him? More likely, she was just playing, as women often did. He shook his head, trying to shake the memory of her sly smile and swishing rump. He couldn't allow himself to get distracted, not even by Gwendolyn. *Especially* not by Gwendolyn.

Even with the ovens shut down, Mack's smelled of yeast from rising bread and fermenting beer. Mack breathed deeply the smell of his own bed and gazed at the plump lump under the blanket beside him. It was all his again, thanks to the mercy and wisdom of the Valoras. He would never risk losing it again.

It was late when a thunderous knock came at the door. His round wife, Wena, rolled over in bed and grabbed him. "Who could it be? One of the old gang?"

"No," he answered. "They all know we're being watched." He crept out of bed in the dark and slipped on a robe and boots.

"Don't answer it," Wena whispered, but the pounding came again.

The narrow stairs creaked under his steps. Wena kept close behind him. He looked through the empty bar to the front door. The knocking had stopped. Mack peeked out the door and found no one, nothing but a large sack on the stoop. He looked around again to make sure nobody was watching, dragged the sack inside, and secured the door. Lighting a lamp, he found the bag full of food and money. Wena's eyes glowed when she saw it, but Mack shook his head. "I've got a bad feeling. I think we're being set up."

The plank that secured the door crashed inward, and Mack grabbed his wife. A glittering knight hugged the back of his white horse as it trotted into the bar.

"Who are you?" Mack demanded.

"An ally," the knight answered. The gold gryphon crest of Valora shone on his chest. "I want the Underground to know they've got a friend in Valora."

Mack breathed heavily. "I can't help you, not like before." He forced his voice down. "I don't know any rebels. Besides, that sheriff is watching me like a hawk. They'll throw me back in prison, take my business, leave my wife a homeless widow!"

The mystery knight spoke with a noble, somewhat familiar voice. "Then you will have to change your tactics. Let someone else stash the loot and house the refugees. I'll worry about the authorities." The knight turned his horse around and ducked under the doorframe again before streaking back into the night.

Mack and Wena stared after him, and his wife asked, "What do you think? Do you believe him?"

"I don't know," Mack answered. "I might be more inclined to trust him if he hadn't broken our door."

CHAPTER 23

THE TOWER

King Aret Valora recognized the two travelers brought before him. He was not at all pleased to see the thieves in his throne room. Anyone in his court could be a spy, and Aret could not afford to be conspicuous in any way.

The thin lanky man was called Brownie, and his partner, Tiny, was a giant with a thick, bald head. They did not know Aret in his public capacity, but it was suspicious enough just to have their sort granted audience with a king. He was curious though, to hear what had brought them to Valora.

"We heard you were looking for the High Necromancer," Brownie said.

Lord Aret raised his hand to silence the thief and then sent his advisor, Purvis, to bring some maps from storage. Once Purvis was away, Aret bid brownie to continue.

"Perhaps I am," Aret said. "You know where he is?"

"The Necromancer's staying in his tower," Brownie said, "Just east of here."

That was only an afternoon's ride from Valora. "Are you sure?" Aret asked.

"We saw his coach heading that direction," Brownie said.

Aret stroked his smooth chin. "Very good." He tossed them two gold coins and rang a bell for Enri. "Evening meal will be served soon. These two are invited to eat in the hall tonight."

Brownie and Tiny smiled at each other. Brownie gave an enthusiastic, "Thank you, King Valora."

King Valora. Aret wasn't used to hearing himself called that. For Aret, *King Valora* would always be his father.

"You are to be on best, law-abiding behavior at my table," Aret said. "The next time you have news for me, you will wait at the public meetings or send a message. I will arrange to meet in private."

"Yes, King Valora," Brownie said, bowing. He slapped Tiny on the back of his bulbous head, and he bowed as well.

To Enri, Aret said, "I will take dinner in my room tonight. Have Rowen, the young stable boy with the scars on his face, brought to me."

Aret's golden mail gleamed in the moonlight. His horse, Snow, trotted off the road and into the trees. Aret dismounted and crept closer to the clearing. Safely concealed in the weeds, he expanded a telescope and scanned the single brick tower that rose into the starry sky.

The tower was six stories high with no doors. The glowing window on the top floor was far above any man or giant's head, leaving Aret to wonder how anyone got in or out of the structure. From the parapet, the watchman had a clear view for miles in any direction. Aret could only hope that darkness and trees had covered his approach. One man, even one in glittering magic armor, could often get places an army could never reach. Aret sat in the brush, watching until the sun came up.

Wheels on the road woke Aret, and he wondered how long he had dozed.

The black coach circled around the tower three times, then spun around to circle again in the opposite direction. Aret waited for the carriage to reappear on the other side of the structure, but only the cloud of dust kicked up by the horses billowed from behind the building.

Aret crept through the trees, crossed the dirt road, and peered around the tower. The coach was gone. There was a worn path encircling the tower, but the fresh tracks of the coach were clear. They rolled straight into the wall. Aret pushed against the structure and banged his fists against the bricks, but the wall was firm. He drew his ivory sword and drove it into the mortar.

Dark clouds gathered in the clear blue sky. Loose dirt from the fresh tracks whipped around Aret in the wind. The alarm had been sounded.

Aret grabbed the hilt of his sword with both hands and tried to pull it from the wall, but it didn't budge. He propped his leg against the wall, pulled with all his might, and finally the blade yanked free.

He retreated back into the forest. Lightning sparked against a tree above Aret, and he stumbled back. A flaming limb fell to the ground in front of him. Aret turned defiantly towards the tower, waving his magic sword high in the air. Lightning sparked against the tip of the blade, but Aret felt nothing. For a moment, Aret seemed indestructible, but the wind threatened to lift him up by his shield. He turned to run again.

If he escaped, he could return again under cover of night. *If he escaped.* The Necromancer was possibly the most powerful wizard in the world. It was one thing to sneak up on him, but now the old wizard knew an intruder was there.

Aret rushed to where he had left Snow, but his steed was gone. The warhorse must have been startled by the lightning.

A murder of crows covered the trees, their black feathers ruffling in the wind. The black birds turned their heads as Aret moved, watching him.

"Snow!" Aret called, running deeper into the trees.

Snow stomped at the dirt nearby, the muscles of his powerful legs twitching with anxiety. Aret rubbed Snow's neck and whispered soothing words.

The crows flocked from their perches and landed in the trees around Aret and his horse. Aret stabbed at them with his ivory sword, but they simply flapped out of reach.

Aret mounted, spurring Snow through the trees and back to the road. They sped into the wind, followed by a cloud of black birds.

Aret couldn't go back to Valora with the crows following him, not if they were the Necromancer's spies. Snow raced down the road at full speed. Slowly the ravens fell behind, but Snow couldn't keep this speed up forever. Aret slowed slightly before coming to a fork in the road. Aret pulled the reins, and Snow veered at a forty-five degree angle. Spurring Snow again to full speed, Aret raced ahead of the dark messengers.

Aret turned his head. The birds seemed to have lost interest, but he couldn't take the chance that they weren't still back there somewhere, fanning out to look for him. Again he slowed his horse, steering into the woods and to a small shack he had seen on his travels. Aret kicked the door open. Hearing no response, he dismounted and led Snow in, pushing aside the owner's belongings to make room for the massive animal. Aret then slammed the door shut.

A shadow fluttered past the window, but did not return. Aret released a sigh of relief, but he was essentially trapped until nightfall. He patted Snow with affection before making himself at home and finding himself some stale bread.

That afternoon, the door swung open, and the blue sky silhouetted an old man with a dead rabbit dangling from his hand. The owner of this shack had finally come home.

Aret rose and flipped him a gold coin. "I mean you no harm. I'm only seeking refuge for the day. As a nobleman it is my right."

The peasant stared at the mess Snow had made of the small shack, then looked at the gold coin in his hand. "I know who you are."

Aret was taken aback. He had never met this man before. Even caught without his helmet, the peasant couldn't have recognized him.

Aret's fears were allayed when the peasant continued, "You are the mystery knight, the one who robs from Hister's men and gives to the poor." The old man bowed his head. "It is an honor to meet you, noble sir. My house is your house."

Aret was surprised by this show of servitude from one ignorant of his true identity. The peasant's description wasn't entirely accurate. Aret stole from Hister and gave to the Underground. Some members of the Underground might be poor. "Thank you."

"No. Thank you." The peasant lowered his voice. "Hister's men've been through here and made a much bigger mess than your horse did. I live alone and don't have much to fear, but, of course, if anyone asks, I'm a loyal servant to the crown."

Aret relaxed. "Of course."

The peasant lifted up the dead rabbit. "Let me cook you up some game and get your horse some water."

Aret and the old peasant played a game of cards and talked until the sun had set. It took Aret's mind off of the coming night, but night at last came. The old hermit had no sense of courtly custom and treated Aret like any other guest. He seemed grateful for the company and a little saddened when Aret led Snow from the tiny cabin.

Aret strapped Snow's headpiece back on. He put on his gloves and flipped the old man another gold coin. "Thank you again."

The peasant bit down on the coin and waved.

CHAPTER 24

FIGHT TO THE TOP

Every rustle of leaves… Every hoot of the unseen owl startled Aret. How could he be sure the animals of the night weren't more of the Necromancer's spies? He thought about giving up the evening, heading back to Valora while he still could. He'd had all day to think… to worry. Even his horse, Snow, twitched with anxiety, reluctant to go back to the cursed tower, but Aret now knew that the High Necromancer was not omnipotent. The wizard had called down lightning from the sky, and it hadn't hurt Aret. There might never be a better chance to confront the Necromancer one on one.

Again, Aret left Snow in the trees while he crept to the tower with no doors. Light flickered in the same high window that it had the night before, and Aret wondered if the Necromancer was there, just out of reach, formulating his malicious schemes.

The black horses that had pulled the Necromancer's coach were tethered outside the tower. The wizard was indeed still here.

Although Aret walked carefully, the sound of his boots in the dirt seemed to echo in the quiet of the night, as did every bump of his magic armor against his gold mail. He made it to the tower wall, apparently without gaining any attention. Running his hand across the bricks, he found the chink where he had buried his sword. He walked around the base of the tower three times, turned, then walked around twice more, as he had seen the coach do that morning. On his second turn, he placed his hands against the wall and found that it had become a cold gray smoke. The smoke congealed as Aret passed into the darkness within. The wall behind him was solid once more. Aret had discovered the combination of movements that allowed entrance into the tower and once again gotten himself into a situation with no idea how to get out.

Dim candlelight showed the silhouette of the Necromancer's black coach. Tracks in the dirt floor led from Aret's entrance to the opposite side of the room, leading into another brick wall. There was nowhere to go but up. Narrow stone steps spiraled the outer wall of the tower.

Every twentieth step or so was marked by a decorative suit of armor from different periods in Gaul's history. A wooden platform above the coach formed the first floor, a room of fine silks. There were chests filled to the top with gold and jewels. The treasure glittered in the lantern light. Aret marveled at the gems. It was more than his whole kingdom was worth, but Aret was not there for treasure; he was there for revenge. Perhaps later, if he succeeded... He tore himself from the sight and continued up into the darkness.

He found his movement impeded. The spider webs were invisible in the dark. Aret pushed through, but the layers of sticky thread became thicker, building on one another. He drew his ivory sword and cut the silky strands, but as he did, a vibration shook his body. The silk threads jerked Aret from the steps and suspended him in the darkness.

The vibrations became more violent. A six-foot-long body of hair scurried from the center of a scaffolding of thread. Eight eyes flickered in the dim torchlight. Eight legs hovered over Aret, and before he could think, two 24 inch fangs butted against his mail. They couldn't penetrate the golden scales, but tiny barbs squirted acid. The acid found tiny gaps between the scales. The inside of Aret's sleeve burned against his skin. Spinnerets on the spider's abdomen wove webbing over Aret's legs at mind numbing speed.

Aret's burning skin took away all reason, and he wildly flailed in the web. He cut one leg free. Aret kicked, pushing the spider away. It spilled its smoking venom over his armor, burning his tunic. Aret kicked again, digging his spur into the spider's soft abdomen while cutting Aret's other leg free from the fresh, wet webbing.

The spider jumped, shaking the web violently. It pounced on Aret, jabbing its fangs against Aret's shoulder plates. Aret's pale blade hacked into the spider. Yellow and red gore glistened in the web around him. Aret slashed off one of the spider's legs. He stabbed at the arachnid again, but it had scampered back along the scaffolding of thread.

Aret tried to still his breathing while the world around him slowly stopped moving. Every time he stirred, the webbing around him reacted.

Aret waved his sword and fell several feet before swinging to a stop on the sticky strings. If he were to cut himself completely free, he would fall down the center of the tower to his death. Or worse, perhaps he wouldn't die. Perhaps he would break his bones and the Necromancer would find him alive the next morning.

Aret's arm was on fire, making it hard to think.

He sheathed his sword, wrapped the organic ropes around one hand, and hauled himself hand over hand until he was slightly above level with the nearest stone step. He then swung his legs back and forth. Once he was above the step, he released the webbing and felt solid stone against his boots. When he was sure of his balance, he cut himself free and dropped to a seat. Aret sat panting on the cold steps.

He ripped pieces of his tunic and stuffed them between his sleeve and his burned skin. At least that would keep the mail from chafing the raw nerves. His wounds begged to be free of the armor and submerged in cool water, but there was no door in or out of the tower. The only way out was up the stairs and through the Necromancer. There could be no turning back, no running away.

A rusty creak directed his attention to the steps above. There was nothing there but one of the empty suits of armor that lined the curved walls. Its arm moved, lifting a mace. Aret jolted up, gripping his sword with both hands. There was a grinding noise behind him, and a sudden weight fell between Aret's shoulder blades, driving him to his knees. An armor shell behind him raised a heavy ax from Aret's back. The suit in front of Aret let its mace fall. Aret rolled on his back, bringing his shield over him like a blanket.

A hard stone step jabbed into Aret's back with a sharp pain. Only Aret's thick gorget had prevented the ax from splitting him in two.

The two lumbering suits brought mace and ax down on the magic shield with muted thumps. Aret stabbed his sword up through a suit of hollow armor. Luminous green smoke leaked where he punctured it. The armor slowed, and Aret pushed against it with his shield, knocking it over the ledge. It fell, but hung suspended in the darkness by sticky webbing.

Aret blocked another blow and slashed at the other metal shell, knocking its helmet off. For a brief moment, a faint green orb hovered above the armor's shoulders, but then billowed away in a cloud of smoke. The armor stumbled, rattling down the steps in pieces.

So much for a quiet ascension.

Metallic footsteps rang over the stone steps above and below. The ghost-driven armors were slow and stupid, but number and gravity were all they needed to knock Aret down the steps to his doom. Aret charged up the stairs with shield and sword raised. He pushed through them before they had a chance to gang up on him. A single puncture of the metal shells was all it took to render them lifeless. Then the only danger was tripping on the pieces strewn over the stairs.

The light above became brighter. At last Aret reached the top level of the tower. The room was lined with books and charts and a bed shrouded in silk.

On a couch lay a man in a black robe. His red sash was identical to Aret's advisor, Purvis. "Get out of here!" the man shouted. He had sharp features and a heavy brow. "This place is only for the High Necromancer and his invited guests!"

Aret, his polished armor covered in sticky tatters and gore, pointed his sword at the man and charged. The man retreated up wooden steps into the night air on the very top of the tower. Aret pursued.

A thin figure gazed out over the landscape. A black robe hung over his bony frame. "You coward," the Necromancer said to his watchman.

The old wizard turned from the edge of the tower and faced Aret. "I see you met my pet. I knew you would return, but never thought you would make it to the top of my tower. I thought that remarkable armor had been lost forever. Where did you find it?" With a wave of the Necromancer's arm, a great brazier sparked aflame, bathing them in an orange glow.

Aret kept his sword pointed at the Necromancer. Aret felt the weight of the blade in his back where the ax had hit him, but a little soreness couldn't stop him now. His heart thundered in his chest. The old man he feared was really here. Aret had made it to the top of the tower, and revenge was truly within his reach.

Aret's confidence was short-lived. A light ignited in the distance. The red and yellow glow was followed by another, then another, creating a web of lights all over Histerland. The Necromancer's towers dotted the country. Each tower had a watchman and a signal flame. When the Necromancer lit the brazier, his watchmen answered the signal by igniting their fires. It wasn't a physical threat, but it was a visible manifestation of the High Necromancer's power. It dwarfed Aret, a tiny king from a tiny province.

The Necromancer must have sensed Aret's fear, even within the concealing armor. His wrinkled mouth creased into a smile. "Who are you?"

Aret's voice shook. "You will know me when you are at my mercy!"

The Necromancer's smile twisted. "Then I will never know who you are…" He shrugged. "Oh well." The Necromancer raised his bony hand to his lips and blew over his palm.

Flames streamed from the brazier over Aret. The spider gore on Aret's magic armor sizzled. Aret felt the heat in his raw flesh before hiding behind the safety of his shield. Once the flame barrage was over, Aret advanced on his prey, preparing to swing his blade.

With a wave of the Necromancer's hand, violent wind tugged at them all, whipping the Necromancer's robes around him in the sudden flash of a storm. Lightning sparked from the sky into Aret's upraised sword and sent a tingle down through his boots. The Necromancer pointed. Electricity arced from his finger, but fell harmlessly on the magic shield.

Aret had never seen any wizard display their power so blatantly. They were more comfortable weaving subtle magics from the shadows. The Necromancer must have been desperate to use his power this way.

Aret continued to advance, ignoring the crows that flocked in his path. His magic armor was more potent than he had hoped. Victory was at hand.

At last there was fear in those evil eyes. The Necromancer backed against the edge of the tower. He raised his black robe as if to shield himself from the sight of his impending doom. Aret almost laughed as he jabbed the ivory sword through the dark fabric. The blade dug into the bricks behind the Necromancer.

But the robe collapsed, empty over Aret's arm.

Aret yanked his sword from the wall and shook the black robe loose, looking for some trace of his foe. He swung his sword around, ready for another attack, but he was alone on the roof.

Aret tossed the empty robe down and howled in frustration. He lashed out with his sword, slicing a leg of the brazier. The bowl tipped slightly, and Aret jumped back from spilling coals.

He stomped on the wood floor and it sagged a bit under his weight. Only near the brazier, over supportive beams, did the floor resist him. He slashed into the platform, drove his sword down into the wood. There was no rationality to what he did; he merely acted. The brazier dipped toward him as the floor bowed.

Aret yanked his sword out of the floor and raised his shield between himself and heat. His tantrum could have gotten him killed, but still his rage was not sated. He cut the rusty bolts that held the brazier to the floor. Aret jutted the narrow end of his shield under the great, flaming bowl. His back throbbed as he pushed up, groaning with all his might. The bowl tipped, and the floor beneath it gave under the weight of hot iron and flaming coals.

Aret stumbled back, panting. The brazier remained embedded in the floor below. Flaming coals had spilled over the furnished top room. Aret smiled at his handiwork. The Necromancer's luxurious hideaway was in flames.

Glowing coals fell through the floor. The smoke was thick, and the wood below Aret started to creak. Aret made his way back down the stairs. He found the silken webbing had ignited into a flickering lattice.

Aret stopped at the floor below that. The treasures called to him. Smoldering pieces of web fell across the silks. Jewels and coins writhed in their chests. Snakes slithered out from the treasures, seeking to escape the heat. There was a thin surface of real treasure in the room, but the bulk of the containers were taken up by venomous snakes and bugs. It was a trap to distract and kill any thief smart enough to get inside the tower.

There was a creaking overhead followed by the crackle of splitting wood. Aret clung to the outer wall of the tower. The glowing hot brazier fell past Aret, accelerated through the platform, and crushed the coach below. The tower became a chimney, thick smoke everywhere. Aret's breath caught in his throat, and there was no door to flee through.

Aret turned back, hoping perhaps to fashion a rope and lower himself from the roof. He tripped over pieces of inanimate armor.

A robed man came through the smoke. "Idiot!" The watchman yelled as he leapt over Aret. Aret didn't know where the watchman had hidden himself and he didn't care. He grabbed the man's ankle and tripped him.

The watchmen rose. He pulled out an amulet that hung from his neck by a long chain. The watchmen extended the amulet in front of him and staggered down the steps. Aret followed, choking on the rising smoke.

A sudden rush of wind blew past the watchman, sucking up the smoke and pushing the man back against Aret. The heat at Aret's back intensified, and he barreled through the man.

Aret fell into open air and kept crawling over the grass. Somehow he had made it outside! A sizzle behind him was followed by a hideous cry. The watchman's face and hands were hanging out of the solid brick wall. The arms of his robes smoldered. The man screamed and flailed. His twisted face was red and sweaty. The watchman's backside was on fire. There was nothing he could do to escape the flames, nothing Aret could do to free him. The watchman's trembling fingers still clung to the amulet.

Aret turned away from the awful sight and made for the tree line. He collapsed, removed his helmet, and took a breath of cool fresh air. He looked back at the burning tower. A tool and symbol of the Necromancer's power in the region had been destroyed, at least temporarily, but the Necromancer himself had escaped.

Aret whistled for Snow. There was a cool stream nearby where Aret could bathe his raw flesh. He worried he would never get the smell of smoke out of his nose.

He had been so close. Only dumb luck had kept Aret alive. All that effort, and the Necromancer had still escaped. But Aret had seen real fear in the old wizard's eyes, and that made it all worthwhile.

CHAPTER 25

THE NECROMANCER FUMES

King Aret's stomach was in knots, but he sat with a relaxed posture. His purple robes draped the throne under him. "Welcome, Lord Necromancer. I wish we had known you were coming."

The High Necromancer squinted up at him. "Do you know why I am here?" the old wizard asked.

"No, Your Honor, but you need no excuse to grace us with your venerable presence. We are already lining up food and entertainment for your pleasure."

"This is not a social visit, and I am in no mood for entertainment. For the last few months, a terrorist in magic armor has been disrupting our affairs in this region."

"Really?" Aret said, feigning ignorance. His skin still had a subtle smoke smell that wouldn't wash away. "I had heard rumors about him, but I'd hoped they were just stories."

"They are painfully real," the Necromancer said. "He stopped a whole platoon of soldiers on the road, tax shipments have been disappearing, and he destroyed my nearest tower. Worst of all, some look up to this brigand. Seditious activities are on the rise."

"That's awful!" Aret said, barely able to hide his glee. Had his activities really inspired others? "He should be stopped."

"That's why I am here. All of these attacks center around Valora. The mystery knight is here somewhere, possibly one of your men. He has a gryphon on his chest, the totem of Valora. You must have some idea who it is."

Aret looked down in imitated shame. "I hate to say it, Lord Necromancer, but I think I know who this knight is."

The old wizard's eyes widened. "Who?"

"Remember how my brother's ghost came back, transformed by his sins to haunt Valora?"

"Yes." The Necromancer barely held back a smile. "Of course I remember."

"I thought we had gotten rid of him," Aret said, "but what if he is still among us… as this rogue knight?" It was hard for Aret not to smile at his joke. He was playing a dangerous game, but it seemed appropriate.

The old man looked away, deflating with a sigh, but then looked at Aret with steel hard eyes. "No matter who this mystery knight is, he will be captured, never fear, and he will pray to me for death. Order in this region is *your* responsibility."

The Necromancer waved his hand and two Histerland soldiers marched up to the throne. One had salt-and-pepper hair and scars on the side of his face. Close behind, the other had wavy blonde hair. They both bowed to King Aret.

"This is General Ulf," the Necromancer said, "and his second, Commander Golga. They will be stationed here with fifty of their men." The old wizard spoke to them all. "See to it this rogue knight is captured or killed."

Aret wasn't happy to house more of the Necromancer's spies, but he couldn't let them know that. Things would be much more difficult with them around. Aret nodded to the newcomers. "Welcome. We are grateful for your assistance, but, Lord Necromancer, what if this knight is a ghost, as some say?"

The Necromancer spoke with complete confidence. "He is as physical as you or me and he can be captured or killed just as easily as *you* can. Don't make us doubt the faith Hister has in you."

Aret swallowed his fear into his stomach and buried it under his role. "Of course not, Your Honor. The Rogue Knight will be dealt with." Aret said it with such conviction that he almost believed he would bring himself in. He hoped the Necromancer found it as convincing.

CHAPTER 26

HAUNT OF THE SHADOW BEAR

Brownie and Tiny nursed their foaming mugs at the bar of Mack's Tavern. They looked nervously over their shoulders at all the off duty Histerland soldiers.

"Anything else?" Mack the barkeep asked.

"What's with all the soldiers?" Brownie whispered.

Mack lowered his booming voice below the level of the crowd. "Ever since that rogue knight came around, Hister's soldiers are everywhere."

A soldier bumped Brownie on his way to the bar, demanding a pitcher of mead. Tiny, the giant, always protective of his little buddy, tensed, but Brownie calmed him with a touch of his hand. A brawl with Histerland soldiers was not a good idea.

The first group of soldiers slowly filtered out, replaced by another group. Tiny and Brownie finished their turkey legs and meat pies. It was the biggest meal they had eaten in weeks. With satisfied stomachs, they dozed over their greasy plates.

At last the bar quieted, and Mack nudged them. "Tavern's closing. Want a room? Ten Histerns a night."

Brownie opened his eyes and looked around the empty bar. "No. No room. We came for another reason, needed to send a message to the Underground."

Mack opened his mouth in horror and looked over his shoulder. "You get out of here! This is an honest business."

Brownie and Tiny stumbled out of the bar into the cold night and leaned against the wall. "No luck here," Brownie said.

General Ulf, the commander of Hister's forces in Valora, appeared in his black leather tunic and mail. He tugged on his ear and cocked his head at them. "Find a place to stay. Vagrants are locked up after curfew."

Brownie gave the General a dirty look and pulled Tiny's sleeve. "C'mon. We're not welcome here."

General Ulf scratched the scar on his face and watched them walk down the road that led out of Valora.

Brownie talked as they strolled. "If our contact wants to be so hard to find, we should just keep the loot. Serve him right."

They passed by shacks, farm plots, and vineyards: all property of the local king. The quiet night was now cold enough that they could see each other's breath. Brownie looked back to make sure they weren't being followed, then dove into the orchard and scrambled up a tree. A few leaves and apples still hung on the branches. With a gleeful smile he threw apples down to Tiny. Tiny caught some, but most bounced against him and fell to the ground. The apples were over-ripe, but the two men didn't mind.

"Hurry!" Tiny said. "I think I hear the woodsman!"

Brownie froze in the branches and listened. Shadows of naked tree branches crawled along the road, but there was no one there. "It's your imagination." He jumped down, and they continued on the lonely road.

Tiny turned around, dropping some of the precious fruit.

"Careful with those!" Brownie said. "What's wrong?"

"I saw something in the woods. It's following us."

Brownie sighed. "You're as big as a castle, but you're scared of shadows."

Rustling in the branches caused Brownie's breath to catch in his throat, and his heart skipped.

"Shadows don't move by themselves!" Tiny said.

The two thieves looked at each other. Tiny dropped all the apples, and they ran down the road. The shadow of a bear on two legs grew in front of them. They turned, running back to Valora, but the bear was in their path. The moon cast the creature's shadow upon them.

It bounded on four legs, charging the two men. Tiny whirled his ax from his back, and his thick sweaty fingers tightened around the handle. He swung the ax into the charging animal, letting the weight of the weapon carry it around in an irresistible arc. But the blade passed through the bear as though the beast were made of smoke. Its claws and teeth, however, were very real to Tiny.

Back at the tavern, Mack washed dishes while his wife, Wena, finished rolling bread dough for the next day's customers. She plopped the balls of dough on trays and covered them with towels, allowing them to rise overnight. Unlike most of the people of Valora, Mack paid the miller for their flour with money. Most Valorans traded produce, usually wheat, to the miller in exchange for milled flour. The miller gave most of the traded wheat to the king that owned the fields and kept a smaller percentage for his own family. A portion of this, he sold to Mack.

Mack's wife was a good, strong woman and a good worker. He couldn't keep this business running without her, especially after he had let their beloved Prince Magna suck him into the Underground. Mack had gotten himself arrested, but he was free. He had to avoid trouble now at all costs.

Wena wiped the sweat from her forehead and made her way slowly up the stairs to their bedroom. He heard their new pig squeal as she pushed it out of their bed and led it downstairs. She led it out the front door and tied it onto the porch. The pig had been his gift to her to thank her for all she had done for him. She loved it, and it was also great for business. Any fleas and bedbugs in their beds would hop on the pig, freeing Mack and his customers to a peaceful sleep. At least that's how the advertisement went.

"Come to bed, dear," she called to him. "I'll finish those dishes in the morning."

Mack shook his exhausted head. "I'm almost done. You go ahead up."

Wena waddled up the stairs, and Mack continued rubbing the glasses in the soapy basin. He heard a faint scratching at the door and stopped washing for a moment to listen.

Thinking it his imagination, he continued washing.

The scratching came again, louder this time. There was no mistake. Someone was at the door. "We're closed!"

Their pig squealed, shattering the quiet night with painful, human-like screams. The piercing squeals stopped suddenly. Mack had no time to adjust to the silence. Something thudded violently against the door.

There was no draft in the tavern, but all the lamps simultaneously blew out. Only moonlight from the window gave any illumination.

Mack's voice was less certain now. "I said we're closed!"

A shadow passed in front of the window, momentarily leaving Mack in total darkness.

Wena called from upstairs. "What is it?"

"Stay in the room. Lock the door!"

The loud crack of splintering wood was heard at the side of the building. Under the tavern, in the cellar where Mack used to hide people and supplies for the Underground, Mack could hear clay pots breaking and shelves being toppled over. Abruptly, all fell silent.

Mack stood frozen, his hands still dripping soapy water. He was afraid to move, afraid to make any sound. The intruder made no sound either. Mack finally released his breath and gingerly moved a foot toward the stairs. As soon as his foot left the ground, a loud thump against the floorboards beneath him filled his heart with terror. He raced up the stairs and into their bedroom. He slammed the door and brought the wooden plank down to secure it.

He and his wife huddled on the bed until sunrise, hyperaware of every tiny sound.

Even after the cock crowed and the sun rose, they huddled in their bed, listening to imagined sounds in the still morning. Mack peeked out the window at smoke rising from the blacksmith's chimney. A thin powder of frost covered a roof of tree bark. Peasants were out in the brown fields. Daily life was starting in Valora.

He changed his clothes and was about to lift the lock when a loud knock at the front door made him drop it back into place. Again, the urgent knock sounded. Mack peered out the window and saw Sheriff Morto in the blue tunic of Valora's personal guard.

The sheriff yelled up to him. "Is everything alright?"

"No," Mack said. "It certainly is not! Wait there, I'll be right down."

The barkeep and Sheriff Morto inspected deep scratches in the bloodied tavern door. If they were any deeper, they would have cut right through the wood. Their poor pig lay on the porch with a broken neck. It would be quite awhile before Mack could afford another.

The cellar door was busted in. Morto drew his sword and led the way down the rickety, wooden steps. The shelves were toppled. Casks and jars lay in pieces on the dirt floor. Thick fumes from hundreds of Histerns worth of spilt wine and beer displaced the oxygen, nearly making them faint. Whatever had done the damage was gone.

"What did all this?" Mack asked.

Sheriff Morto made no expression on his face. "Have you been hiding people down here again?"

Mack shook his head adamantly. "No! No, sir. I'm a loyal citizen. I only did it before because the prince asked me to. You know that! You watch my place like a hawk."

Morto nodded. "I know. Probably just a wild animal looking for food. I'll have the woodsman come by and take a look." Morto marched up the creaking steps into the sun.

"Thank you, Sheriff. Thank you." Mack looked at the toppled shelves and splintered barrels, lost inventory and lost income. "Thanks for nothing," he added quietly, knowing the sheriff was out of earshot.

CHAPTER 27

HUNTING THE SHADOW BEAR

Garnet and his father, Gruff Woodsman, strode past the hammering of metal at the blacksmith's shop. Mack's Tavern and Inn was still closed after last night's visitation. The town carpenter was waiting for them to inspect the scene before he installed a new door to the cellar.

Garnet and his father examined the ground carefully. "What do you see?" his father asked.

Garnet shook his head, confused. "I see bear tracks, but they don't make sense."

"Why?"

"They appear by the door, here and there, but then they just disappear. They don't lead anywhere. They don't come from anywhere." A thin powder of snow had fallen. If tracks were there, they should have been obvious.

His father examined the ground. "You're right. And the prints have no weight. It's like he flew."

"Like a ghost," Garnet added.

The innkeeper's wife overheard them from the window and exclaimed, "A ghost bear!"

Garnet's father scowled at her. She frowned back at him and returned to her business.

Gruff turned back to Garnet. "Bears don't have ghosts, son. We'll have to get the royal hounds in on this one."

Garnet wondered why a bear couldn't have a ghost.

They met Sheriff Morto in a thatched hut at the edge of the forest. This was the home of the healer woman, Miss Bonnie.

The giant victim lay on a bed much too small for him. Miss Bonnie was not quite fifty years of age. She mixed a salve with mortar and pestle and dabbed it onto the giant's open head and chest.

"If it isn't a ghost and it isn't a bear," Miss Bonnie said, "then maybe it's something in between."

The giant moaned, even under the influence of sleeping potion. Garnet's father inspected the red gashes and mottled bruising. "It was a bear, alright. No doubt about it."

Miss Bonnie waved her hand over her mixture, and Garnet asked, "Is that magic?"

She looked to him fearfully and then to his father and the sheriff. "There are no magicians left in Histerland that don't work for Hister. I'm just a simple folk healer." Her voice quaked. "The right plants and oils in the right proportion, that's all."

Garnet began to follow his father and the sheriff outside, but Miss Bonnie placed a hand on the boy's shoulder. She lifted a silver arrow out of a cauldron and said, "This might work when normal weapons don't."

Garnet took the arrow. He looked up into Miss Bonnie's nurturing eyes and remembered his long dead mother. "Thanks."

His father called from outside, and Garnet rushed out to meet him.

His father looked back at the healer's cottage and squinted. "I don't trust that folk woman."

Garnet wondered why, but didn't ask. His father was a man of few words and fewer explanations.

They accompanied Sheriff Morto to Castle Valora, and Garnet wondered aloud, "If it was a hungry bear, why did it kill the innkeeper's pig but then not eat it?"

His father ignored Garnet's ponderings and bade him wait by the heavy, oak door.

King Aret Valora eagerly motioned Gruff Woodsman and Sheriff Morto into his council chamber. Old Purvis dipped his quill in ink, preparing to document the meeting.

Aret was deadly serious when he asked his woodsman, "Is it the Husk?" He had buried his cursed brother himself, but when it came to magic, nothing was definite. He had seen his brother die twice, after all.

Gruff Woodsman shook his head. "Definitely not. The Husk had tiny, sharp hooks for claws. These are much bigger, not as sharp, but with massive strength behind them. I'd say they come from a large bear. Bears are known to be curious and brave enough to come into a town from time to time. It was probably attracted by the smell of food at the tavern. This one must be very brave: dangerous, but hard to miss. I'll get him, Lord."

King Aret sighed with relief. "Just an animal. Very good. Maybe it will make a good rug."

Purvis looked up from his writing. "Perhaps we should invite the other nobles, make a sport of it. It's been quite a while since we had a hunt."

Aret shook his head. Valora didn't need any more attention right now. "Our woodsman can handle it." He nodded at Gruff and said, "You may begin."

The woodsman bowed slightly. "Yes, Lord."

Aret then turned to Morto. "I want to talk to the giant's partner."

Sheriff Morto nodded and they went to the castle's seldom used prison.

Brownie was in the back of a dim cell. It seemed like the over-sized manacles on his thin wrists could slip right off. "Let me out," he said. "I didn't do anything. We are the victims!"

"What were you doing with all that money in your bag?" Morto asked.

"I'm a traveling salesman," he said.

Morto snorted back a laugh. "Then where are your wares?"

Brownie hesitated before saying, "We sold out. That's how we got all the money."

"And the orders with Hister's seal?" Morto pressed.

"Enough," Aret interrupted. "Tell us about the attack last night."

At that, Brownie broke protocol and looked up at his better. A flash of recognition crossed Brownie's face, then confusion.

"Your king is talking to you," Morto demanded.

Brownie bowed his head in submission. "The monster was big, black. Tiny, that's my friend, the real big guy, buried his ax right in its gut, but nothing happened. Tiny's a tough customer, but it was like he was cutting shadows. I didn't know what to do. I just stood there. After it was done with Tiny, It came after me. I fell down and covered my eyes. Nothing happened. When I looked up, the bear was gone, like it was never there."

"How is Tiny?" the prisoner asked. "He's, a bit slow but he's the most decent… He never… He's the only friend I've got."

King Aret was touched by this show of affection. He had thought of the two thieves as subhuman, like animals he could use without guilt, as Aret had been used by his betters. "Your friend is with the folk healer. He is alive, but his wounds are serious."

Brownie dropped into the straw on the floor and held his head in his hands.

Aret and Morto left together.

"They were carrying lots of money and official documents," Morto said. "Probably spies, part of the Underground, like Mack the barkeep is, or was. If I didn't know this bear was just an animal, I would almost think the victims were targeted."

General Ulf and Commander Golga waited in the hall. "How is the prisoner?" the General asked.

"He'll be fine, physically," Aret said. "He is upset about his friend."

Morto added, "I'm surprised to see you so concerned, General."

General Ulf scratched his ear. "If he is hurt too bad, I can't question him."

Aret shook his head. "This is an internal matter. Morto and I will interrogate them."

"With all due respect," Ulf said, "Hister has put me in charge of stopping the Rogue Knight. This prisoner may work for him."

"Hister assigned you to me," King Aret said. "Sheriff Morto will tell you anything we find out from him."

Ulf bowed his head as though in submission, but his eyes remained trained on Aret.

CHAPTER 28

DEFEAT

Garnet's father finally emerged from the heavy, arched door. "Are we going on a hunt?" the boy asked.

His father gave a thin-lipped smile. "Yes. Where do you think we should start?"

"The bar," Garnet suggested.

"Very good," his father agreed. "The dogs can pick up the scent."

While Mack waited impatiently, Garnet and his father led the hounds around the tavern. The dogs sniffed intently outside the cellar. In the course of their activities, Mack and the carpenter had obliterated all visible signs of the bear, but the dogs got the scent of something. They took off running. Instead of heading for the woods, they ran to the castle and howled around the soldier's barracks.

Garnet's father shook his head with disappointment. They leashed the dogs and dragged them out into the forest. The days were growing shorter and the shadows of the forest were thick and gloomy. When released, the hounds again returned to the castle.

General Ulf strutted into their midst and the dogs backed away, the hair bristling on their backs. "What is this racket?" the General asked. "You interrupted my nap."

Garnet's father answered immediately. "I'm the woodsman of Valora and I—"

"If you are the woodsman," General Ulf interrupted, "shouldn't you be in the woods?"

Commander Golga and the other soldiers chuckled. Gruff Woodsman spat on the ground, leashed the dogs, and dragged them back to their pens. Before he could lock them up, the hounds suddenly tensed and became alert.

Father and son looked excitedly at each other. Gruff released the hounds once more. The dogs ran into the forest and the woodsmen chased after them. They were completely unprepared for the immense black shape that towered above them on hind legs.

It was surreal, a fuzzy dark blur. The monster's deep roar vibrated in their chests. The dogs surrounded it. Gruff Woodsman pushed his son back and loaded his crossbow. One, two, three arrows flew into the beast's chest and neck. The shadowy bear leapt upon Garnet's father, tearing into him with teeth and claws. His father's last act was to pull his dagger from his coat and lash out at the nebulous fur above him. The attack did not stop.

Garnet backed against a tree, frozen. His father, the man whose strength was the standard by which he judged all other's, screamed.

A soldier yelled in the distance. "The Rogue Knight! The Rogue Knight is here!"

Garnet tore his gaze away from his father. The Rogue Knight erupted from the far off stables on a white horse. It was as though he had been hiding there all along. The gold antlers on the horse's headpiece made it appear that the glittering knight was riding a giant stag.

A soldier in black was casually strolling down the path when he saw the knight. Before his blade was fully drawn, the Rogue Knight had already sliced through the soldier with a sword of polished ivory. The alarm was out. There was no sign of soldiers yet, but there would be. The Rogue Knight was a fool to appear in the open like this. Garnet didn't know what had driven the knight to such desperation and he didn't care. He did care that the knight was coming straight at him, following the sound of the baying hounds.

The bear had finally left Garnet's father. The hair on the dog's backs stood up as they surrounded the 10 foot tall bear. The hounds were fierce, but their howls were filled with terror. A dog charged, but was easily batted away by the bear. It yipped as its back broke on the cold ground. The other dogs backed away, and their barks became higher in pitch.

The knight's steed charged into the fray, and the dogs cleared a path. The Rogue Knight's ivory sword cut through the bear, and Garnet briefly found himself cheering for the villain. The bear did not bleed. Its claws sparked against the horse's armor as it knocked the knight from the saddle.

Garnet crouched next to his father, who stared blankly into the sky. Steam rose from his glistening neck and chest.

The Rogue Knight staggered to his feet while the bear's limbs battered uselessly against his shield. Unexpectedly, the bear grabbed the sides of the magic shield as a man might do. The bear hurled the shield away. The knight's sword sliced through the bear as uselessly as slicing through air. The bear's claws slashed the knight's tunic. The force of the blow knocked the knight painfully to the ground, but the claws didn't penetrate the golden scale mail.

The bear grabbed the knight from behind in a tight embrace. Its teeth clamped down on the knight's shoulder. Hairy arms tightened around the knight's ribs, and the criminal's feet lifted from the ground. The magic sword fell from the rogue's hand.

The knight kicked wildly and desperately wheezed for breath.

The wild baying of the dogs still pounded in Garnet's ears.

The gold gryphon crest on the knight's chest glowed brightly, then pulsed dimly as his life weakened. Miss Bonnie's silver arrow reflected the ethereal light.

When the shadows reclaimed the forest, Garnet stood defiantly before the combatants. He aimed his father's crossbow and let the arrow fly. The silver shaft dug into the creature's eye. With a painful roar, it dropped the knight and melted into the shadows. The silver arrow fell to the ground. The bear was gone, but its roar still echoed off the trees.

The dogs circled, wild and directionless.

Garnet struggled to reload the crossbow with his shaking hands. He cautiously nudged the Rogue Knight with his foot. The knight groaned and grabbed his ribs. The boy would be a hero when the soldiers arrived. The Rogue Knight removed his helmet, gulping irregular breaths.

Garnet gasped when he recognized the face of his king, Aret Valora, lying helpless before him. When the soldiers found him standing over his king, would they consider Garnet a hero, or a traitor?

After a short time staring down at his king, he ran after the knight's white horse and grabbed the reins. He led the horse to his master and struggled to heave the knight up over the saddle. King Aret grunted, and Garnet winced as the king's bruised and broken ribs jarred loose. The boy led the horse deeper into the woods.

From his hiding place in the trees, Garnet saw soldiers arriving on horseback. They shouted with glee when they found the knight's magic sword and shield. They barely took notice of Garnet's father face up on the sticky leaves. The dogs still roamed nervously, untended, but the animals ignored Garnet.

Commander Golga plucked a silver arrow out of the dead brown leaves.

CHAPTER 29

HERO'S END

"Where is General Ulf?" Aret asked from his throne. "He was injured in a fight," Golga said. "Nothing serious. He asked me to present you with this gift. The Commander bowed to Aret and held the ivory sword flat in the palms of his hands.

Aret's eyebrows sagged with failure as he accepted his own sword. "Thank you. You have done a wonderful job of disarming the Rogue Knight." The sword seemed light and lifeless without the rest of the armor. "Is his sword as sharp as they say?"

The Commander shook his head. "No. We've tried sparring with it, and it's actually quite dull. I don't know how it managed to cut down so many of Histerland's finest."

"What about the mystery knight himself? Where is he?"

"We don't know, Sire. He vanished like a ghost, just like the bear."

Aret shifted his weight and grunted in pain. "A ghost bear and a ghost knight. Where has the kingdom gone?"

The commander looked up at the king for a moment, but then looked down respectfully again. "Are you well, Sire?"

"I'm fine. The king's health is not your concern."

"Yes, Sire."

"Keep up the fight," Aret said. "If the Rogue Knight still lives, I have no doubt you will have him soon." He nodded to young Enri, who gave the commander a bag of money and a case with 25 bottles of Valoran wine. "Share this with your men and give them my thanks for a job well done."

Commander Golga smiled with pride as he took the bounty. "Thank you, Sire. The men will be pleased with your generosity."

As soon as the Commander was away, the king released a look of unrestrained pain.

"Are you alright, Lord?" Purvis asked.

"I'm fine. The stress of kingship has made me old before my time."

"It's obvious this is no mere beast," Purvis said. "I think we should request the Necromancer's assistance."

"No!" Aret said. "Definitely not. We can handle our own problems." Aret would never call Hister's wizard for help, but a wizard might be their only way out of this. He had discreetly sent inquiries for the Gatekeeper, but no one had heard or seen anything from Gabriel in months. Aret feared the worst. "Leave me be. I will see no one else today."

Purvis bowed. "Yes, King Aret."

Aret slumped into the throne. The woodsman's son had taken Aret to the folk healer, but Miss Bonnie could only do so much. Any miracle-workers remaining in Histerland were either in hiding or working for the Necromancer. After facing the old wizard himself, Aret had thought his magic armor unbeatable. He had been wrong.

Lady Gwendolyn strode confidently before him, and Aret tried to sit up straight. "I told Purvis I didn't want any more visitors today."

Gwendolyn ignored him. "Permission to speak, Your Highness?"

Aret looked up into the wooden rafters. Lady Gwendolyn was not the average, submissive lady of court. She would say what she was here to say whether she had permission or not. "Granted."

"It's plain to see you are injured," she said. "I'm worried about you, King Aret."

There was something musical in the way she said his name. "You don't have to worry about me anymore. Things are going to get back to normal now that the Rogue Knight is dead."

"Is he?" she asked.

Aret shook his head. "We have his shield and sword. He has crawled off to die."

She nodded, sadness in her eyes. Did she suspect the truth? It didn't seem possible, but she was a clever princess. Once she had left the room, Aret struggled to stand. It was a long, humiliating trip up the stairs. Aret used the banister for support.

Once in his bedchamber, Enri helped Aret remove his robes and the boy saw the blue and purple bruises. "What happened?"

"I fell from my horse this morning. I'm fine." Aret downed a vial of Miss Bonnie's sleeping potion. He eased his battered body and spirit into bed.

Shouting awakened him. He told himself that he was dreaming and tried to go back to sleep, but the damage was done. His aching body was awake. There was a loud slam and a scream. He attempted to sit up, but the pain was too much. He took the bell from the table next to his bed and shook it. In a few moments he rang it again more insistently.

Finally, Enri poked his head into Aret's chamber. "Sire?"

"What's going on out there?" Aret asked.

"The ghost bear is back!" Enri answered. "It's in the stables, but the horses escaped, and they've got him cornered. Looks like we've got him this time!"

Aret furrowed his brow, knowing this animal couldn't be cornered. "In our own royal stable." Aret's heart raced. The stable was connected to the castle by one known means and another secret means. He jerked up with a groan. Something inside him seemed to slip out of place and he collapsed back to the bed. "Go, Enri. You are my eyes. Find out all you can and report back."

Enri dashed out with a smile, pleased to be given such an important and exciting assignment.

Light flickered onto the ceiling from the window. The smell of smoke and burning manure stung Aret's nose. Valora was coming apart and there was nothing Aret could do but lie in bed.

A long painful hour later, Enri returned. "They set the straw in the stable on fire, hoping to smoke the bear out, but it disappeared again.

Aret groaned. Of course it had disappeared. "Is the fire out?"

"Yes, Sire." Enri tried to hide his yawn. Ruby rays of the rising sun peeked in the window, and the excitement of the night was more than the boy was accustomed to.

"Fetch the healer," Aret said.

"Yes, Sire. Right away." Enri hurried off.

Time passed painfully slow.

At last Enri returned, face pale and distant.

"What is it?" Aret asked.

The door opened wider and Sheriff Morto, still not completely dressed, entered. "The healer woman is dead, mauled by a bear. A silver arrow was found next to the body."

Aret turned his face into his pillow. She was dead because she had helped him.

At last Aret struggled to his feet. Enri put a loose fitting robe on his master and the three of them went out to the blackened, smoldering stable. The horses were housed in a temporary pen on the great lawn. Aret surveyed the damage. The fire had been carefully controlled. The straw was scorched black, but the timbers and stone of the building, though stained with soot, remained sturdy. In a corner, he saw where the bear had been when it had disappeared. There were scratches at the secret entrance and the dirt at its base had been dug up. The creature had tracked Aret back to the castle.

Aret had brought such pain to Valora by using that magic armor. How could he put an end to it?

Perhaps he could turn the rest of the armor in, tell them they found it discarded. Perhaps Aret could lace the armor with blood so it would look like the Rogue Knight had died. Perhaps the only way out for his people was for Aret to turn himself in as well as the armor.

The healer wasn't the only person that had helped Aret last night. "Has anyone heard from the woodsman's son?"

"No," Morto answered.

"Conduct a search," Aret commanded. "We must make sure he is safe."

A frigid wind filled Aret's nostrils with the smell of burnt wood. Histerland soldiers guarded the smoking stable and the rickety, makeshift horse pen. General Ulf bowed to Aret. One of his eyes was missing.

"What happened to your eye?" Aret asked.

The General smiled fiendishly. "A fight with a rogue. I killed him."

"Very good." Aret couldn't take his eyes off the glistening, pink socket. "Looks serious. Did you have the healer look at it before she . . . ?"

Ulf's smile broadened. "I saw the healer-woman. Yes."

Aret looked at the General firmly. "Quite a loss."

"Yes, Sire. With all the excitement in Valora, Perhaps you should courier for a new healer."

Aret's voice was flat. "An excellent idea, General."

Once Ulf was away, Aret asked, "Morto, have you ever seen General Ulf during one of the bear attacks?"

Morto looked inward, thinking back. "I don't believe so, but then I wasn't really looking for him."

"Tonight I want you to watch him," Aret said. "All night. If you like, you may tell him I've assigned you to help him track the bear."

"Yes, Sire," Morto said.

Aret smiled to himself. "And place the Rogue Knight's sword under guard. I believe he may come after it. Have it guarded by Ulf's men."

"Yes, Sire. What about the shield?"

"I'll lock it in my personal collection."

The light had faded in Aret's window, and a tray of barely touched food sat next to his bed. Aret sat up using his arms to help support his back.

Enri was out of breath when he bowed to his king. "I just met Sheriff Morto outside the soldier's wing. He says that General Ulf is sleeping in the soldier's barracks. The sheriff wanted to know how you were feeling."

It made Aret sick to be the object of everyone's pity. Their suspicion should probably have bothered him more than their pity. "I'm better. I will be fine after a good night's sleep. I know it's been a long day for you, Enri. I suggest you go to bed. I won't be needing you again tonight."

"Yes, Sire. Thank you, King Aret."

Once Aret was shut in his room, he rose stiffly and entered the secret passage behind his closet. He took up the magic shield and crept down into the abandoned, burned-out stables. He limped into the cold night, through the fields, and out toward the forest. The trees cast so many shadows. Any one of them could be a ghostly bear. Aret's breath left him in heavy clouds.

The mattress in the healer woman's hut was stained with blood. Her giant patient was gone. He had been moved to the prison, relocated for his protection rather than as a punishment.

Aret scooted an old chest out from under the blood stained bed. Opening it revealed arcane ingredients for forbidden spells and medicines. Aret painfully lowered himself to the floor. With a click, he pulled out the false bottom in the chest. Within were the pieces of his magic armor. Aret paused, panting from the exertion.

He rested his back flat on the dusty floor to keep it immobile while he slid the gold mail pants up to his waste. One painful arm at a time went into the hooded mail shirt. He put the thick purple coat with the gryphon insignia over the mail and had to rest again before buckling on the metal plates. He took a slow breath. His ribs were bound, and he could not fill his lungs to capacity.

He left the hut with his empty scabbard in hand. The shadowy woods gave way to the great lawn, all viewed through tiny eye slits in his helmet.

CHAPTER 30

MORTO IN THE MIDDLE

Sheriff Morto saw the moon glinting off metal. He stared unbelieving at the man in polished armor slowly marching across the great lawn. Finally Morto drew his sword and shouted, "Guardsmen! Soldiers! The Rogue Knight is here!"

The Rogue Knight took no notice, maintaining his slow march toward Morto. This did not seem like the knight Morto had heard about, the swift ghost knight that moved into battle and was gone before anyone could react. This real man before him was more frightening than the stories. A man who marches casually into impossible odds is either too confident for his own good, or stupid. Either way, it was the profile of a very dangerous man.

The Rogue Knight lifted his empty scabbard high into the air. Was he surrendering?

A shout emanated from high in the castle. The ivory sword flipped out of the castle window. The blade fell neatly into the scabbard in the Rogue Knight's hands. The knight then buckled the scabbard securely to his waist.

"Where is General Ulf?" the knight demanded.

"What business is that to you?" Morto asked.

Commander Golga emerged from the barracks along with Morto's reinforcements. Startled by the impudence of their enemy, they surrounded the Rogue Knight with short swords drawn.

"You are under arrest," Morto announced to the mysterious knight. "Drop your weapon and you won't be killed."

"Where is General Ulf?" the mystery knight repeated.

His reply was a dark shadow creeping along the ground. The beast reared up in front of the castle walls. Morto's Valoran guard scattered, but Commander Golga and his men relaxed their weapons. Their strange behavior mystified Morto, who was even more puzzled when the mystery knight addressing him by name.

"Sheriff Morto," the knight said. "Where is General Ulf?"

The bear's claws sparked against the Rogue Knight's shield. Morto saw that the knight had retrieved his shield from King Aret's collection, and a startling possibility occurred to him. He turned to Commander Golga. "Where is General Ulf?"

"What does it matter?" Golga said. "The bear is fighting for us."

Morto barged his way into the barracks and found General Ulf sleeping peacefully on his bed. "General!" Morto yelled. "The Rogue Knight is here! Along with the bear!" Getting no response, Morto shook the man. Ulf moaned woozily. Morto heard his men exclaim and he looked outside. The shadowy bear wavered in and out of sight.

Commander Golga and one of his men pulled Morto away from Ulf.

Morto's loyal men in blue saw the scuffle and Morto called to them, saying, "Get these men off of me!" Flynt, the old veteran in blue, pulled Golga and his man off Morto, but Ulf's men in black came to the aid of their fellows, and soon swords were drawn against one another. Morto dragged General Ulf from his bunk, but he would not awaken. He dragged Ulf out onto the lawn through the tense standoff.

The bear had easily ripped the Rogue Knight's shield from his arm and pounced on him. The Rogue knight lay under the black mass, barely even putting up a struggle. Morto thought he heard the Rogue Knight moan.

Morto again tried to wake the general, but to no effect.

Just as the bear was about to sink its teeth into his victim's neck, the Rogue Knight screamed, "Kill General Ulf!"

The bear looked over its shoulder. Light glinted off its one black eye, and it snarled a threat to Morto. It then looked down to

Aret and reluctantly abandoned its conquered prey. The bear crept ominously in Morto's direction.

Morto began to understand what this bear was. He pulled his dagger and jabbed it quickly into the sleeping General's throat. General Ulf came to and grabbed his throat. A gurgle of blood erupting from his neck and mouth. As he did this, the bear grabbed its throat. A dark vapor billowed from a sympathetic wound. The bear stumbled back, but summoned all its strength into one gurgling roar. It leapt into the air at Morto.

Morto ducked behind the mortally wounded General, but before the bear landed on its victim, it faded into a cloud of frigid darkness. The darkness dissipated around Morto like black smoke.

Commander Golga pointed his sword at Morto. His face was red. "You murdered a loyal Histerland General in his sleep!"

Morto's loyal guardsmen surrounded him defensively with swords raised. Morto looked where the mystery knight had been and found that he had already vanished. He rested General Ulf's corpse on the ground, stood, and said, "I am the sheriff of Valora. General Ulf murdered innocents here and prevented us from taking the Rogue Knight." Morto pointed to the spot where the knight had been. "Take your grievances to the king in the morning. I will abide by his decision."

Commander Golga looked at the line of men in blue and Morto knew what he was thinking. Morto's Valoran guard was about equally matched with Golga's own men. Even more numerous in Valora were the other soldiers in black, not part of Valora's personal guard or Golga's unit. The question was whether Golga would gamble on their unknown loyalties. Where would their allegiance fall if all out conflict broke out? Ulf would have taken the gamble, but Golga was in charge now.

Finally Golga waved his men to stand down. They took charge of Ulf's body. "We will see what your little king has to say."

Early the next morning, General Ulf's body was draped in the Histerland flag and loaded on a coach. The body was destined for Histerland City where it was to be interred in Valhalla, Hister's hall of heroes. Golga's men saluted as the coach sped off, but most Valorans didn't pay any attention to the fallen general.

Commander Golga marched before King Aret. The king was pale with dark circles under his eyes. He moved stiffly, as though much older than when Golga had first been assigned to Valora.

"King Aret," the Commander began. "Sheriff Morto murdered General Ulf. I demand that—"

King Aret interrupted. "You are in no position to demand anything! You knew all along General Ulf was a were-bear. Do you know how many innocents he harmed? The entire fief has been terrorized, the children of Valora afraid to sleep at night!"

"Lord Aret," Golga said. "General Ulf never harmed an innocent. All the people he terrorized had ties to the Underground."

"Did they?" Aret said. "I am king here. I judge innocence and guilt. Not you. Not General Ulf. I should have been informed that he was the bear. You are supposed to be working for me. Because of my lack of knowledge, the Rogue Knight was allowed to escape again. You call Morto a traitor? Who is the real traitor here?"

Commander Golga had thought King Aret a weak leader and a fool, but he could see the king was deadly serious. "I'm sorry, King Aret. It will not happen again. I will see that you are informed of everything we do."

"You are General now," King Aret said, "in charge of Hister's forces in my lands. See that you don't disappoint me."

"Yes, Sire. Thank you, Sire." Perhaps King Aret was right. Perhaps they would have won the day if they had trusted the king in the first place. It was difficult to trust anyone here. The Rogue Knight could not operate so freely without help. A national hero was dead, and Valora had not heard the end of it.

CHAPTER 31

THE TRAITOR

The uncertainty on the old man's face pleased Aret. Purvis was not accustomed to being called before the throne at such a late hour. It would unbalance him, make him nervous.

"Yes, My Lord?" Purvis said in a high, tired voice.

"Am I really?"

Purvis was confused. "*Really* what, Sire?"

"*Really* Your Lord?"

"Of course! I don't understand."

Aret pulled an envelope out of his shirt. Purvis averted his eyes. He knew what it was.

"This was found on a private courier. Along with detailed notes on our finances and inventory, it contains suspicions about my loyalty. You included a list of my disappearances and my wounds."

"My Lord! You know I wear the red sash. Sending reports to the Necromancer is part of my duty, my obligation. This has never been a secret."

"And did you send these reports on my father... my brother?"

"Of course, but—"

"Did you get my family killed?"

"No! I only made reports, as any member of the order would. I had no idea what they would do with that information. I downplayed your brother's activities. He was just going through a phase."

Aret burrowed his stare into the man.

"I raised you children," Purvis said. "The Valoras are my family."

Aret shook his head. "That's what hurts so much."

Purvis slowly lowered his gaze and wiped his eyes on his sleeve. "What do you intend to do with me?"

Old Purvis was so much smaller than Aret remembered. "I haven't decided."

"The High Court is already suspicious," Purvis said. "If my reports stop, they will investigate."

Purvis was slimier than Aret had suspected. "Trying to save yourself?"

Purvis straightened himself and met his master's gaze. "The safety of you and Valora is my only concern." He paused. "If you want me gone, the best course would be to make my death look… accidental."

Aret was truly perplexed by this statement. Was Purvis still playing the advisor?

"But they will send a replacement to your court," Purvis continued, "and my replacement will be much worse. I kept things out of my reports. If not for me, you would have been dealt with long ago, like your brother." He averted his eyes again. "Your father was more than my king. He was my dearest friend. My fate is yours to decide."

Aret couldn't believe what he was hearing. "Are you actually trying to say that you *helped* me?"

"In my small way."

Aret waved the envelope. "*This* was helping? *This* would damn me!"

"Things have gone too far. I've done all I could. You will note that I make references to *suspicions*. In actuality, I have known with complete certainty about your activities for quite some time."

Aret could feel his temper rising. He wanted to grab a sword and cut the old man in two, but there would be no honor in that.

"You will be kept around for the time being, but your mail will be monitored. You will only write what I tell you to write."

Purvis furrowed his brow. "Yes, Sire. But it may already be too late."

CHAPTER 32

THE FALL

Prince Brigham rode into Valora with a hundred Histerland soldiers at his back. A boy stood in the road waving the Gryphon banner. The thundering hooves pounded closer and closer to the boy, but Brigham did not slow down or make any attempt to announce their purpose. The flag bearer finally dashed off the road, barely escaping being trampled in the deafening stampede. Brigham looked back to see the boy literally choking on their dust.

Sheriff Morto and General Golga awaited them at the great oak doors of Castle Valora. Brigham had made his way into town so swiftly that the sheriff barely had time to gather a few guards together.

Prince Brigham stopped his horse abruptly before them, and his men followed suit. He tossed Morto two envelopes sealed with the imprint of Hister. The prince watched coldly as Morto tore the seal and read.

"I expect no resistance," Brigham said.

Morto looked to the castle and his guard, then to the Prince and his force. With no trace of emotion, Morto waved his guard back.

Prince Brigham sneered and rode his horse right into the main hall.

The traitor was on the stairs. The look on his face was priceless! Aret hadn't seen this coming.

Brigham dismounted and marched up the stairs with drawn sword. "Stop where you are!"

Aret backed away. "What is the meaning of this?"

"You are under arrest."

Brigham smiled when Aret pulled a decorative sword from the wall. This wouldn't be fun if it was too easy. Aret blocked Brigham's strikes. The traitor was a better fencer when taken by surprise than in formal competition, but resisting Brigham with that display piece was hopeless.

Aret knocked a decorative suit of armor into Brigham's path and dashed into the master bedroom. Brigham leapt over the obstacle. The traitor was trapped, actually seeking to hide in his closet! What a humorous anecdote this would make! Brigham opened the wardrobe, but found his quarry gone.

He gave voice to his frustration as he knocked ornate clothing to the floor. The sides of the wardrobe were smooth, but the back wall made a full thump when rapped upon. This was no magical escape.

Brigham's men finally caught up to him. He turned and pointed to the open wardrobe. "Batter this wall down!"

King Aret Valora was warm and comfortable in a quilted doublet. His ribs still ached, but they had healed, more or less. A delicious dinner of roast lamb sat in his content stomach. He was strolling up the steps to his bedchamber when he heard a racket below.

Someone had ridden a horse into the main hall! Prince Brigham, followed by a group of Histerland soldiers, marched up the stairs.

Aret backed away. "What is the meaning of this?"

"Stop where you are!" Brigham called out. "You are under arrest."

There was no way to talk his way out of this. Aret grabbed a decorative sword from the wall. He blocked Brigham's sword strokes while continuing up to the balcony. There was no way Aret could fight them all off, and the decorative sword would never penetrate mail.

Aret knocked a suit of armor into Brigham's path. With his pursuers momentarily delayed, Aret darted into his room. He leapt into the wardrobe and shut the door.

In the secret chamber behind the closet, Aret quickly slipped the gold scale shirt over his head. He covered the mail with the reinforced tunic. A loud bang at the secret door startled Aret, and he dropped the metal gorget. The clang of metal on stone excited his pursuers, and they battered the wall with more fury.

The buckles were stubborn and his fingers unsteady. A king should never have to put his armor on unassisted.

The wood panel splintered, nearly caving in.

Aret pulled his shield onto his arm and braced himself behind the secret entrance. The brass-tipped battering ram pounded into the secret room and came against Aret's magic shield. The men behind it jarred suddenly and painfully to a stop, as though they had struck a stone wall. The heavy battering ram fell on their boots.

Aret wrapped the remaining plates in a sheet and slung it over his shoulder.

Brigham's men piled into the narrow passage, confronting Aret one at a time in the darkness. One by one, they fell before the ivory sword. For every soldier down, another took his place. It was as though the entire Histerland army were here to take him. At last, Aret had no choice but to retreat down the secret stairs.

He emerged in the stable with the soldiers steps behind. A smile crossed his lips when he saw Snow already decked out in brass horned armor. Rowen saluted and ran into hiding as Aret leapt onto his horse.

Aret and Snow tore down the road into the setting sun. General Golga and his men guarded the road, but Snow leapt over them. Golden horseshoes knocked the soldiers to the ground.

The road turned slightly, momentarily hiding Aret from his pursuers. This was his chance to leave the road. Snow slowed in the thick brush, but the trees would conceal them, especially as the sun sank lower. Snow flew down a streambed, splashing through the frigid water, breaking the trail of hoof-prints and their scent.

Deep in the forest, Aret dismounted and led Snow behind an ancient, ruined wall. The mossy, crumbling stone was overtaken with weeds. Aret crouched behind the wall, trying to silence his breathing enough to listen for pursuers. Frozen vapor puffed from his mouth in longer and longer clouds.

Dogs barked in the night. The baying echoed in the distance and finally faded. Aret's life was safe for the moment, but his role as king and the fate of his kingdom was very much in doubt.

CHAPTER 33

A COMMON THIEF

The next morning, a nobleman's coach stopped before a gleaming knight that blocked the road. The Rogue Knight easily killed the noble's defenders, and the noble crawled out of the coach on all fours begging, "Spare me. I have money. You can have anything."

Aret Valora, the Rogue Knight, searched through the coach and finally found a pack of food and wine. He loaded it onto his snow-white horse and sped away, ignoring the noble's offers of money and jewels.

Aret washed his face in a cold stream while Snow drank. The water along the edge of the stream had a thin layer of ice, but the motion of the water kept the rest from freezing. Aret stared at his reflection in the water. Clouds floated in the blue sky above him.

He had truly lost it all. A king just yesterday, now he was nothing but a common thief. He led Snow through the woods to the overgrown ruins where he had made camp. Aret unbuckled the horse's armor. He untangled burs from Snow's mane and brushed through the knotted hair. At least Aret still had this one loyal friend.

The glow of the fire was hidden by the crumbled walls. Aret reclined against the stones and buried his face in his hands.

His father had been right. Gabriel had been right. The riddle of the Sphinx had been right. His quest for revenge had hurt him and the people he cared about. His enemies were not only unhurt, they had prospered.

A snapping twig startled Aret out of his misery. He drew his ivory sword and slowly peeked around a corner of the ruined stone wall.

The intruder was not there.

"Good day, My King."

Aret whirled around at the sound of the voice behind him. Garnet, the old woodsman's son, bowed to him. Garments of leather and wool protected him from the chill of the woods.

"I'm nobody's king anymore," Aret said. "How did you find me?"

"I'm officially the new woodsman of Valora," the young man said. "Forgive my impudence, but I know these woods better than you do."

Aret pointed his sword threateningly. "I can't let you tell anyone where I am."

"The dogs would have found you last night if I hadn't covered your trail."

Aret lowered his weapon. "You helped me... again?"

Garnet lifted a dressed rabbit. "You are still my king, no matter what that cruel man in your castle says."

Aret sighed with relief and collapsed against the wall. "Sit," he said with a bit of his old authority. "What's going on in Valora?"

Garnet hung the rabbit over the fire. "As I said, I've been officially appointed the new woodsman. The false king increased taxes to raise the transition of power tax and to pay a penalty for any help the Valorans may have given you against Hister's interests. People are having a hard time getting by."

Aret sat across from Garnet. "How is Sheriff Morto?"

"Gone."

"Gone? You mean they..."

"Sent him into the Histerland Army."

"And Purvis?"

"Still in his old spot. Wishes he wasn't though. He's the subject of all the new king's jokes."

"Serves him right." There was a long pause before Aret asked what was foremost on his mind. "What happened to Lady Gwendolyn? Did they send her back to Lyon?"

The woodsman shook his head and poked at the roasting meat. "No. They married her off already, got quite a treasure for her."

The thought of her with another man sent a shudder of revulsion through Aret, and he could no longer bear to sit. "Who did they marry her to?"

The young woodsman showed no real interest as he answered, "King Bulba, the troll king."

Aret looked up to the sky and clenched his fists. He strapped Snow's saddle back on without a word.

Garnet looked up at Aret and raised an eyebrow. "Where are you going?"

"I have to get her back."

"Why? They're married."

"I don't care anymore," Aret said.

"What are you going to do, storm Troll Keep alone? You're a wanted man."

Aret ignored him, spurring Snow over the forgotten forest path.

CHAPTER 34

RESCUE THE DAMSEL

Snow bounded across the bridge. The smell of the stagnant moat made Aret dizzy. A surly giant, at least 12 feet tall, stood guard at the opposite end of the bridge. He had a bulbous nose and only three visible teeth. Aret pulled back the reins, slowing Snow. The giant lifted a massive club, thicker than Aret's waist and as long as Aret was tall. The giant swung it forward.

The tremendous impact reverberated off the ruinous walls of Troll Keep. It should have broken every bone in Aret and his horse. At the very least, it should have knocked him from the saddle and into the fetid mud below, but Aret's amazing shield absorbed every bit of the blow.

Aret drew his sword and struck back. The giant was caught off guard by the quick recovery of his foe, but, with his long stride, he easily stepped away from Aret's blade. The giant brought his club down on the sword, ripping it from Aret's hand and sending him off balance.

Aret rolled into the fall, his armor clanging against the stone bridge. He stopped just short of the edge, looking down at the bubbling mud below him. An ominous webbed fin wound across the slimy surface.

The shadow behind him signaled Aret to raise his shield once more as the club came down on him. Aret wished he would have brought a lance. The long reach could have speared the giant as Aret charged on horseback, and the giant wouldn't have had time to strike. There was no point in thinking about that now.

Aret struggled to his knees and positioned his shield to the side, deflecting the next blow.

Aret stepped towards his sword, but the giant made movement impossible. The giant's large fingers curled around the edge of Aret's shield, pulling it to the side as he raised his club high. Aret had no choice but to let the shield slip away so he could roll from the giant's club and dash towards the keep. The giant tossed the shield to the ground and charged his prey with pounding footsteps.

Aret turned to face his foe and raised his empty scabbard into the air. He had maneuvered the giant between himself and his sword. The magic blade answered Aret's call. It flew home, but the giant was in its path. It sliced into the giant's side as he was raising his club to strike.

With the giant off balance, Aret ploughed into his legs, knocking him backwards off the stone bridge.

The giant managed to catch hold of the ledge and dangled above the bubbling mud. His muscles twitched and his neck knotted as he pulled his massive body up.

Aret again raised his scabbard, calling his sword. The giant howled with pain as the ivory blade twisted out of him and flew into its home.

The giant lost his grip and splattered into the mud below. The mud was deeper than a normal man was tall, but not deeper than a giant. He rose to his feet and wiped brown slime from his eyes. The giant hurled mud up at Aret defiantly, not noticing the fin sliding around him until he was pulled down into the muck.

Aret turned away from the muddy struggle and retrieved his shield.

Snow had wandered into the courtyard of Troll Keep and had found a bountiful banquet of weeds. The horse seemed oblivious to the trouble they were in. Aret wiped his blade clean and gripped the sword tightly in both hands. He proceeded into the courtyard, scanning from side to side, expecting another attack. Troll Keep seemed to be abandoned. Spider webs hung in every corner. Weeds and vines intruded into every crack in the stone walls.

Aret cautiously climbed narrow stone steps. The stairs were open to the sky. Anyone wandering in the courtyard would see Aret, but the place appeared deserted.

He found Lady Gwendolyn sitting on an elaborate bed, still in her veiled wedding gown, an angel in white, still untouched by earthly sin. She looked up with startled surprise. "Aret?"

King Bulba emerged from an adjoining chamber. Fur draped his broad shoulders and his stringy bangs were combed forward. "My son guarded the bridge. My last son. What did you…?" Bulba was shaking, his oily face red with anger. "The girl is mine. We were married by the Necromancer himself, perfectly legal. You have no right to—"

The sound of the Necromancer's name filled Aret with burning anger. He stabbed at Bulba, who dodged the blow.

"I don't honor the Necromancer's bargains," Aret said.

"Then you have no honor," King Bulba said. "You are nothing but a villain."

Bulba pulled his ax from its mount on the wall and swung, but Aret easily blocked it. The ivory blade slid into Bulba's chest like he were made of butter. Bulba stumbled back against the wall, wheezing for breath as he dropped the ax.

He snarled up at Aret. "We could have been friends." He struggled to breath. "Together, we could have… Not even Hister could have stood against us…" his voice trailed off and he fell dead.

Together we could have… Still panting from excitement, Aret stared down at his defeated foe and found himself empty. Bulba may have been ugly and uncouth, but what had been his real crime? The trolls had suffered under Hister as much as anyone. Could Bulba have been an ally?

"You shouldn't have come here," Gwendolyn said. "I'm their queen now."

Aret pulled Gwendolyn up from the bed. "I know," Aret said. "But I couldn't stand the thought… It's my fault you're here. I wanted to rescue you."

She looked away from him. "I was going to be married off to someone eventually. You knew that."

"Yes, but..." Aret looked down at King Bulba's body once more. "Is *he* what you wanted?"

"Of course not, but this is the life of a noblewoman. If you wanted me for yourself, you should have said something."

"I never said—" He stopped himself. It was true. He wanted her. Why else would he storm Troll Keep alone, kill her rightful husband? He was behaving like a villain, it was true. He grabbed her by the hand and pulled her to him. His helmet provided an extra barrier between her scrutiny and his heart. She couldn't see the sudden realization and fear on his face. "What if I *had* said something? Would you have wanted a life with me, or would I be no different to you than King Bulba?"

"Oh, Aret." She turned away again.

He felt like such a fool. He had not thought any of this through. "Do you want me to leave you?"

She wrapped her arms around him, burying her cheek against his purple tunic. "Of course you would have been different."

His chest swelled with renewed purpose. He grabbed her hand and turned towards the steps, almost bumping into a mud-encrusted face. King Bulba's giant son had successfully freed himself from the bog and had crawled up the narrow stairs like a normal man climbs a ladder.

"Daddy!" the giant moaned as it landed on Aret. With his knee in Aret's stomach, and a single minded fury in his eyes, the giant tightened his plump fingers around Aret's neck. The giant rang Aret's head into the stone floor, again and again. The world inside Aret's helmet bounced back and forth. His spine threatened to pull apart every time the monster lifted his head.

Suddenly it stopped. All was still and silent, but the sound of metal on stone still echoed in Aret's head. Bulba's ax stuck out of the giant's skull. Lady Gwendolyn, her white dress splattered with blood, released the handle of the ax and backed away from what she had done.

The giant, ax still hanging from his head, snarled at her.

Aret grasped at the stone under him. His hand found his sword hilt and he stabbed up through the giant's neck.

The stained blade poked out the top of the ogre's head, and his face changed from fury to sadness as he looked upon his father's dead body. Tears of blood dripped from his eyes. The giant toppled down the steps and off the ledge, landing with a thud and a cloud of dust.

Below Aret and Gwendolyn, a gray woman strolled through the courtyard with a heavy pot. Her only clothing was her gray hair, which was tied around her like a dress. She dropped the pot of stew, probably meant to be part of the newlyweds' dinner, and rushed to the dead giant. She looked up at Aret, her new queen behind him, and wailed like a banshee. The mournful sound echoed off the stone walls.

It was a cry that could wake the dead, and whatever forces were hiding in the keep would surely be after them now. Aret removed his helmet and looked into Gwendolyn's eyes, pulling her close. "Do you want to stay, or do you want to come with me?"

She did not hesitate. "Let's get out of here."

Aret nodded, put on his helmet, grabbed her hand, and led her down the stairs.

The gray woman pointed at her queen as Aret led Gwendolyn across the courtyard. "Traitor!" she screeched. "We knew you were trouble! I warned King Bulba not to marry you!"

Gwendolyn looked behind her as Aret pulled her forward. "This wasn't my intention."

"Don't talk to her," Aret said. "You will only make things worse."

The troll woman shrieked and moaned. "You will never be safe! You hear, witch? Your names will be cursed and hated by all trolls until the end of time!" The gray woman continued to shout, but the words became indistinct as they put more distance between them.

They interrupted Snow's repast when Aret helped Gwendolyn onto the saddle and then quickly mounted behind her. They bounced down the road, but then dove into the forest, following narrow trails not meant for horses. Branches slapped against their legs and tore Gwendolyn's wedding dress, but Snow ploughed on, oblivious. Lady Gwendolyn's soft hands clung tighter to Aret, and he wished he were free of the armor so he could feel her touch.

At last Snow trotted to a stop; he knew the way as well as his master. Aret leapt down and lifted Lady Gwendolyn to the soft grass next to an ancient stone wall. The wall had been invisible behind weeds and vines.

"These are the ruins of an old castle," Aret said. "Magna and I used to play here as kids. We'll be safe here for awhile."

Her doe eyes blinked up at him. "Thank you, Lord Aret."

He removed his helmet and shook his head. "I'm no one's lord anymore."

"Why did you do it?" Gwendolyn asked. "You could have been killed, most likely should have been killed. King Bulba may have been disgusting, and his people cruel, but I was given to him."

Aret looked up at the sunlight through the leaves. "I couldn't bear to see you hurt because of me. I love you." He looked into her eyes. "If I ever become a king again, I want you to be my queen."

The corners of her mouth twitched, not sure whether to stretch up into a smile or down into a frown. Aret's heart seemed to stop, waiting for her to give some reaction.

"Why now?" she asked. "Why didn't you say this earlier, before all of this?"

Aret said nothing. There was nothing he could say, no excuse he could make. He should have told her when he was a king, when he was deserving of her. Now he was nothing but a common thief.

"Why wait for what might never happen," she said. "Why not marry me now?"

Aret put his hands on her shoulders. "Do you know what you are saying? If you marry me now, you will give up all right to title and property. If I am captured or killed you will become a beggar."

"What did you think I would do after you took me from King Bulba? If you send me back to Lyon, or to my brother, I will only be traded off again."

She was right. He had no plan. "You could go back to Troll Keep. You had no part in what happened. I could even send them a ransom demand, make it convincing. Or you could seek asylum in the Golden City."

"Better a beggar wife or widow than a bargaining chip to be traded for this or that."

He drew her shoulders towards him and gently pressed his lips to hers. The gentle kiss became prolonged, more aggressive as their lips became accustomed to each other. Aret never imagined this could happen, especially not now. He removed his glove so he could touch her silky cheek.

She pulled away. "What about Valora?"

He shook his head and shrugged his shoulders. "Lost. Nothing I can do. Your brother raised taxes to pay for my crimes. The people are living in poverty, just like my father always warned would happen if we openly rebelled."

Aret changed topic suddenly. "Would you like some food? I stole some supplies from a troop of soldiers, and we have rabbit meat, a bit cold now, but we can build a fire and—"

"We have to help them," she interrupted.

"What can I do?" he asked. "All my most trusted people are either dead or assigned to other baronies."

She furrowed her brow. "When you were working in secret all that time, were you working alone?"

"Not exactly. My brother had friends. They would come and go."

She smiled faintly. "Then there is an organized network of resistance. We have allies. We just have to make contact with them."

CHAPTER 35

GATHER THE MERRY MEN

Young Garnet Woodsman sat alone at a table in the corner of Mack's tavern. He waited as Mack took Sheriff Golga's order.

"We don't have any bread or meat right now," Mack said. "Porridge and beer is all we got."

"Are you refusing to serve a loyal Histerland sheriff?" Golga said.

Mack shook his head. "Of course not, Sheriff. We are just running a little short right now after paying our taxes. I tell you what I'll do. Bowl of porridge and a beer... on the house." He lowered his voice. "Don't tell anyone and I'll even give you a pinch of salt for your porridge."

As Mack made his way to the kitchen, he saw the new woodsman and said, "I'll be right with you." He brought the sheriff his meal and then approached Garnet. "Porridge and a beer?"

Garnet spoke in a low voice, "Beer," then he lowered it even further, "And our king would like to talk to your contacts in the Underground."

Mack looked over his shoulder at the sheriff, making sure he wasn't within earshot, and whispered, "King Brigham?"

"No." Garnet said. "Our *real* king."

Snow trotted to a stop at the crossroads. There was only one other person there, a crooked old beggar sitting on a tree stump. His hair was a gray tangle and his arm curled around his walking stick in an unnatural way. Perhaps Aret's contact had seen the beggar and left for lack of privacy.

Aret dismounted and dropped a single flower on the sunken earth. This is where Aret's brother had been buried in a shallow grave. Magna's grave should have been covered by flowers and accolades, yet here he was, one lone flower and not even a stone marker.

The beggar stood straight. "So, you are the deposed king we've heard so much about."

"Who are *we*?" Aret asked.

The dirty man extended his no longer twisted arm. "I am Arim. You wanted to see me?" The lines on the beggar's face were no more than dirt embedded in the small creases of his skin. He had bulldog jowls and a slender nose.

At last Aret realized his foolishness. An agent of the Golden City would not look like an agent from the Golden City. Aret extended his hand and found Arim's grip strong and vital.

"I am Aret Valora. I am here to offer my services to the Underground."

Arim moved Aret's cloak aside and looked over the glittering gold mail and silver plates. "Is that armor everything people say?"

"More." Aret could not help but respond with pride at hearing his magic armor complimented, but he wasn't sure what to make of this man touching his cloak. No beggar touched a nobleman, but then this man was no beggar, and Aret was no longer royalty.

"Good," Arim said. "It will have to be. We used to have a pretty extensive spy network in Histerland, but it's breaking down. People are becoming complacent. They don't remember the better life they had before Hister and his wizard. For years, we have been planning to raid the Bastille. It houses political prisoners that are mostly forgotten, including Rollo, heir to the throne of Norman. If we can get him on our side, we might be able to rally the people of Northern Histerland against the barons there."

"Unfortunately," Arim continued, "The Bastille is damn well guarded. We would need an army to get in and out, but we can't get an army that deep into Histerland. We only have a small band."

"Sounds like you don't think we have much chance of success," Aret said.

"No," Arim said plainly. "Are you in?"

The plan was ridiculous. Nothing beyond Histerland City itself was as well guarded as the Bastille. But then, a year ago, the Necromancer's tower had seemed impregnable too. It was better than stealing trinkets and food like a common thief. "What have I got to lose?"

Arim smiled. "Meet us in two days at the fork in Bonne River."

CHAPTER 36

THE BASTILLE

Aret rode into a small camp at the river's fork, but instead of finding allies, he found four Histerland soldiers. Without slowing, he dropped from his horse and drew his sword. One of the soldiers raised his hands in submission. Aret blinked in confusion and realization. The jowls and slender nose were unmistakable. It was Arim, but not the Arim he had met before. The gray tangle of hair was now a silky reddish-blonde. He had a high forehead, and his clean face appeared twenty years younger, making him around Magna's age. Arim and his men wore stolen Histerland uniforms.

Aret's new allies were full of surprises. Arim made introductions, and Aret was disturbed to find that these four men were the entire group: four men for four floors of the Bastille. Aret dared not show his reluctance, not when the others showed no hesitation.

They rowed a small boat upstream. Soon, they neared a stubby tower about four times as wide as it was tall. The Bastille. Anyone who saw them assumed they were Histerland soldiers on business, and no one questioned Histerland soldiers on business. Unable to disguise his armor, Aret hid in the bottom of the boat under a blanket. It was humiliating, but Aret was becoming accustomed to hiding and sneaking.

Once they docked at the Bastille, Aret immediately pushed off the blanket and jumped to shore with brandished sword. He sliced through the two guards at the dock before they could raise the alarm. Arim's small group dashed into the brick tower and up the steps of the Bastille, killing guards and stealing keys. They split up. Each of them took a different floor of the Bastille.

Aret ran up the steps behind Arim and charged onto the third floor. He tried his stolen key in the first cell, but the catch wouldn't budge. He tried to pull the key from the lock, but it was jammed inside the rusty mechanism. The success of this venture depended on getting in and out quickly.

At last he gave up on the keys. He hacked through the lock with his ivory sword and yanked the door open. Aret hoped the others weren't having the same problem. They didn't have the advantage of magic swords.

The smell of urine and mold hit Aret like a wall. The old man inside the cell was withered, his muscles atrophied. Aret moved on to the other cells, hacking them all open. The prisoners that could run darted past Aret and down the steps, but the first man still lay in his cell.

"Wait!" Aret called to the escaping prisoners. "This man needs our help." But the escapees ignored their savior and continued to run. Aret pulled the old man's withered arm over his neck and hauled him towards the stairs.

Another man crawled out of a cell. He was young, but both of his legs were missing. "Wait," he called to Aret. "Help me!"

Aret gently put the first man down and dragged the other prisoner across the wood floor. Then another prisoner called to Aret from a shadowy cell, begging for help.

"What can I do?" Aret said. "I can't carry you all!"

Arim called from the stairwell. "Where are you? We've got Rollo. It's time to go!"

"These prisoners can't walk!"

"Reinforcements are coming!" Arim shouted. "We are leaving now! With or without you!" Arim disappeared down the steps, leaving Aret alone with the helpless prisoners. Even with his magic armor, Aret couldn't fight all of Histerland by himself. He dropped the legless man, trying to block out their cries as he ran from them. Their cries would haunt him for the rest of his life. His decline was complete; a nobleman doesn't run away.

The open air was crisp and refreshing after the stale mustiness of the Bastille. Their boat was in sight.

"Stop!" A single guard pointed his sword at the docks.

Arim's band froze in place. The guard cautiously unbuckled his chinstrap and removed his helmet.

Aret's heart swelled. "Sheriff Morto!"

"Captain Morto," Morto corrected him. "You may have tricked the other guards, but I'm not so easy."

Arim raised his sword, but Aret waved him back. "If he was going to sound the alarm, he would have done it already."

Morto looked over his shoulder and nodded, lowering his sword. "Get out of here."

Aret removed his helmet so he could be face to face with his former sheriff. "Come with us!"

Morto shook his head. "I have a family to think about." He marched from the docks, and Aret stared after him. Morto had been a good sheriff, the best, and loyal to the end.

"Come on!" Arim yelled. He had already kicked the boat off.

Aret jumped onto the boat as it drifted away and smothered himself in the blanket. It was hard to be suddenly still after so much exertion. Aret peeked out from under the stifling fabric. Soldiers on shore chased after escaping prisoners, paying no attention to a boat of fellow soldiers.

The new man with their group had a gray handlebar mustache. He was not nearly as filthy as the men Aret had seen on the third floor. Though slender, Rollo was not starving, and his garments, though frayed, were once fine and had been cleaned recently. Most of the other escaping prisoners would be caught or killed. Aret hoped this one man was worth their lives.

The High Necromancer approached the throne of Valora, but this time there was a different man sitting on it. The entire mood of the fief had changed. Purvis was chained to the seat beside King

Brigham and, as always, he chronicled the official proceedings of Valora.

"Brigham," the Necromancer began.

"*King* Brigham," Brigham corrected him.

The Necromancer narrowed his eyes. "Don't forget you are here by the grace of Hister. No one else wants you here. Your subjects certainly don't."

"What's wrong?" Brigham asked. "Did you come to Valora just to insult me? Have a drink of Valora's oldest wines with me."

"You let Aret escape. With no kingdom to lose he is fighting Hister's interests full time. No one knows where or when he will turn up next."

"Histerland's been around over half a century," Brigham said. "One villain in magic armor won't change that. You can handle him."

"We don't have to. Aret is your problem. I have important business of my own to attend to. Handle him or we will appoint a new king who will."

Brigham stiffened slightly and nodded. "Yes, High Necromancer." He stared up at the wooden support beams, thinking aloud. "No one knows when or where Aret will turn up. What I need is something to lure him out…"

CHAPTER 37

THE PRISONER OF VALORA

A heavily guarded coach rolled up to Castle Valora. Soldiers unlocked it and yanked out a manacled man. The prisoner's face was covered by a burlap sack. Queen Mimi and her maids saw them march this obviously important prisoner through the main hall.

Mimi followed them to the prison wing. A guard bowed, but stopped her at the door. She raised her head high. "Who is that prisoner?"

The guard stared ahead, no sign of emotion. "I don't know, My Lady."

"You don't know?" she probed.

"No, My Queen. None of us were told except for the king and possibly Sheriff Golga."

She nodded. "Thank you, soldier."

Her maidens waited for her while she entered the king's office. Mimi found a maid sitting on Brigham's lap. Camille, the same maid that had serviced her younger brother in his youth, was kissing Mimi's husband.

"Don't you people knock?" Brigham said before seeing that it was his wife. "Oh, it's you. What do you want?"

Mimi was accustomed to his infidelity, but wished he would at least pretend to hide it from her. "I just saw them escorting a new prisoner in. Who is it?"

Brigham motioned with his head and slapped Camille on the bottom as she left. "That is none of your business," he said to his wife.

Camille kept her head bowed but shot the queen a sideways glance as she passed her.

"I am queen here," Mimi said.

"Queens are best seen and not heard," Brigham said. He then gave a fiendish smile. "If you must know something, if you won't leave without some tidbit of gossip… that prisoner is my secret weapon to lure your traitorous brother to me."

She furrowed her brow. "What prisoner is that important? And how would his presence lure Aret here if no one knows who this prisoner is, not even me?"

Brigham laughed and took a long drink of century old Valoran wine. "He'll know." Camille entered with a plate of fruit of cheese. Brigham smiled at her then scowled at his wife. "You are dismissed."

Mimi turned and marched directly back to the prison, her ladies barely keeping up with her. Again the guard bowed, but remained staring straight ahead. "Let me by!" she demanded.

"I'm sorry, Milady," the guard said. "I have orders."

"I am your queen. I order you to let me by."

He looked down at her for a moment, not sure what to do. Finally he moved aside. Mimi pulled the keys off the wall hook, and one of her maidens lit a lamp to illuminate the shadowy halls.

She raised her light at the faces in the cells. Until recently the jail had almost always been empty, but now it was full. Some cells even housed two or three prisoners, though they were only meant for one. At the end of the hall, the light fell on a dirty, haggard profile. His face was sunken and sallow, but still familiar. She stared in disbelief. "Magna?"

He looked up at her and some of the light returned to his eyes. "Mimi? Is it really you?"

Tears filled her eyes. "Shouldn't I be the one in doubt? You're supposed to be dead!"

"Where have they taken me?" he asked. "Am I in Lyon?"

"You are back in Valora," she said. "But not the Valora you remember." She grabbed the keys and fiddled with the lock. Her hands were shaking

"What are you doing?" Magna asked, a hint of fear in his voice.

"Freeing you, of course."

"No!" he said. "You can't do that!"

She ignored him, continuing to unlock the door. "Don't worry about King Brigham. I can handle him." To her surprise Magna pulled the door back shut.

His voice was weak and raspy. "You can't let me out. I'm dangerous. What time is it?"

She looked at him with pity. "Dangerous? Not now you aren't, but with a bath, some food, and some clean clothes… you will be dangerous again. Not even Hister himself will be able to stand against you."

She unlocked the door and hugged him tightly. He resisted at first before cautiously returning his sister's embrace.

Something sharp scratched at her hip. Magna's fingernails sliced into her shoulder. She looked up to see her brother's terrified face shrinking around his skull. Her handmaiden screamed, and the Husk that was once Magna lashed out with meat-hook claws.

He dropped his sister and started down the hall, but Sheriff Golga charged in with a lance, spearing him in the chest and forcing him back into his cell. The Sheriff then slammed the door shut.

The lance fell from the Husk's punctured chest, but there was no blood. Claws scratched and scraped at the prison bars, darting out towards Golga and King Brigham, who had followed the sheriff in. Leather wings poked out from the Husk's back and flapped uselessly in the small space, doing nothing but blowing up dust and straw.

King Brigham looked down at his bleeding wife and laughed. "I knew you would try something like this. You're a whole family of traitors!"

Queen Mimi opened her mouth as if to speak, but she didn't know what to say. Her hip and shoulder stung, and her dress was sticky with blood.

"What's that?" King Brigham held his hand to his ear. "I can't quite hear you. I guess I finally got you to shut up!" He raised his arms and looked to the ceiling. "At last I'm a free man!"

Her maidens rushed to Mimi's side, crying.

Sheriff Golga looked to his king. "My Lord," he said. "Perhaps we should get her to a healer."

King Brigham interrupted him with a scowl, drew his sword, and pointed it at his queen. Her ladies gasped and shielded her body.

"King Brigham!" Golga shouted.

With a crooked smile, King Brigham sheathed his sword and commanded, "Carry her to her rooms and fetch the healer."

CHAPTER 38

THE TRUTH LEAKS

Magna awoke on a bed of straw over hard stone. In a strange way, he was content. He was home and locked securely away so he couldn't hurt anyone.

The scraggly serf in the next cell asked, "Who are you? What happens to you at night?"

Magna laughed at the thought of a peasant not recognizing his former king. His neighbor crept into the shadows in the back of his cell, as far from the hysterical were-man as he could get, which just made Magna laugh even more.

"Barkeep!"

Mack looked away from the customer he had been talking to and saw Sheriff Golga with his head propped on his arm. There was an empty mug next to Golga's elbow, and his free hand waved in the air. "Barkeep!"

Mack fearfully abandoned the customer he was talking to and rushed a sixth mug to the sheriff. "If you will forgive me saying so, Sheriff Golga, I've never seen you drink like this. Is everything alright?"

"Alright?" Golga chuckled. "There's a monster in the jail… the queen was almost…" He stopped himself by chugging his ale.

Sensing something important going on, Mack sat across from Gogla. "I don't like seeing you like this, sir. You are a good, brave man and a good sheriff. If you tell me what's wrong, maybe I can help."

Golga looked up at him with bloodshot eyes. "You? Help? You're a barkeep."

"Exactly," Mack agreed. "I'm nobody." He raised the empty mug. "But I serve happiness by the pint."

Golga's chuckle ended in a burp. "I envy you, barkeep. You don't have to worry about anything but serving your drinks."

Golga, of course, could never learn how wrong he was on that count. Mack had come close to losing everything by serving Magna, and with Brigham's regime he could barely afford to stay open. He had tried to put his past with the Underground behind him, but was in constant fear that someone would exploit that connection for political gain or to confiscate his tavern.

"No mad kings," Golga continued, "or monsters, or their poor queens."

That was the second time Golga had mentioned the queen. Mack lowered his voice. "Is something wrong with Queen Mimi?"

"She's fine. The new healer-man fixed her up."

"A healer? Did the king strike her?"

Golga looked Mack in the eyes, and Mack looked away. He had overstepped his station in asking such a direct question, but the sheriff answered. "No. Almost. It was her brother that cut her."

Mack gasped quietly. "Lord Aret…?" He covered his mouth and corrected himself. "The traitor?"

"No," Golga said. "The other one." He pushed the empty mug at Mack. "Get me another."

Mack nodded and jumped from his seat with the empty mug. He paused for a moment behind the bar. The queen only had one living brother. The other, their beloved Magna, was supposed to be dead. Mack and his wife were among the few who knew that Magna had returned from the dead once before.

CHAPTER 39

LIFE IN HIDING

The thatch roof was mere inches above the loft where Gwendolyn and Aret slept. She could hear mice tunneling through the straw above her. Sunlight streamed through cracks in the wood walls, signaling morning. The rough canvas dress she wore had caused her to break out where the fabric chafed against her pale skin.

She rose without a word and climbed down the ladder. A wet nose against her leg startled her. Snow, who slept under the loft, was saying good morning. Flies buzzed around his night's waste. She shoveled it out the front door and rooted for eggs in the henhouse. She only found one, but along with some oatmeal warmed in the fireplace, it would serve as their breakfast.

Aret emptied out their bedpans and relieved himself in the bushes before joining Gwendolyn. They ate on a bench in the cool morning air, not bothering to say a word.

Gwendolyn thought about the day she and Aret had killed the troll king and their talk in the woods. She wondered what her life might have been like if her answer had been different.

While Gwendolyn rinsed the morning dishes, Aret brushed Snow and dressed the horse in armor. She was jealous of the attention he paid to that horse. He still looked at her tenderly, still huddled against her at night for warmth, at least when he was home for the night, but there was no passion anymore. How could he love what she had become? Aret may no longer be a king, but he was still able to ride over the land having adventures. Gwendolyn had longed for a life of freedom, a life outside castle walls, but she was as trapped as ever. Life in the castle was now nothing but a fantasy, with servants and maidens to care for her and talk with her. When Aret left her, she was more alone than she had ever been.

Aret called to her, and she buckled armor plates over his gold mail. He kissed Gwendolyn gently on her once ivory-smooth hand, now raw and calloused from toil. He then mounted Snow and spurred the horse away, leaving her alone once again. She wondered what would happen to her if he did not return. Would Garnet and the Underground still look out for her?

How could they consider bringing a child into a life like this?

Riding Snow was the only time Aret felt free. He would ride from the time he awoke until he went to bed at night if he could. Sometimes he did. This ride was over much too soon.

At the crossroads was a tailor's cart full of mended garments. Arim was a tailor today, in slick clothes and a puffy hat. He was not alone. There was a mustached man, tall with dark features. A pointed and feathered hat sat on his head.

Arim beamed as Aret dismounted. He slapped Aret on the back and held his shoulder tightly. "Have you heard?" Arim didn't wait for a response. "The Necromancer is gone!"

"Gone where?" Aret asked.

"Gone!" Arim said. "Disappeared! Banished from the world by the new Gatekeeper. The southern kingdoms have already seceded from Histerland. They call themselves the United City-States of Hellena. Histerland is falling away at the edges!"

"Really?" It was a lot for Aret to accept. His friend, Gabriel, replaced by a new Gatekeeper, never having said goodbye; the High Necromancer, his greatest enemy, gone, never giving Aret the satisfaction of seeing him suffer. But if it were true, could Hister's downfall be in sight as well?

"Yes," the tall stranger answered. "But the Hellenans have a unifying cultural identity."

Arim motioned to his dark friend. "This is Alonzo, special agent of King Luis." King Luis ruled Iberia, a large kingdom beyond the mountains west of Valora.

Alonzo bowed and extended his arm to Aret. "Iberia has lived in the shadow of Hister for far too long."

Aret took Alonzo's arm and said, "I've heard your king's wizard is almost as powerful as the High Necromancer."

Alonzo flashed a smile of perfect white teeth. "The Moor is even greater."

Aret doubted that. If their Moor was so powerful, why had he never stepped foot in Histerland before?

Alonzo pulled a wineskin from the cart and handed it to Aret. The wine was bitter, not sweet like wine from Valoran grapes.

"King Luis would love to send men across the mountains to help liberate Gaul," Alonzo said. "But we will be massacred if we do not have allies already in place here." The tall Iberian took the wineskin back and tipped it above his mouth.

"Valora would be the first province on their path to Histerland City," Arim said. "We need to find out how many people in Valora are still loyal to you."

Aret wondered that as well. He knew he still had a few friends at home, but would they be willing to fight … and possibly die for him? Moreover, would Aret be willing to take responsibility for their deaths? He had already cost them so much. "I will think about it."

"What's to think about?" Arim asked. "Liberating Valora, taking down Hister; isn't this what you wanted?"

Aret turned his back on them and jumped on his horse.

The Necromancer gone.

The Gatekeeper replaced.

The world had changed.

He left the road, taking a forest trail to the humble, thatch-roofed shelter he shared with his peasant wife. The hut was filled with smoke and the smell of a hearty stew on the fire. He found the once noble Gwendolyn scrubbing at a copper pot, work that should have been beneath her. Garnet, the woodsman of Valora, sat at their table sipping a bland tea. They always had meat when Garnet came to visit, and Aret knew Gwendolyn was grateful to have someone else to talk to.

When she saw Aret enter, Gwendolyn stared up at him with pleading eyes. Something big was going on.

"What's wrong?" he asked her.

She turned back to the wash basin, but Garnet answered him. "King Brigham has locked your sister in the east tower with her maids."

"She's a prisoner?" Aret said. "She is his queen. I suppose it is his right to keep her. He won't harm her. Having a Valora as his queen gives his reign legitimacy."

"I'm not so sure," Garnet said. "She was wounded. I spoke to the healer that treated her wounds." Garnet then added, "Brigham is also holding your brother."

Aret stared at him in numb silence for a moment. "My brother is dead. I buried him myself."

"No. He is being held in the castle prison. It is supposed to be a big secret."

Aret dipped the ladle into the thick stew and picked out a juicy piece of meat, probably rabbit. He was surprised by how numb he felt as the details washed over him. He had buried Magna's dead body, but where magic and curses were concerned, anything was possible.

Lady Gwendolyn dropped the copper pot she had been scrubbing. "Why are you so quiet? What are you thinking, Aret?"

"I'm thinking that I'm going to have to go back there and get my family out." He said it matter-of-factly, no inflection, no passion. It was simply what he had to do.

Gwendolyn shook her head. "Can't you see it's a trap? They'll kill you! How would you save them anyway? Do you think your sister would be happier here in this squalor than with her maids in the castle?"

That provoked a reaction from him. Aret turned to her. He could see in her eyes she regretted what she had said, but it was the truth. She wasn't just talking about his sister. Gwendolyn regretted living here with him. He could only blame himself. He pushed out the door, but was stopped by Gwendolyn's hand on his shoulder.

"I'm sorry, Aret," she said. "I love you. Given another chance I would have made the same decision, would still have run away with you."

He wrapped his arm around her waist and looked back into the dark cabin. "No. You're right. This is no place for a lady." He placed a hand on her stomach and the life growing inside. "Or our children." He kissed her on the forehead. "I have to do this. I am still a noble. I've faced greater odds and come back to you." He turned to Garnet Woodsman. "Take care of her."

Garnet bowed. "Of course, Lord."

Aret dared not look back to see the look on Gwendolyn's face.

Aret stopped at the crossroads where he had buried his brother the previous year. A single dry flower marked a depression where Magna's body had been. Had the dirt collapsed because the body under it was missing?

Aret stabbed into earth hardened by melting snow and spring sun. He dug his fingers into the dirt. Magna's body had been gone for quite some time.

Aret imagined the Husk crawling out of the shallow grave the very night he had been buried. Perhaps the Necromancer had found Magna there, dug him up to do his bidding.

Aret mounted again, wondering what Magna's life had been like all that time, killing night after night as the Husk, living like a beggar in the day while Aret squandered the life that should have been his.

CHAPTER 40

THE TRAP

Snow's hooves pounded the dirt road into Valora. Two guards were taken by surprise. One got in Aret's way and was immediately cut down. The other was smarter, retreating to spread the alarm. Citizens got out of the road, and two boys waved a happy greeting to their former king as he rode past them. It seemed not everyone in Valora hated Aret.

A rope pulled taught in his path, and before Aret could react, he found himself knocked from the saddle. Aret slammed into the dusty road as Snow continued on.

He forced his sore body to its feet as soldiers piled on. There were no more knights in the blue tunics of Valora. The few of the old Valoran Guard still remaining were forced to adopt the black garb of the Histerland soldiers.

One… two… three… blows were easily deflected by Aret's magic shield, and the soldier's gray mail was pierced by the ivory sword, but long arms finally pulled Aret down.

He struggled to his feet, waving his sword, but another body landed on him, pushing him to the ground, followed by another and another. Soon, Aret was buried under a mass of men. They pulled his shield away. Firmly grasping his sword arm, they twisted it back. At last his hand lost strength and the sword fell. They flipped him on his back, and King Brigham pulled off Aret's helmet.

Aret looked up at him with a sweaty brow, trying to mask his fear and frustration with defiance.

Brigham spat in Aret's face and gave him a fiendish smile. "Pull off that cursed armor."

Aret struggled. As long as he wore the armor, there was a chance. A crowd of citizens watched buckles undone and metal plates removed.

As long as Aret wore the armor, he was more than just a common man.

The golden scale mail fit Aret as though it were forged around his body, a second skin. It took much effort, but the soldiers managed to peel the mail shirt painfully over his shoulders and his head. A punch to the gut stunned Aret, and they slid the shirt off his arms.

Aret lay panting in the dust, wearing nothing but underclothes, his impotence plain to his people.

Brigham picked up the ivory sword and commanded, "Clear a space and give this traitor a sword."

The men pushed the crowd back and someone tossed a sword on the ground in front of Aret. Aret rose to his knees, still panting.

"Well," Brigham said. "Pick up the sword. I want to even out your ears."

Aret fumed with a sudden fury that overcame his exhaustion. He picked up the common sword and slashed at Brigham, who easily deflected the blow with the ivory sword. Again and again, Aret attacked. Each time his blow was deflected.

Aret's blows came slower, and Brigham finally jabbed the point of the ivory blade into Aret's ribcage. Aret recoiled from the pain of the thrust and stumbled backwards. To everyone's astonishment, there was no blood. His skin, bruised by the force of the blow, was not cut.

Brigham ran his finger along the edge of the blade and exclaimed, "This blade is as dull as a spoon!" He kicked up the scabbard, sheathed the ivory blade, and threw it to one of his burliest men. "Put it in the vault. At least it will make a worthy tribute to Hister." Brigham stared down at his defeated foe. "All our debts will be over, and peace will finally reign in Valora, thanks to me."

As two soldiers dragged Aret away, the soldier with his magic sword tried to pull the ivory blade from its sheath. The blade would not budge from its home. The soldier noticed Aret watching and looked to make sure no one else saw his failure. The sword joined the rest of Aret's armor on a cart.

The thought of his last and greatest treasure in someone else's hands made Aret sick to his stomach. He had truly lost everything.

The jail, once empty under the rule of Aret's father, was now full of ragged peasants who, for offenses real or fabricated, had been arrested and their property confiscated.

Aret was tossed onto straw covered stone and locked away.

This was how it ended. It was over.

"Aret?" a voice called from the neighboring cell. "You look like crap."

Aret looked into the sunken eyes of Magna, his brother, and a smile crept across his defeated face.

Purvis took dictation while Brigham lounged with his feet on the desk. "The traitor is captured," Brigham said. "He lies safely in my jail next to his elder brother. I await your orders, blah blah blah..."

Purvis paused in his writing, but King Brigham continued, "His magic armor is a worthy trophy for you, High King Hister... Your humble servant, King Brigham of Valora..."

Aret had been like a son to Purvis, but now that he was in custody, perhaps things could get back to normal. Not normal perhaps, but safe. Purvis sighed. Normal here was a Valora on the throne, and that would never be again. There was no way Purvis could have avoided an investigation after Ulf's death. There was nothing Purvis could have done to save Aret. Aret didn't believe that, though. Aret hated him.

Brigham looked to Purvis, whose quill still waved back and forth on the parchment, changing the king's *blah blah blah* into something more presentable.

"Come on, man! I haven't got all day!"

Purvis handed him the letter, ink still wet. King Brigham proofread it, stamped it with his seal, and commanded, "Courier this immediately to Histerland."

"Yes, Lord," Purvis said. "Perhaps with the bounty on the traitor, we can pay our debts to Histerland and the people of Valora can get some relief from the high taxes."

Brigham slapped his glove against Purvis's face hard enough to sting his old cheek. "I will decide when the people deserve relief!"

CHAPTER 41

LOCKED UP WITH A MONSTER

Captain Morto's two kids screamed with glee as their father picked them up, one-at-a-time, and tossed them in the air. "We missed you, Daddy." They said it in unison, even Morto Jr., who had barely begun to talk when Morto had last seen him. When had he started speaking so clearly?

"I missed you too," Morto said. They were growing up without him.

His plump wife, Reyna, stirred the evening stew. "How long are you home this time?" She turned and noticed that her husband was not alone.

Morto was conscious of his heart beating, and a lump in his throat made it difficult to speak. "You remember Garnet, the woodsman of Valora?"

It was obvious that she did. "What is he doing here?"

Morto let out a worried breath. He would rather face the Necromancer himself than provoke his wife. "You must go with him. We will finish the stew, and then you will take a light pack and bundle up the kids."

"What do you mean?" she asked. "You aren't going to do something stupid, are you?"

He sighed again. "Probably."

She wagged the spoon at him. "Morto... what have you got planned?" She waved the spoon around the room. "Look where helping those Valora kids has gotten us! Were they thinking of you when they started playing their adventure games? Or their people? I'm not moving again—"

"You will do as I say!"

Reyna turned away from him in silence, and Morto was afraid. He had never ordered her to do anything.

"Please," he said. "The less you know, the safer you will be. If I'm worrying about you, I can't do anything. I'll be helpless. These are troubled times." He touched her shoulder, and she flinched. "I will send for you as soon as it is safe."

"It may never *be* safe." Reyna beat the spoon against the iron pot, still not looking at him. "Eat your stew before it gets cold."

Morto gave a sigh of relief and motioned for Garnet to take up a bowl. She was going to cooperate. She had little choice, really. He was her husband and had the final say, but she could make his life miserable. If he returned to her alive, her cold shoulder would melt for him again.

A guard Aret did not recognize came by with a bucket. He ladled mush onto the fly infested plates of the prisoners. The guard seemed surprised to find Aret and Magna laughing as he dispensed their gruel. The two princes were reminiscing about old times in the castle.

Soon, King Brigham marched down the dark corridor and smiled down at his prize prisoners. "You are happy to be reunited? Good. Perhaps you would like to be closer. Perhaps you would like to share the same cell tonight."

Magna stopped smiling and looked to his brother. Aret knew what he was thinking; anyone who shared Magna's cell at night would be dead by morning.

Brigham focused on Aret. "Tomorrow you will tell me all you know of your allies in the resistance. If not ... one of you will be dead by the other's hand. Enjoy your time while you can." Brigham marched away, obviously satisfied to have stopped any pleasure the brothers felt because of their reunion.

Aret and Magna looked at each other in silence, wondering how they would escape.

"I don't care about my own life anymore," Magna said, "but you must survive. Tell him what he wants to know."

Aret shook his head. "He will still kill me. If not, he will keep me in prison for the rest of my life. Betraying my allies is not an option."

"If he locks you in my cell," Magna said, "you must kill me before nightfall."

Aret shook his head and forced a smile. "We tried that once already, but you're still here."

Magna's demeanor relaxed and he shook his head, "This is serious, Aret."

Aret made a stern face and mocked Magna as he had when they were children, "*This is serious, Aret.*"

Magna smiled despite himself, but his skin seemed to shrink in the torchlight. His breathing had become shallow and labored. He looked at Aret with a wide, horrified grimace. Fingers and toes sprouted narrow, curved hooks that slashed wildly at the bars of his cell, trying to get at Aret. Long appendages jutted from his back and spread into leathery wings. The Husk hissed, and his limbs flailed against stone and iron.

Aret huddled in the far corner of his cell. He stared at the creature in wonder and helpless terror, then covered his eyes and ears tightly with his arms. No matter how he tried, he could not shut out the sight and sounds of the neighboring cell.

The creature that was once Magna thrashed, hissed, and scraped against its cell for hours. It did not rest. Aret forgot all about his brother. All he wanted was quiet. Aret threw his food bowl at the Husk, but that only made things worse. It tossed itself against the bars and jutted two hook–clawed hands at Aret. Its flapping wings blew straw and dust around the prison as it rammed against the walls of its cage, over and over again. All Aret could do was cover his face and wait.

At last the Husk took a wheezing breath and stumbled.

Startled by the sudden silence, Aret looked up and saw the Husk's wings shriveling. Its skin became pink and soft. The monster's chest rose and fell, taking in deep breaths. Recognition returned to Magna's frightened eyes. A bit of rosy sky was visible outside the tiny window slit. Dawn had finally arrived.

CHAPTER 42

THE VALORAN GUARD

The Old Veteran, Flynt, smiled and grasped Morto's arm tightly. "It is good to see you again, Sheriff."

"I'm not a sheriff anymore."

"You will always be Sheriff to me," Flynt said. His voice was like gravel, with a calm that comes with age.

Another soldier slinked into Mack's tavern long after closing time.

Morto assessed the interior of Mack's Tavern, only lit by one dim candle. "We are still missing a couple people."

One of the men said, "Merrill is dead."

Flynt added with a defeated voice, "Rene was relocated to another fief, and Percy... I fear he can't be trusted."

The former members of the Valoran Guard nodded in agreement. The Guard had been disbanded. They were just soldiers now, but Morto knew where their loyalty lay.

"Things are bad," another added. "The people are hungry. Brigham barely feeds us, his soldiers and our families, but the serfs are truly starving."

Mack the barkeep said, "I have to feed the soldiers for next to nothing. I pay more money in taxes than I take in."

"It was never like this under the Valoras," someone said.

"Our true king is in jail," Flynt finally said, causing a momentary silence over the group. They had all been thinking of Aret Valora.

Morto nodded. "Are we alone? Do any of the other soldiers feel the same way?"

"No one talks about this sort of thing," a man said. "We could be killed for even bringing it up."

"I know the serfs support us," another soldier said, "but serfs are useless in a fight among nobles and soldiers."

"You would have to be blind not to see the injustice in Valora," Flynt said. "The Queen locked away in her rooms… I have seen people's faces, heard accidental remarks. We have friends, but there are many cruel men from here and abroad who will remain forever loyal to Hister and whoever he places on the throne of Valora. I've seen them mock the peasants as they collect taxes and chase starving families from the lands they farmed all year."

Morto shook his head. The men in this room were good, strong, skilled, but they were few. He looked to Mack then back to his men, wondering what might happen to his own family. "The rightful king sits in our jail. We don't have much time to act. If they don't kill him soon, then they will move him to Histerland City, out of our reach."

Old Flynt shook his head. "What can we do? Even if we can overpower Brigham's men, Hister will send his high necromancer after us. He will turn us into demons, like our poor King Magna."

Morto's voice became hard. "We don't speak of that."

A younger guardsman grabbed the Old Veteran's shoulder. "Haven't you heard? The Necromancer is gone!"

Flynt shook his head. "So they say. But how do we know he will *stay* gone."

Morto spoke over them. "Do we do this or not? I will not risk my life unless we are all committed."

An odd, animal moan alerted them. It was the woodsman's signal. Morto motioned downward with his hands. "Everyone, hide!"

They dove into the shadows behind the bar and halfway up the stairs. A silhouette blocked the window for a moment, then passed. There was a methodical knock at the door.

No one moved.

Again the knock, louder this time, more demanding. No one in the tavern dared to breath. The visitor pounded against the door, loud enough to wake anyone from a dead sleep. At last Mack emerged from behind the bar and shouted, "We're closed!"

The muffled voice said, "I saw your light on. I'm a soldier. Open the door."

Flynt's bulky frame was squeezed next to Morto behind the bar with obvious discomfort. He recognized the voice and whispered, "Percy."

"It's late," Mack said. "Come back tomorrow."

Percy slammed his fist hard on the door. "In the name of Hister, I order you to open this door!"

"I'm coming." Mack removed his apron, untucked his shirt and messed up his hair before finally cracking open the door. "Yes?"

A lean soldier pushed his way in and scanned the shadows. "I saw your light. Perhaps you could bring me a late night snack and ale."

Mack sighed. "Of course, kind sir, but it is very late. I was in bed."

"A candle is lit," He said, still scanning the room back and forth. "I smell freshly cooked meat. You haven't had good meat on the menu in ages."

"I was preparing for tomorrow's breakfast. With the traitor caught, I expect taxes to be lowered. I felt a special meal was in order… to celebrate."

"I thought you were in bed?"

Mack tried to smile. He pulled down a chair and motioned for Percy to sit, saying, "Tomorrow's special meal was supposed to be a surprise, but I suppose giving you an early taste won't hurt anything."

Percy licked his lips as he sat. "Indeed. I don't think that would hurt anything."

Mack went behind the bar. His eyes met Morto's as he carefully stepped around him and poured Percy a drink. Old Flynt grimaced, and his bones creaked as he changed position.

Percy sipped slowly, but stopped and stretched his head to the side when a stair creaked. "You know that several off duty men aren't in the barracks tonight, all of them former companions of mine in the Valoran Guard. Why don't you light some more candles so I can see what I'm eating?"

Mack bowed. "Of course, sir."

There was a sound of motion, and Percy jumped up, drawing his sword, but old Flynt's knife buried itself in his chest before he could make a sound. Flynt held his hand tightly over Percy's mouth to make sure no dying scream emerged. He then looked to the others peeking out at him. "I'm with you, Morto! Always!"

Morto peered out the door to make sure no one else was there. Garnet Woodsman briefly emerged from the shadows and waved the all clear sign, then backed away into darkness like a ghost. Morto Shut the door quietly and carefully lowered the plank of wood that secured it.

"Gather your companions that you trust," Morto said. "We meet on the great lawn tomorrow afternoon. We must act before the sun sets." He took out his knife and cut Hister's insignia from the left breast of his leather tunic. Then he sliced the red cloth tied around his arm. The others followed suit, and all took a large gulp of cheap ale.

CHAPTER 43

THE COUP

Aret slept morning into late afternoon on smelly straw over hard stone. He turned his body over again, trying to get comfortable. If not for his traumatic night, he would never have been able to fall asleep in this place.

There was a faint rustle of straw, and his food bowl scraped against the floor, nudged by some small rodent in the dark. Aret marveled at how easily his brother slept. Magna's life since they last saw each other must have been one long nightmare.

The guard made his daily trip down the hall. He very slowly and deliberately dipped his ladle in his bucket of gruel and let it plop into Aret's bowl, not the careless splatter of the usual guard. Aret didn't look up. The guard waited. Such insolence, a guard expecting to be acknowledged by a king, even a deposed king.

At last Aret looked up, ready to scold the man for his impudence, but the familiar face stole the angry words from his lips. Enri gave a subtle bow, brought a tiny slip of paper out of his tunic, and dropped it next to Aret's bowl. Then he continued on, giving a nod of recognition and loyalty to Magna as he dripped gruel into his bowl.

Once Aret was sure that Enri was gone and no one was looking, he struggled to read the note in dim light from the narrow window.

"TONIGHT." He whispered as he read and asked Magna in a hushed voice, "What does it mean?"

King Brigham marched down the dark corridor, followed by Sheriff Golga and a guard. Aret quickly wadded up the tiny paper and put it in his mouth, swallowing it with a gulp of bland gruel

"Have you thought about our discussion yesterday?" Brigham asked.

The brothers made no response. Aret spooned more white mush into his mouth.

Brigham was perturbed at being ignored and added, "I trust the night was very motivational."

Still, they ignored Brigham as though he were not even there.

"Talk!" Brigham demanded.

"Did you hear something?" Aret asked his brother.

"I didn't hear anything," Magna said. "Must have been the wind. Lot of hot air this time of year."

Aret suppressed a smile. A little of his brother's old humor had returned. It was good to be together again.

Brigham fumed, nodding to Sheriff Golga. "Very well." The rusty locks clicked open. Aret was dragged into the corridor and shoved into Magna's cell. The door clanged shut with finality.

"You know," Brigham said. "I really didn't want you to talk. I will enjoy watching your brother kill you tonight. Perhaps I will give you one last chance before the sun sets."

Magna boiled with fury. "My brother says you consider yourself a fencer. Why not try me?"

Brigham looked Magna up and down through the bars. "You might have been something in your day, but there would be no challenge in fighting you now. No. I would rather watch you kill each other tonight."

Brigham turned to march away, but paused. He reached into his belt, pulled out a dagger, and tossed it into the cell. Looking at Aret, he said, "Just to give you a fighting chance." Then he continued down the dark hall and out the heavy door into the castle proper.

"Now we've done it," Magna said. "I hate myself enough already. I don't want to have your death on my conscience."

Aret stuck his finger in the bowl of sticky gruel, put it in his mouth, and forced his throat to swallow the bland mush. "If something is going down, we will need our strength. We should try to eat this crap."

A thin smile crossed Magna's face. "You have grown wiser and a lot less picky since the last time I was in Valora."

Morto watched the great lawn from a window above Mack's tavern. It was three o'clock in the afternoon before the gathering began to seem out of the ordinary. No one had yet noticed any guards missing from their posts.

He took a deep breath. Controlling one's breath was the first step in controlling one's emotions. Everyone expected Morto to be a rock, and they needed him to be that rock now more than ever.

It was time for him to join them, and once he was seen, there would be no turning back.

There was no other choice. A tyrant on the throne and two Valoran heirs held prisoner: it was a slap in the face to all Valora. Even Aret, who hadn't been a perfect king, was still a Valora, still his father's son. Aret hadn't been perfect, but he hadn't been a bad king either. He had been far braver than Morto ever would have thought. If Aret hadn't gotten caught… Aret had grown much in the last year and a half.

Morto was doing what he had to do, what Aret's father would have wanted him to do, but the outcome was far from certain.

Mack's voice startled him. "Are you okay?"

Morto turned away from the window and wiped his hands on his pants. "It is time."

If anything happened to Morto, Garnet would see to Reyna and the boys.

Mack followed him down the stairs and to the door.

"Lock yourselves inside," Morto said. "If this goes bad, you won't want to have been seen with me."

Mack simply nodded, but his wife gave Morto a kiss on the cheek. Morto's stone face blushed. He bowed to them both and marched out the door.

A peasant child carrying buckets of water stopped when she saw Morto pass. Morto heard her drop the buckets and take off running. The secret was already out.

"What's going on?" a woman asked old Flynt.

"Wait," was his only response, but her eyes grew wide when she saw Morto come up from behind, marching to the head of the loose group.

He ordered, "Get inside," and she immediately obeyed.

Morto's group huddled into a tight, unified group. Men on the edge faced outward. A few more men had joined their ranks, but they were still few, far outnumbered by the bulk of Brigham's forces.

Golga came out of the castle, followed by two of his men. Other soldiers loitered around the great lawn, awaiting a call to action.

When Golga saw Morto at the head of the group, he seemed to shudder slightly. "Arrest these men!" he commanded.

To Golga's chagrin, no one moved. The two soldiers that flanked Golga looked from their Sheriff to Morto, not sure what to do.

Peasants gathered around the great lawn, awaiting the sight of noble blood.

"Arrest them!" Golga demanded.

One of Golga's men drew his sword, but instead of striking at his former sheriff, he cut Hister's insignia from his breast.

His companion drew his short sword and pointed it at him, yelling, "What are you doing? Are you a traitor?"

"We are all traitors," Morto's new ally said. "We abandoned our rightful king when he needed us most."

Golga's loyal soldier charged his companion, and their swords clashed.

Golga drew his sword, and a few of his men followed his action, but he looked at the faces of his men and hesitated. They stood back and awaited the outcome of the duel.

A man fell. In the confusion, no one was sure which one.

Two others forced their swords together, but half-heartedly, almost as though they were merely sparring. Most of the soldiers hung back, hesitant to fight their friends.

Golga's shoulders slumped as he watched. At last he dropped his sword, surprising everyone. "I don't care anymore. Fight amongst yourselves. I will be here to serve whoever is left." He made a hand washing motion and headed off to Mack's tavern, leaving the men to look at each other awkwardly.

"Up the steps," Morto finally said. Perhaps it would be easier than he had thought. They could storm in, release Aret—

"What is the meaning of this?" Brigham was at the top of the stairs. His presence was electric, and the men stiffened.

Aret wanted to say something to make his brother feel better, but what could he say?

Magna stared at the narrow ray of light creeping up the stone wall. Night was only a couple hours away, and with it, Aret's death by his poor brother's hand.

Aret sighed.

There was shouting in the streets beyond the window… the clang of blades and a scream. More voices joined the cacophony.

A clanging of keys and light, hurried footsteps trailed from the corridor. Enri and Rowen unlocked the cell door.

"We've come to free you, lords," Enri said. "They're fighting on the castle steps."

The brothers immediately jumped from the straw. Before Aret knew what was happening, Magna had pushed him out of the cell and pulled the door back shut.

Aret looked at his brother through the bars with pity and pride. Then he looked to the neighboring cells. "Unlock all of these doors." He looked once more into his brother's cell. Magna held out Brigham's dagger by the blade.

Aret took the hilt. "We will be back for you."

Enri asked, "What of your sister?"

"She will be safer in her rooms for now," Aret answered.

Aret and the other prisoners charged into the castle proper and raced for the clamor beyond the great door.

Aret paused for a moment when he saw Brigham in the doorway. He was barking orders to his guards. With his back to Aret, Brigham didn't see them coming. Aret sneered and his hand tightened around the dagger as he charged full speed at his enemy.

A lesser man would have stabbed Brigham in the back, but Aret was a king. He shouted, "Brigham!"

Brigham whirled around and drew his sword while dodging the fierce attack. His guards backed away, not daring to interfere in a duel among kings. Aret's dagger didn't have the reach of Brigham's sword, but the fervor of Aret's swing forced Brigham down the steps. Gravity aided Aret's push, but he dared not take his eyes off of Brigham.

Aret nearly tripped on the steps, but regained his footing and even managed to use the near fall to surprise Brigham with a low lunge. They reached the great lawn, and everyone else stopped fighting. All eyes were on Aret, and the citizens of Valora cheered. Aret sliced the air furiously with the small blade, keeping Brigham on the defensive, but wearing himself out.

A familiar voice shouted, "Aret! A sword!"

Aret revolved around Brigham, keeping him in sight while seeking out the voice. Morto, his former sheriff, tossed Aret his sword and bowed.

Brigham tried to snatch Morto's sword from the air, but surprise and the setting sun in his eyes slowed his reaction. Aret caught the sword by the hilt. He had no idea how his former sheriff had returned to Valora, but he was overjoyed to see him there.

Tired of being on the defensive, Brigham struck back. Aret blocked the strike with his sword and then another with the dagger. He was already breathing hard. The initial fury of his attack had worn him out. Aret kept the setting sun at his back, keeping the light in his enemy's eyes, but that wouldn't be enough to win this fight. Aret was slowing down.

Brigham had defeated Aret easily in the past. Aret's people believed might made right and they would accept the winner of this duel as their true king. Trial by battle was an old tradition that died hard.

Brigham taunted Aret. "I was looking forward to seeing you and your brother slaughter one another tonight. Too bad. I may have to kill you before the show."

It was ridiculously obvious that Brigham was trying to infuriate Aret, make him fight stupid. Had Brigham always used this tactic when they fought? Aret's temper was his greatest weakness, but it also spurred him to action.

Aret attacked with new vigor. Passion reignited weary muscles, putting Brigham back on the defensive. Aret struck with the sword and blocked with the dagger, swinging his blades in one last gasp of energy. The taunt had worked, but Aret remained in control. He would either win or lose, but he would fight with his head as well as his heart until one man was victorious. He felt the steps against the back of his heel, moved aside and stayed on the defensive.

Brigham's foot then hit the steps. He stumbled. Aret's sword slid off Brigham's blade and into the false-king's neck.

Brigham became perfectly still. He grabbed Aret's blade, steadying it in his neck as he dropped to his knees, never taking his hateful eyes off Aret. He grimaced, showing red stained teeth. His lips moved, trying to voice one last taunt, but no sound came out. He finally went limp, the blade ripping skin as he fell.

Even with the mighty cheer that went out for him, Aret didn't take his eyes off his prostrate foe. Aret fell panting to his knees, unable to catch his breath, still staring at Brigham as though he might spring up again.

Enri and Morto helped Aret up and raised his hand in triumph. Aret was lifted into the air by his cheering people, all wanting a chance to touch their once and future king. A river of hands brought him into the castle where Morto and Enri rushed him to his chambers to recuperate from his ordeal.

CHAPTER 44

ROGUE KINGDOM

Gwendolyn tried to ignore the little boy sitting beside her in the carriage. Morto Junior had been staring at her most of the journey. He finally asked what must have been on his young mind all that time. "Is she really our queen?"

Morto's other son sat across from Gwendolyn with his mother, Lady Reyna. "Leave her alone," Reyna scolded. "You don't pester a queen. She could order you beheaded."

Gwendolyn smiled at the boy and nodded at his mother, but she could not bring herself to respond in any other way. Gwendolyn was grateful that Reyna had loaned her a dress to wear, but Reyna still looked more like a queen than she did. It was humiliating, being snuck into Valora this way.

It reminded Gwendolyn of the first time she was brought to Valora by carriage. It was a nervous time, being brought to live in the castle of her future husband's family. Magna had seemed nice enough, but she had no way of knowing how he would really be, how life in Valora would be.

But her ladies had been in the carriage with her and they would live with her in the castle. That gave her new world a touch of safe familiarity. Some of those ladies had been with her since early childhood. She wondered where they were now. Two had gotten married and left her to start their own families. Two had remained at Castle Valora to be near suitors, but two others, along with two new maidens, had accompanied her to Troll Keep. They had been left there when Aret took Gwendolyn from King Bulba. She hoped they were safe, sent back to Lyon or Valora, married off to good husbands. Now that she was to be Queen, perhaps she would finally be able to find out where they ended up.

There was no way to know what being Queen of Valora meant now. Valora was a rogue kingdom.

Gwendolyn peeked out a curtained window. A peasant bowed as the coach passed, evidently recognizing that someone important was on board. No one paid too much attention to them though.

The coach stopped by a door, not the main door, and Gwendolyn lowered her veil. It wouldn't do for her subjects to see her like this. She had considered using the secret passage into the castle, but it had probably been sealed. Aret didn't need it anymore anyway, not now that everything was out in the open.

Her two remaining handmaidens were joined by the matrons who had been with her from the beginning. They joined hands and cried when they saw what had become of their lady.

Purvis solemnly brought a scroll to his once and future master. Aret read the details with a sinking heart. A century of wines from the cellars was gone as well as most of their stores of food and the gold and jewels from the treasury. Aret clenched his eyes shut. With no more than what they had and no support from Hister, his people would grow to hate him as much as they had Brigham.

Purvis humbly interrupted his master's thoughts. "It is truly good to have you back where you belong."

Aret looked him over with suspicion. "Is it?"

"Of course, Sire. Brigham was a monster."

Aret wasn't sure what to make of his old advisor anymore. Gwendolyn had insisted they keep him, and after all she had done, he couldn't refuse her. It had been her idea to ask Morto for help. Perhaps, if Aret had taken her into his confidence sooner, things would have turned out differently.

Aret again scanned the scroll in his hands and commanded, "Distribute some wine to my people. They deserve it. And slaughter some meat."

Aret continued his inspection. As he entered the kitchen, Cook fell at Aret's feet. His white hat flopped back and forth as he kissed Aret's boots. "I knew you would return to free us from that tyrant," Cook said. "He wouldn't know good food if it bit him back."

"Rise," Aret said. "I need a stew for the entire city. But we haven't got much meat."

Cook rose, but bowed again. "For you, I would jump in the oven and serve myself!"

King Aret smiled. "Let's hope it doesn't come to that."

Aret was appalled at the decor along the halls of his castle. The portraits of his ancestors and the displays of their arms were gone, possibly lost forever. In the master's chamber, he found his bear skin replaced by a Persian rug. He tore the lacy curtains from the walls and caught sight of his scruffy, dirt-lined face in a mirror.

Gwendolyn startled him. "Perhaps it is time for a bath and a trim."

She was radiant, already wearing the pearl-embroidered gown of a queen. Her hair was clean and golden again, done up in a tight braid. He kissed her, long, deep and passionate, a kiss he had kept pent up since they were married, waiting to be released on this day.

Aret and his queen exited onto the steps overlooking the great lawn. Valora cheered. For a moment, Aret's heart rode the wave of his people's accolades. He raised his hands to quiet them, but they cheered even louder. At last they quieted enough for Aret to speak, and when he did, they all fell silent.

"Thank you," Aret said. "You have risked much and made my ancestors proud. Today you did more than free me and my siblings. Tonight we are no longer part of Histerland."

The flag of Histerland was cut dramatically from the castle tower, and the crimson banner drifted slowly to the ground, leaving only the blue flag with the gold gryphon insignia. A murmur passed through the crowd as if they had only now realized the extent of what they had done. There was no turning back now.

"This can't be good for business." Mack's face flushed and Wena tightened her grip on his arm as all eyes turned to him. He had not expected everyone to hear him in the sudden silence of the crowd.

Aret thought of the poor barkeep's embarrassment and suppressed a chuckle. The crowd saw his amusement and released a collective laugh. Aret was reminded of his father. The people had loved his good humor, and the just never feared his wrath.

"You great people have given me back my lands," Aret said. "I will rule in the tradition of my father and grandfather. You have my word that I will never abuse your allegiance or your loyalty."

Wena dabbed her eyes, and she wasn't the only one moved to tears. His people still loved him.

Aret continued, "Tomorrow there will be work to do. We will build fortifications and make ourselves safe… but tonight we celebrate."

The people cheered and small portions of wine and stew were passed throughout the great lawn.

That night, Aret slept in his own soft bed at last. He could stretch out as much as he liked on the enormous mattress. After their cramped loft, it seemed unnatural to have so much interior space above and around him. His room seemed foreign to him now. Aret's land was not secure and neither was his rest.

Lady Gwendolyn followed Morto through the dark prison. The pitiful man in the cell perked up his head and forced himself to stand.

The Queen could hardly believe this was the suave man she almost married. His long hair, once an immaculate frame to his firm face, was now a scraggly mat over sunken cheeks. Magna collapsed on his knees and pulled her hand through the iron bars, kissing it gently. A tear dripped from his eye onto her porcelain skin.

Lady Gwendolyn looked down at his lips pressed against her hand. "I'm married," she finally said.

Magna forced a smile. "I know. Does my brother treat you well?"

She smiled, blinking the tears out of her eye. "You taught him well."

They looked into each other's eyes for a long moment before she said, "I didn't know—"

Magna put his finger to his lips and shook his head. "I was... I *am* dead. I'm a ghost. I wish you happiness together."

Magna looked at the sun dipping lower in the tiny slit of a window. "Thank you for coming. I didn't think I would ever see you again. You are a ray of sunshine in the darkness my life has become." He backed away from the bars. "But please leave now. I don't want you to see what I become at night."

Gwendolyn straightened and nodded. Morto followed her out of the jail. She could feel Magna's eyes following her down the corridor and knew if she looked back at him, the tears would flow freely. She stared straight ahead until reaching the main hall. "Thank you, Sheriff," she said in her most formal voice before retiring to her room.

CHAPTER 45

PREPARE FOR WAR

Brownie and Tiny drove a supply laden cart on a meandering path into Valora. Portions of the road were being dug into deep trenches, with men shoveling the earth into large mounds.

"Why are we doing this?" Brownie asked himself aloud.

Tiny bore scars on his neck and bulbous head. "You said to. We been helping the Underground ever since we met the guy in the magic armor."

"That wasn't just any guy, Tiny. That was King Aret Valora."

Tiny was unimpressed. "Oh."

"Working with the Underground served us well. We never ate better. I've even managed to hold a little gold back for us, but look around. They are preparing for a war. I don't want to fight somebody's war. We were better off just hanging out by the road and stealing from travelers."

Tiny shrugged. "But now we go all over the place telling other thieves what to do."

Brownie swayed his head back and forth. "That is a perk. No one ever did what I told them to before."

"Except me," Tiny said.

Brownie smiled. "Except for you."

"Maybe if we win a war, *we* can be kings."

Brownie laughed, and Tiny frowned, saying, "I'm stupid."

"No," Brownie said. "You are pretty smart, Tiny. We might not get to be kings, but I've stockpiled a little gold for us. We'll have

that no matter which way this goes. If we can get some land too…
We just need to choose the winning side."

"Are we on the winning side?" Tiny asked.

Brownie shrugged. "We're already here, and they've been good to us so far. We can always switch sides later."

Tiny smiled and shook his little buddy's shoulder a bit too forcefully. "You're smart."

Enri announced that Alonzo was waiting in the throne room, and Aret nodded, sending for Arim.

"I don't like it," Gwendolyn said to Aret. "Foreign troops in Valora."

"Alonzo was in the Underground with Arim," Aret said. "We can trust him." He put an arm around her and drew her close. Her stomach bulged under her gown, life growing within it. "Besides," Aret said, "we need them if we are to stand a chance."

She nodded with a hesitant smile. Aret relished a quiet moment with Gwendolyn's silky hair against his cheek.

Arim entered the room. His clothes were a typical courtly cut, but of a drab earthy color. This was probably the first time Aret had seen Arim without some disguise.

Aret led them into the throne room where Alonzo was waiting. Alonzo wore a light chest plate over leather. Under one arm, he carried a helmet topped by a metal comb.

Alonzo bowed to Aret and presented a long list of supplies the Iberians had brought across the mountains with them. "I see you have been beefing up your defenses," he said with a smile.

Aret scanned the list. "Excellent!" He did not want to reveal how desperate his kingdom was after Brigham had squandered their resources. These supplies, along with the other gifts they had received, would be salvation for Valora, at least for a time. He gave a calm, "Thank you," and motioned Enri to take the list. "Distribute these supplies. What we don't use now, put in storage with the other gifts."

Alonzo cocked his head. "Other gifts?"

Aret nodded. "When Valora formally declared its independence, the underground network of rebels started bringing me their plunder. We may just make it through the year."

Alonzo nodded. "You will make it much longer than that. The time is right. Did you know that your neighbor, Vincennes, has not paid his taxes in over two months?"

Aret's curiosity was piqued. "What has Hister done to them?"

Alonzo flashed his white smile. "Nothing."

"Nothing?"

"He can't afford to," Arim explained. "Hister's stretched himself too thin. The Underground has broken his supply lines. He can't pay or feed his armies. Without the Necromancer to maintain order, he is ripe for a coup."

Aret looked to Arim and then to Alonzo. "Where would we find enough men to wage a military campaign against Hister?"

"I've brought fifty of King Luis' cavalry with me. One hundred more are in the mountains awaiting my call. If you call volunteers from the Underground and the surrounding fiefs, we will have more than enough to bring Hister to his knees."

Arim agreed. "You won't be alone. An army of Rollo's Normans and knights of the Golden City have taken control of Northern Gaul. They are ready to sail down the Rhine into Histerland City. The nomadic hordes to the east of Histerland were kept content with land and money and in fear of the Necromancer. Without that, they have allied themselves with the Tsars of the east. The Tsars have a long list of grudges against Hister. They may or may not be with us, but we know they aren't against us."

"Perhaps," Aret said. Listening to these two, it was all too easy to believe that war with Hister would be simple, but both foreigners had their own agenda. Aret would not act rashly again.

Enri returned to the throne, and Aret bid him wait while he wrote a quick but formal note on several scrolls. Aret sealed them one by one with a drop of wax and pressed his ring into the soft wax. The sign of his ring proved they were his official correspondence. "Have these letters delivered to the surrounding fiefs."

CHAPTER 46

THE GATEKEEPER'S NEW WEAPONS

Golga and Morto brandished their swords, springing between the stranger and Aret. The young man came into Aret's throne room with a large canvas bag over his shoulder. His thin, loose, button-down shirt had a weave so tight that the fibers were almost invisible. By contrast, his pants were almost skin-tight. The stranger's shoes resembled leather, but were white with a bright swooping design and red laces.

"How did you get in here unannounced?" Morto asked.

A gold key dangled below the stranger's dark goatee. Aret raised his hand. "This must be the new Gatekeeper."

The stranger's eyes were crowned by thick, black eyebrows. He looked to Morto and then to Golga. The men backed away from his confident gaze, giving the Gatekeeper room to drop his bag and bow.

"I would have been here sooner," the young wizard said, "but it took awhile to get to your chapter in my predecessor's chronicles."

Aret rose from his throne. He knew the former Gatekeeper as a wise old man, but this new Gatekeeper, despite the facial hair, looked younger than Aret himself. "The High Necromancer, is he really…"

The Gatekeeper seemed to hesitate. "You are out of each other's reach. He won't be bothering you again."

The answer was vague, what one would expect from a wizard. Aret clasped the newcomer's hand. "I considered the old Gatekeeper a friend. I owe him much."

Aret was about to ask about old Gabriel's final fate, but the new Gatekeeper cut him off. "I hear that quite a bit." the young wizard said it with a detached, almost bored tone. "Things have progressed much in Valora since the last time he was here."

Aret wasn't sure what to make of this young man in his old friend's role. "Yes. I have raised an army. We are considering marching on Histerland City. I have been assured that we will find allies once we reach the capital, but even if that is true, we have to cross half of Gaul to get there. We have no way of knowing for sure how many allies we have and how many will oppose us."

The young Gatekeeper nodded grimly. "You have allies. Some of them are still afraid to speak out, but they are there. Unfortunately you have made enemies too. News of the troll king's death has spread around the world. Trolls from many distant lands have enlisted in Hister's army. They have taken residence in Vincennes, directly in your army's path."

"So much for Vincennes' short-lived defiance." Aret saw Gwendolyn listening from the hallway. Taking her from King Bulba had made him many enemies, but without her, he never would have gotten this far. "So it is impossible then?"

"No," the Gatekeeper said, crouching next to his large bag. There was a small chip of metal on the bag. The Gatekeeper dragged the chip across a line of metallic teeth, zipping open the canvas. Inside were a series of black metal tubes, each embedded in pieces of curved wood. The young Gatekeeper took one of the tubes in hand. He pulled a piece back and forth with a click-clack and then raised the wide wood end of the tube to his shoulder. He took careful aim at a decorative suit of armor.

There was a tiny click. The empty armor bounced against the wall and fell with a clatter. The clatter was dwarfed by echoing thunder. The brave men in the room jerked at the sudden, deafening boom.

The men gathered around the damage. If they uttered a syllable, no one knew, for the explosion still echoed off the stone walls, drowning out their words. Sulfurous smoke hung in the air.

Guards and servants from throughout the castle rushed to the throne room to investigate the thunder.

The Gatekeeper lowered the hollow tube and pulled on his earlobe. He said something, but Aret's ears still hadn't recovered from the noise. The young wizard inspected his target. A hole had burst through both the chest and back plates, even chipping the stone and plaster behind them.

The Gatekeeper presented the weapon in his flattened hands and bowed to Aret.

Aret picked it up cautiously and looked into the open tube.

The Gatekeeper seemed like he was about to yank the weapon away, but restrained himself. "Careful, King Aret, you don't want it to go off in your face."

Aret froze at the thought, again looking at the devastated armor at his feet. The young Gatekeeper pushed a button on top of the tube, saying, "This is the safety. It will keep it from going off, but it is still a very bad idea to point the barrel at yourself or your friends. I have brought five of these *guns*. Their magic will only work nine times each. This one has eight shots left. When they are spent, they will be useless to you and absolutely *must* be returned to me. Agreed?"

Aret looked to his men surrounding the pierced armor and damaged wall, then to the gun in his flattened hands. He imagined what this weapon would have done to a man inside that armor. "Yes. Yes, of course."

"You agree they will all be returned to me when the battle is done?"

Why would it matter to Aret what happened to them once they were spent? He would agree to anything to get these magic weapons into the hands of his men. "You have my word."

"Good." The Gatekeeper smiled. "Good." He looked at the punctured chest plate. "Honestly, I had been aiming for the helmet.

I hadn't thought aim would be that important with a weapon like this."

Aret ran his finger along the polished metal tube. He couldn't wait to fire it. "I will use this one."

The room fell silent, but no one looked Aret in the eyes. He thought he had been generous to take the one with the least shots left.

The Gatekeeper cleared his throat. "As you wish, King Aret. With only nine shots, there won't be much leeway for practice. Probably best to let your best archers use the rest."

Queen Gwendolyn gave Aret a kiss on the cheek and whispered, "Let someone else play with these toys, Lord, unless you plan for another to use your sword and shield."

Aret pressed his lips against her white cheek and held them there for a time, taking in the scent of her skin. She was right. They had all thought it, but only his queen dared question him. He took another long look at the new weapon in his hands, then handed it to Golga. "You take charge of them."

The room seemed to breathe a collective sigh, and Golga bowed, eying the prize in his hands.

"I already have magic weapons," Aret said. "Just keep carful account of them." He nodded to the young Gatekeeper. "They will all be returned, as I agreed."

The Gatekeeper bowed to Aret with a slight smiled.

Aret emerged from the stable. He was hand in hand with his queen. The great lawn was full of people. Men, wagons, and carriages lined up for the campaign. Aret commanded 400 armed soldiers, but these men were dwarfed by support people and supply carts. They could be gone a long time.

Snow nuzzled Rowen's neck affectionately as the boy brushed through his mane. Rowen took extra care today, as though this would be the last time he groomed the mighty horse. Perhaps it would be. This campaign could be their last.

Aret and his queen watched the boy toss a blanket over the sinewy warhorse, then the sheet of golden scales over that. With one foot on a stool, Rowen heaved on the ivory and leather saddle and buckled it securely beneath the creature's belly.

The boy again stood on the stool to fasten Snow's silver headpiece in place. Gold antlers projected from the animal's shielded brows. Snow was a magnificent animal all on his own, but in the armor he became a creature of myth.

Aret held Queen Gwendolyn's hands in his and stared into her strong eyes. "You are in charge," he said. Her fair skin had a puffy fullness and seemed to shine. Aret would almost certainly not return before his child was born.

Morto interrupted. "I should be with you, Sire." It was insolent to interrupt his king and queen, but Morto had earned the right, and this was serious.

"No," Aret said. "I need a sheriff here I can trust… a sheriff who will protect the fief and see that my queen is obeyed."

Sheriff Morto bowed. "You can count on me, King Aret."

Aret then put his hand on his loyal woodsman's shoulder. "I'm counting on you as well, Garnet. Nobody knows these lands like you."

Garnet Woodsman bowed, knowing he could best serve Aret in his woods.

Aret kissed Gwendolyn gently, but she grabbed him by the neck and pulled his face down, probing his mouth with her tongue. At last she pulled away, hands still gripping his cheeks. "Come back to us, Lord." She released him, and her reserved demeanor returned. Aret was speechless. He would hold onto that kiss until he either returned to his queen or he was dead.

Aret had already said goodbye to his siblings. He gave one last look at his hereditary castle. Within the walls, Mimi sat outside their brother's cell.

King Aret brought his foot up to his waist, placing it in the stirrup. With his hand on the saddle horn, he arched his other leg over the saddle in a fluid motion. With a wave and one last look to his queen, he kicked Snow into motion and the procession of soldiers, servants, and laborers marched down Histerland Road.

The road was flanked by the Valorans who stayed behind. They waved goodbye. Young maidens stood atop the freshly dug mounds. They threw scarves and garlands to the men they favored.

CHAPTER 47

MEN FROM THE GOLDEN CITY

Ultor folded his enormous arms over his gold-plated chest. His gilded boat led the charge into the river delta. Five more narrow boats followed. All Ultor had ever wanted was to serve as a knight of the Golden City. He had been made a general for this invasion. It was an honor he never dreamed possible, but also a great responsibility. The boats in his rear were laden with supplies for the Normans, their allies in Northern Histerland. His failure would mean their failure as well.

Three black sailboats with red sails waited for them. Ultor's pulse quickened. The black vessels loomed large, over twice the size of Ultor's craft. Arrows flew deck to deck, piercing warriors and sailors on both vessels.

The bow of Ultor's ship crashed into the hull of a black vessel. The deck jerked under Ultor. The Histerland craft splintered from the impact. General Ultor leapt to the enemy's deck. His gleaming warriors followed.

Ultor may have been a general now, but he was not one to stand idle while others fought. His over-sized sword hacked into black-garbed soldiers. Many of Ultor's men were struck down by the shorter, leaner Histerland blades, but another gold boat pulled alongside and lowered a plank to the Histerland vessel.

The golden warriors piled on. Histerland soldiers jumped into the water below, foolishly seeking safety in the waves. Their heavy mail dragged them to the bottom. A few lucky ones were plucked from the water and taken prisoner. The rest were fish food.

The first battle was won, but Ultor could not relax. He scanned the water as his men searched their captured ships. One of Ultor's boats had been sunk, as had one of the Histerland ships, but the remaining vessels were all his.

Ultor set anchor in the shallow waters and his men streamed onto shore. They fought their way inland and found King Rollo and his Normans already engaged in battle. With reinforcements from the Golden City, Rollo's victory was quick.

The sudden cessation of fighting was unsettling after so much action, but there were preparations to be made. The Norman king immediately delegated control of the region to his loyal supporters. By no coincidence, these men were also loyal to the Golden City. Supplies were distributed, and Rollo's men bolstered the crew of Ultor's captured vessels.

The next morning, Ultor's fleet left the delta firmly in control of themselves and the Normans. They rowed against the current while King Rollo led an army by land. If all went as planned, they would meet up at Hister's capital City.

Ultor watched the fisherman and traders on the river banks. Any one of them could be a spy or a saboteur. As they rowed deeper into enemy territory, Ultor was certain Hister knew they were coming. Spies travelled faster than ships. At least the river was wide enough to keep them safe from any archers on either shore.

A captured Histerland ship took the lead in front of Ultor's Golden boats. Ultor hoped the black vessel would confuse any enemies they encountered along the way.

They passed surprisingly little resistance on their journey, and Ultor found himself strangely disappointed. It gave him too much time to contemplate the fighting yet to come and the uncertainties that went with it. It was better to fight than to think about fighting, better to be woken up and told to fight rather than to sit and plan and tell others to fight. Perhaps Ultor was unsuited to leadership.

Farmers watched them from shore, and traders abandoned their cargo when Ultor's small fleet came into sight. Ultor only encountered one military vessel. It was abandoned of all men and cargo, but the boat itself was in perfect working order, a fine addition to Ultor's collection.

Torches within Histerland City cast its long walls in black silhouette. Ultor commanded the anchors dropped while they waited for Rollo's army to catch up by land.

A great brazier on the stone wall blazed to life. Ultor's boats had been spotted. The flames of the brazier were visible for miles. They signaled Hister's allies, telling them invaders were at their door.

Histerland City would soon be surrounded, but an enemy was always most dangerous when it was cornered. Ultor sent scouts to assess Hister's defenses and to find King Rollo. Again, all Ultor could do was watch and wait.

CHAPTER 48

THE TROLL ARMY

Kay moved quickly, not hampered by mail like most of the Histerland soldiers. He hesitated when he found Glarg at the bar with his head buried in a bowl. When the troll general finally came up for air, his green warts were covered in white porridge. He washed it down with a cup of wine. Rich red liquid dribbled over his pointed chin.

"Meat!" Glarg shouted. "We need more meat!"

The barkeep bowed his head submissively. "There is no more meat, sir."

The troll's yellow eyes looked the barkeep up and down like a butcher studying livestock. Glarg licked his lips. "There must be some meat we haven't slaughtered yet."

The barkeep saw Kay behind the troll and sighed with relief. Kay wondered how close the barkeep had come to being on the menu.

"An army approaches," Kay said.

Glarg rose and pulled Kay close with rough hands. Glarg's breath smelled of the gristle decaying in his teeth. "Is the Troll-Killer with them?"

Kay nodded. King Aret had killed the troll king and at least one of his sons. "King Aret leads them."

Glarg released Kay, and the young scout stumbled backward. The troll banged his fist on his shield and gave a howl that raised the hairs on Kay's neck. It sounded the call to battle throughout Vincennes.

Since Glarg's army had arrived, Kay's own soldiers had become second class, little more than servants to the trolls. King Vincennes himself refused to leave his castle, afraid to walk his own kingdom.

Aret had fallen back and rode in the royal coach with Arim and Enri. "This is taking forever."

"It takes longer," Arim said, "with an army. You have grown accustomed to traveling alone. Even when you came here in an official capacity, you only had a few carriages and an armed escort. Now you have over four hundred soldiers, two healers, cooks, launderers, carpenters, a blacksmith, the list goes on. Some of the men even brought their wives and children to assist them."

Alonzo rode up alongside the coach and knocked on the door. He wore the sweeping brimmed helmet and light chest plate of the Iberian cavalry he commanded. "King Aret," he called over the sounds of wheels and horses. "A wall of men and trolls in Histerland uniforms lies just beyond the next hill, between us and Vincennes."

Aret called for his horse, and Snow was led up alongside the still moving coach. The landscape rolled past them while Snow and the coach seemed to be standing still. The speed of the coach was like that of a snail to Snow, who trotted along casually.

Aret placed a foot in the stirrup and brought the other over the saddle. He urged Snow to greater speed and shot to the head of his army. The men cheered.

Soon they saw the road blocked by a line of men and trolls. The trolls ranged in size from dwarves to giants. The two armies appeared to be evenly matched in manpower.

Aret waved his ivory sword, signaling Golga and his three gunmen to his side.

Aret shouted over the sound of hooves on dirt. "Wait until we are in range. Forget these weapons are magic; think of the guns as mere crossbows."

A loud bang and a puff of brimstone resounded from Golga's gun. Aret felt Snow's skin twitch at the sound. Golga pulled back on the gun with a click-clack and fired the weapon again. The other gunmen followed with another explosion, then another. One, two, three, four times the thunder boomed, but the enemy did not fall.

Kay rode behind the line and reported to Glarg that King Aret's army was coming over the hill. Something whizzed by him, and a crack of thunder split the clear blue sky. The dirt in front of Glarg himself exploded with a second boom.

Glarg's fingers dug into Kay's leg, nearly pulling him from his horse. "What is that?"

Kay shrugged. Smoke hung over the approaching army. "They carry thunder with them!"

Again the sound echoed, four times in regular succession. One of Glarg's men fell from his horse. Another grabbed his suddenly bloodied chest.

One, two, three, four times came the thunder again… Glarg's men broke formation and began to scatter.

"Hold the line!" Glarg yelled.

The trolls scattered at the rush of men. The smell of sulfur stung Kay's eyes and throat. Aret might actually win this battle. Vincennes could actually be free of the trolls!

Glarg frantically pulled at his men and pointed at King Aret.

Kay pulled out his dagger and urged his horse closer to the troll general. The frantic troll was completely preoccupied by the battle.

Kay buried his dagger into the soft space under Glarg's leathery arm.

Glarg turned, but Kay was already riding away. Kay waved his red armband in the air as a sign of surrender.

Others followed Kay's lead, and trolls scurried from slashing blades.

Kay witnessed one of the magic weapons firsthand. Its bearer, Kay later learned his name was Golga, brought a front piece back and forth along the metal tube. Something ejected from inside the weapon and fell to the ground, but Golga took no notice. He aimed, but instead of thunder, the weapon only made a tiny, barely audible click. Golga pulled the front piece back and forth once more and aimed again, but the weapon was spent of magic.

Kay and the others who surrendered were herded together. King Aret's men rode past them into the trees, slaughtering scattered foes and rounding up riderless horses.

King Aret rode around Kay and his fellows. The king's armor gleamed in the sun. Gold scales peeked out though the metal plates, folding like skin over his muscles. His sinewy white horse had gold antlers, like a giant stag.

When Aret circled to the front of the group once more, Kay raised his hands in submission. "We pledge allegiance to you, King Aret Valora. We will serve in your army and follow your orders without question."

The king removed his silver helmet, revealing a mortal man with trim brown hair. King Aret wasn't that much older than Kay himself.

"You have knowledge of Hister's forces along our path?" King Aret said.

Kay nodded. "Everything I know is yours."

"I accept your offer," Aret said. "You will march ahead of us."

Golga rode to Aret's side. "Two of the guns stopped working, Sire. They are out of magic. We still have two that may work."

Aret nodded. "Have the dead ones put in my coach. We must return them to the Gatekeeper as promised."

Kay raised his eyebrows. Aret had gotten the magic weapons from the Gatekeeper. If things didn't work out in Aret's army, this information could get himself back into Hister's good graces.

Golga bowed to Aret and rode off to follow his orders.

Golga's weapon had not been the only one to eject fragments. The ground was littered with these pieces, but Aret's men didn't seem concerned with them. Kay bent at the knees and scooped one of the fragments from the dirt, a deformed tube with metal at one end. Kay could discern no significance to its shape or size, but he tucked it into his tunic. It might prove valuable one day.

A foreigner with high forehead and red-blonde hair, who Kay later learned was Arim from the Golden City, raised a finger. "Didn't the Gatekeeper say there were *five* magic guns?"

Without moving his head, Aret eyed Arim. "No. There are only four."

Only four magic guns, and two of them spent. Aret's advantage was mostly in surprise. These weapons wouldn't be much use if he truly planned to march on Histerland City.

Once Aret's men had assembled again, his army rode into an undefended Vincennes. Kay and his men marched in front.

Kay was happy to see King Vincennes waiting for them with outstretched arms. King Vincennes seemed small alone in the street, more beard than man. The gray-bearded king gave King Aret a kiss on the cheek and offered the men lodging. Fresh bread was passed among them, and Kay was allowed to sleep in the same room that night as though nothing had changed. Perhaps fighting for Aret would not be so bad after all.

CHAPTER 49

SIEGE

Aret's army swelled as it made its way across Gaul. Every place they stopped, they were joined by dissatisfied men and older boys ready for change.

The long, gray walls of Histerland City rose above the hills, looming larger as they neared. No one in Aret's party spoke. They only stared grimly towards their imposing destination. They had all been raised to think Histerland City sacred, untouchable.

Ragged skeletons hung in cages on the road, a warning that further reinforced their trepidation. Perhaps it was a blessing that there was no time to dwell on it.

Histerland soldiers in black leather tunics and gray mail spilled from the castle gates.

Aret ploughed his army through the black-garbed soldiers. His horse, Snow trampled all in his path. Blows slid harmlessly off Aret's shield, and his ivory sword cleaved the weapons of all who opposed him.

There must have been around two hundred enemy soldiers that made it out of the gate before their egress was clogged with men. The enemy gave ground, and Aret's army pressed after them.

A rain of arrows from the sky bounced harmlessly off Aret's shield, but punctured his men. Aret sheltered the men near him with his shield, but the rest of the men were unprotected.

Golga raised the magic gun to his shoulder and took aim at one of the narrow wall slits where Histerland's archers perched. There was an explosion of smoke. The stone wall chipped and fragmented, but the aperture was too small a target. An arrow whistled through Golga's mail.

The Gates to Histerland City slammed shut, and the enemy was beyond reach. "Fall back!" Aret screamed above the cries of his men. He raised his shield over Golga, leading him back beyond the range of Hister's arrows.

They laid Golga on the cold ground. He had one arrow in his chest and another in his shoulder. "Hold on!" Aret said. "A healer is on the way."

Golga shook his head and tried to speak, but no sound came. At last his face relaxed, and he stared peacefully into the sky.

"You are a good soldier!" Aret shouted into Golga's deaf ears. "Do you hear? You are a good man." Aret shook his head and looked at the dead and dying littered before the stone walls. There must have been nearly a hundred men, side by side, regardless of their loyalties in life. More good men had died for Aret. Some of them moaned; they still had a chance for life.

Without being asked, some of Aret's men had already gone into the woods to chop down trees for fires and building material. They were setting up camp within sight of the imposing gray walls and towers.

Aret rode alone through the field of bodies and shouted up at the walls. An older soldier with graying hair shouted back. "I am the high general of Histerland."

It was Verney, who had been kind to Aret so long ago. Aret shouted up at him, "I know you. We propose a short cessation of fighting to collect our dead and wounded while you do the same."

The high general agreed, "Two hours."

Aret hated to admit it, but the number of bodies belonging to his army far outnumbered those of Hister. Most of the casualties were from the arrows that covered Hister's retreat. "Three hours," Aret countered. Most of the dead were not well-known to Aret. The newer recruits, the ones who had joined Aret in Vincennes and Gaul, bore the brunt of the losses. It seemed morbid, but Aret was grateful for this. He had lost enough friends and was running out of people he could truly trust.

The high general agreed to Aret's terms. The gates were opened just wide enough and long enough for a band of men in black robes to collect the fallen Histerland soldiers. Aret then sent a small group of unarmed servants to load his bloodied men onto a wagon. They also retrieved a spent gun from the blood-soaked mud.

CHAPTER 50

MEETING OF GENERALS

A strange breeze moved through the camp. It moved here and there with direction, with a pattern. A faint humming became louder, and Aret grabbed his sword, fearing enemy sorcery.

The buzzing stopped, and an adolescent boy suddenly appeared before them removing a helmet. The helmet was brimmed all the way around and now hung behind the boy's neck by a strap.

The boy wore no armor, only a simple toga and cloak over his tan skin. A curved sword of pale gold and a polished shield hung at his back. Aret pointed his sword at the stranger.

"Greetings," the boy said. "I am Skylar. Agamemnon, Principal of the United City-States of Hellena, has sent me to meet you. Our army camps south of the city.

Aret sheathed his sword, removed his glove, and extended his hand.

Arim added, "Tell Agamemnon that we are proud to work with his people." It was the sort of thing one expected to hear when meeting a new ally. Arim seemed taller somehow and a little broader in the shoulders because of the cut of his jacket.

Aret eyed the wings on the boy's sandals. "If you can magically appear out of thin air, why don't you do us all a favor and unlock Hister's gates from the inside."

"I've tried," Skylar said. "Apparently the Necromancer set up some mystical protections before he disappeared. I will have to go in through the gate with everyone else."

A young man with thick, dark hair and goatee appeared. The gold key around his neck signified he was the new Gatekeeper. "I see you've met the flying Hellenan. Don't let his age fool you. I hear he is quite a warrior."

Hearing the compliment, Skylar stood up straight and stuck out his hairless chest.

"Well," Aret said. "It appears I'm surrounded by wizards." Under the jealous hand of the High Necromancer, it had been rare to see sorcerers in Gaul.

The Gatekeeper asked, "Did my presents help you?"

Aret nodded. "Yes! Thank you. Unfortunately, their magic is all used up. They are in my coach, ready for you to reclaim as we agreed." Aret lowered his voice. "Their magic seemed to come from the projectiles inside. If there is any way you could get more—"

The Gatekeeper scrunched his eyes and raised his hands. "No. No way. You don't realize how risky it was to get you those guns. If just one of them remained here, if someone learned the secret of their manufacture, the entire balance of power in your world would forever be altered. Letting you have them even for the short time I did went against everything it means to be the Gatekeeper!"

Aret was surprised by the intensity of the Gatekeeper's refusal and regretted asking. The new Gatekeeper was young, but still had reasoning beyond Aret's scope. "I am sorry, Gatekeeper. My people are forever grateful to you and your predecessor for your help. There will come a day when you need me, and I will be there for you."

The Gatekeeper nodded. "I know."

The young wizard's confidence was somehow chilling, and Aret looked to the sky, ready to change the subject. "The sun is high."

The Gatekeeper looked at a device strapped to his wrist. "It is time."

Aret let out a long breath. "Where is the Hun's representative?"

"I've heard they aren't very reliable," Alonzo said.

"Stavros made a pact with Agamemnon," Skylar said. "We can count on them."

Arim spoke first. "We estimate 1,100 armed men currently manning Histerland City."

The Gatekeeper spoke next. "I just spoke to my friend from the Golden City, General Ultor. He has five boats docked in the river north of the city with about 20 men on each vessel. They also have three captured Histerland ships. King Rollo has over 200 warriors camped on shore."

Skylar nodded. "Agamemnon has an army of 800 men south of the city. We have siege engines and battering rams, but we haven't been able to get them close enough to the walls to use them. We have begun to construct catapults."

Aret raised his eyebrows, impressed. Aret was the de facto leader of his army, but Alonzo and Vincennes were in charge of their own contingents. Only about 250 men were now loyal only to Aret, and twenty of those were too wounded to fight. Their initial losses made their numbers even less impressive. "We have around 520 able-bodied warriors. About sixty were injured, unable to fight. We'll have to wait and see how they heal."

Skylar almost seemed not to hear him. "Agamemnon recommends we each send men and supplies halfway to the next contingent, creating additional camps to ensure the entire city wall is watched and to aid in communication between the main armies."

Aret was about to dismiss the idea, but the other leaders all nodded in agreement. It was a good plan. Aret wished it had been his and hadn't come from a boy half his age. These Hellenans were organized. He should try to learn from them, not be jealous of them.

"Everyone here is in agreement," Arim said. "We all stay at our posts until Hister surrenders."

The representatives from the different armies all nodded.

Aret served wine from the regions of Gaul they had traversed. He raised his glass and closed the meeting. "When this is all over, I will have a drink with you and your leaders in Hister's throne room." The thought of a celebration in that gloomy chamber amused Aret.

Skylar and Alonzo chuckled, and they all drank. With the meeting over, young Skylar put on his helmet and faded from sight. There was a buzz and a breeze out of the camp. Young Skylar had magical tools as impressive as Aret's armor. When Aret looked up from where the adolescent had been, he found the Gatekeeper already gone as well.

"Surrounded by wizards," Aret said. "I'm glad they're on our side."

The chilly air blew in Skylar's face and his cloak billowed behind him as he skated through the sky. Balancing on the winged shoes came much easier now. When the Gatekeeper had first led him to his ancestor's toys, one of the winged shoes flew out from under Skylar and landed him on his butt. Now, he found the less he thought about it, the easier it was to remain upright.

Tiny campfires dotted the eastern side of Histerland City. Circling over one of the Hun camps, Skylar could see Stavros lounging on a carved jade chair. A pointed fur hat rested over his silky black hair. Skylar's attention was drawn to two scantily clad women kissing at the warlord's feet. The women pressed their naked breasts together, and the light of the crackling bonfire cast orange tones on their skin. A cook stirred meat on a sizzling metal disc, filling the camp with pleasant smells.

Stavros grabbed the end of a turkey leg with his bare left hand and pointed the index finger of his gloved right hand. The glove was leather and fur covered by a single plate of armor on the forearm. A razor-sharp blade shot out of the finger and stabbed into the bird's roasted carcass, releasing the turkey leg for Stavros to stuff into his mouth.

The flames wavered in Skylar's sudden breeze, and the horses whinnied, disturbed. Stavros stopped chewing, and his muscles stiffened. He knew someone was there.

Skylar removed his helmet and appeared before him.

Men in heavy fur grabbed their swords.

"Greetings," the young intruder said. "I am Skylar, from the Hellanas. I just met with the leaders of the other contingents. We missed you."

Stavros waved his men back and continued to chew while he spoke. Grease clung to his wispy black mustache. "You will bow to the lord of the Huns."

Skylar dropped to one knee. One of the women crawled towards him with a mischievous grin and grabbed his sun-brown calf muscle, gripping it hard enough to hurt. She pulled at his toga, and Skylar stepped back, his heart beating faster. Stavros and his men laughed at Skylar's discomfort.

"One of my wives likes you," Stavros said. "She could put some hair on that chest of yours."

Skylar felt his face turning red. The woman had a raw beauty, but her sadistic expression and attitude made her ugly. Skylar didn't have much experience with girls and he certainly didn't want to be part of a show for Stavros and his men. He went straight back to business. "Why didn't you send someone to the meeting?"

"Why should we help you?" Stavros said. "Hister gives us land and money."

"I thought we had an agreement," Skylar answered. "You were to receive land after—"

"It's not enough," Stavros said. "With Hister gone, this land will be ours anyway. We want more. We want Histerland City."

Skylar couldn't believe what he was hearing. "You want to keep control of the city itself?"

"Why not? We have as much right to it as anyone."

Skylar had not expected this and wasn't sure how to respond. There was no way anyone would let Stavros keep Histerland City. "I will relay your wishes to the other leaders. They say we will share a drink in Hister's throne room together."

Stavros smiled. "That, I would like to see."

Skylar added, "The other leaders plan to share camps at halfway points between our main armies."

Stavros sighed. "We already have camps everywhere, all along the eastern side of the city."

"Have you met anyone from Rollo's army?"

Stavros sneered. "I think they are scared of us."

A few of his men chuckled.

"Perhaps it would be best to make peace with them," Skylar said, "as the Hellenans have done with you. We need them."

Skylar bowed, returned his helmet, and faded from sight.

Stavros' woman looked up at her master. "You don't *really* think they will give us control of Histerland City?"

Stavros shook his head. "No. But we can't let any of *them* have it unchallenged either. They won't give us what we ask for, so we have to ask for more than we expect. Assuming they actually pull it off, I think we can expect to keep everything east of the city, but anyone who controls the city will eventually try to take it all back from us."

Skylar lifted his leg, and his winged sandals hummed. The sandals supported his weight as he skated into the sky with a shift of the breeze.

Verney, high general of Histerland, was a practical man. He had risen through the ranks because he knew when to keep quiet when others did not. He unrolled a map on the table in front of Hister and his three generals.

Verney made a mark on the edge of the map. "King Luis has sent cavalry to reinforce our former subjects from southwest Gaul. They have gathered here. The armies of Hellena are at our south. The Tsars have unified the Huns to our east and The Golden City has reinforced Rollo's army at our north."

"Bring me the High Necromancer." Hister's eyes were distant. Some color had returned to his skin, along with an edematous plumpness. "He will scatter the invaders with plagues and storms."

The high general squirmed uncomfortably. "The Necromancer is gone, Sire, banished by the new Gatekeeper."

"Then bring me another wizard," Hister commanded, "any wizard, all the wizards of my kingdom."

"There are no other wizards," the general answered. "The Necromancer had them all killed."

Hister seemed frustrated. "Why don't you just simply kill these invaders?"

Hister's question was simplistic and immature. "We've tried," the general said. "They've moved out of range of our arrows and, combined on all fronts, they outnumber us two to one."

"Send word to Latia and our loyal subjects for immediate reinforcements. All the men of Histerland will come to my aid."

With a sigh, the general answered, "Yes, Sire."

"But we won't wait for them. Get out there and fight those traitors."

"They outnumber us," the high general repeated. "We can't fight them on all fronts at once."

Hister squinted at the map. "Then pick a single front. Where are they weakest…? The Gaul front. Their armies passed through miles of my loyal subjects before they arrived. This little King Aret of Valora, his army is made of my subjects. Undoubtedly, some of them are loath to strike at their high king. They will see the error of their ways. Send the full might of my army against them. The rest will fall like dominos."

The generals looked at each other and hesitated.

"Do it!" Hister demanded

High General Verney bowed, "Yes, Sire. At once."

CHAPTER 51

HISTER ATTACKS

The gates suddenly fell open. A river of men in black streamed out. Aret's watchman blew the horn, stirring everyone out of their tents.

Aret gasped at the sight of so many soldiers shooting towards them, and the lines had not stopped. They were still pouring out. "I thought their strength would be divided."

"It is," Alonzo said. "If they are all here fighting us, then there is no one guarding the rest of the city."

"How does that help us here?" Aret asked.

"It doesn't," Alonzo admitted.

Arim grabbed Aret's face in his hands. "The men need to be inspired, Aret. Your pessimism could lose this war!"

Aret nodded and leapt upon his warhorse, Snow. He rode before his men, shouting, "They are *not* invincible. They attack because they are desperate! This is the last gasp of a dying city! Defend yourselves! Charge through that army and we will spit in Hister's face!"

Aret put on his helmet and waved his ivory sword in the air, charging into the midst of the Histerland soldiers, riding the cheers of his men. Arrows fell harmlessly off his shield and bounced off Snow's armor. Golden horseshoes smashed over men in black while Aret sliced through chain mail and swords like they were paper.

Arrows from Aret's Iberian allies whistled by, impaling his enemies through their mail. The crossbows had enough range to keep the Iberian archers out of immediate danger while Aret and his men occupied the advancing Histerland soldiers.

Aret's fellows weren't blessed by magic armor. Histerland short-swords hacked and stabbed the men of Gaul, staining the snow red. At last, just when Aret thought it was all over for him and his allies, a deep horn was blown. The Histerland soldiers fell back behind their walls.

"They are on the run!" Aret yelled. "Keep at them!" But his men had lost their enthusiasm for battle. While most were catching their breath, few braved the rain of arrows only to have the city gates slammed shut before them.

Aret and his men fell back to camp. Moaning bodies littered the frozen ground. Many were his foes, but many of the dead and dying had fought for Aret. This is what it meant to be a king. Aret had promised to never take advantage of his people's loyalty, but here they were, dying in his name.

Smoke and flame licked the sky from behind the city's southern walls. The Hellenans had gotten off a volley while Hister's forces were distracted with Aret's men, but the walls of Histerland were still intact. One more attack like that, and Aret would have no army left.

High General Verney reported to his emperor. "The armies of Gaul suffered significant losses, Sire, but so did we. We lost a fourth of our men, and the Hellenans were able to launch firebombs into the city while our army was busy."

Hister fumed. "Has Latia sent a reply yet? Where are our reinforcements?"

"We haven't heard anything from them," the General answered. "Perhaps our courier was killed by—"

"No!" Hister barked. "The Latian Emperor is ignoring us. He talks of reclaiming past greatness, but he is a coward and a traitor. Their time is long past, but ours is not yet done. Where are our allies from cities loyal to me … where are the trolls?"

Verney hesitated, fearing the fate of messengers with bad news. "Dead or deserted, Sire."

"Bring me the High Necromancer," Hister said. "He will scatter the invaders with plagues and storms."

The high general looked at the other generals with a look of horrified helplessness. "The Necromancer is gone, Sire, banished by the new Gatekeeper."

"Then bring me another wizard, any wizard, all the wizards of my kingdom."

Again the General paused. He had already been through this with Hister, but any failure would be considered his, not Hister's. "There are no more wizards, Sire."

This time it was Hister's turn to pause in thought. "How did I come to be surrounded by such incompetence? It doesn't matter. I still have a few tricks up my sleeve. We will be safe behind my walls while my minions pick at them one by one. We have enough food to last years."

The high general cleared his throat. "Before the siege, our supply lines had already been cut. I've had an inventory done. We can't feed the whole city for more than a week. If we allow the peasants and servant class to starve, we might last a month—"

"Then starve them," Hister said. "What good are they to us anyway? They're all a bunch of traitors. Cut the army's rations to the minimum. He grabbed the high general earnestly by the arm. "We will go on. A month is all we need. A soldier owes a certain period of his year to his king for large campaigns, but after that time… A month from now, our enemies will have all gone back to their homes, and we will plan our revenge."

Aret wrote by lantern in his tent. He rubbed his forehead and called Enri to copy the letter for each noble who died under his command. Then, he took another parchment and wrote his queen. He kept optimistic, but didn't sugarcoat reality. Gwendolyn was a strong lady. She would want the truth.

My beautiful, perfect, Queen Gwendolyn,

Hister and his men sit trapped within their walls. They fought a desperate battle today, and we suffered many losses. I hope this attack was the last scream of a dying regime. Another battle like that could finish us.

I just finished composing a letter to the families of the high-born that died under my leadership. Their deaths bring honor to their families. Losing them is difficult, but harder still is seeing all the serfs and commoners who died in the fighting. I know it sounds strange that I should think of them. I don't even know most of their names, and I never will. Their families, if they have any, will never know for sure what happened to their loved ones. Father always said there can be no nobility without serfs and peasants to support them. I think I finally understand what he meant.

I can't fault the survivors who desert our army. I have sent scouts into the countryside to find, or force, if necessary, food from surrounding fiefs, but some of them will not return, preferring to seek safety in the countryside. Luck has aided us, however. Tribute on its way to Histerland City has instead ended up in our hands and mouths.

Before, I fought to avenge my family and my people, but now I have you and our child to fight for. I am nothing without you. My every victory is yours. You are beautiful… perfect… willing to sacrifice so much.

I will be worthy of you in life or death.

Eternal Love,

Aret Valora

The river stank with a mixture of fish, mud, and decomposing vegetation. General Ultor stood on deck, peering intently at the walls of Histerland City. The river flowed under the walls. If they could sneak past the archers, some of Ultor's men could swim under and open the gates from the within, but there was no way to evade the sight of the archers on the wall, even at night.

One of his sailors shouted in terror, and Ultor's heart skipped. His men looked down at the water, and the color drained from their faces. Ultor grabbed the hilt of his heavy blade in both hands. "What is it?"

"Bodies," someone answered. "The water is full of bodies."

Ultor pushed past them and looked over the deck. Hundreds of corpses floated past his anchored ships. Ultor's heart sank as he followed the horrific image to its only possible source. "Rather than surrender to the siege, they are allowing their people to die and tossing the bodies in the river."

One of his men howled. "This place is cursed! My fields need planting. My term of service was over weeks ago, same with most of us. Why are we still here?"

Another man, afraid to speak up on his own, was happy to voice his opinion now that he was not alone. "We aren't doing any good here anyway. All we do is sit around."

Ultor raised his hands trying to silence the men, but to no avail. He worried he would have a full mutiny on his hands. His arm muscles flexed in a sudden fit of frustration, and he punched the first man that had spoken, bloodying his chin and knocking him to the deck. All fell silent as Ultor looked up and down the ranks, waiting for another man to tempt his anger.

Ultor's heart pounded. "You are not here because of a term of service to your king. You are not here because you have to be. You are here because you believe in the Golden City and its values, because you want to ensure its safety. Hister ordered the killing of our dragon, our magnificent Lady, and his men burned our city. Have you already forgotten? These aren't ancient crimes, although there are many of those I could list. You want to go? Leave his crimes against us unavenged? You want to wait for him to attack us again?"

The men looked at each other in shame, but still hesitated.

"It won't be long," Ultor added. "Hister's men are stewing behind their walls." He motioned to the water. "Look at the corpses in this river! Look at them! Why would a people do that to themselves? Their end is near. All we have to do is wait for it. Would you rather leave with our job unfinished?"

A man raised his hand and shouted, "Death to Hister!"

The rest followed, chanting, "Death to Hister. Long live the Golden City!" But for all their posturing, they still glanced periodically at river. Dead men, women, and children bobbed past their ships.

CHAPTER 52

BLACK FOREST GHOST

The smell of breakfast entered Aret's subconscious, and he flipped stiffly onto his back. He tried to scratch an itch on his elbow, but his fingernails were frustrated by gold scales. He picked between the armor and the sleeve of his mail shirt, shifting the shirt in an attempt to let the mail itself sooth his itch, but the rubbing of the mail was probably what had caused the itch in the first place. He hadn't completely removed his armor in days. The mail shirt was truly like a second skin to him now.

There was a commotion outside, and when Enri pushed aside the curtain to his tent, Aret already had his scabbard in hand.

"There's been an attack," Enri said. "It appears these woods really are haunted, Milord."

Aret followed Enri out of the tent. Their camp, expected to be a temporary base, had started to look more like a permanent settlement. Barracks of canvas had been replaced with log buildings. Shelters for the horses had grown four walls, turning into barns. Their original latrines had been buried over, new ones dug. Aret didn't like it. This was not supposed to be their home. When Aret had agreed to this campaign, he expected action until the war was won or lost. Instead, there was endless waiting and watching. Would this siege ever end?

On the edge of camp, they came upon a prostrate guard, his intestines strung over the snow. The guard's flesh had been opened up by big heavy claws. Aret's men had left boot prints in the snow all around the body, but no animal tracks were visible. It was possible that the man was attacked by a normal bear and the men had marred the animal's tracks. Aret didn't think so.

Hister had once sent a shadowy were-bear to kill Aret, and the beast nearly succeeded. Even Aret's magic armor was little use against it. They had only stopped it by killing its human host, General Ulf. If Ulf had somehow been resurrected, they had no way of getting to him. If this was a different creature, then they had no way of knowing who or where its living body was, and by the time it attacked, it would be too late. They had no weapons that could hurt a living shadow.

"Send couriers to our other contingents," Aret commanded. "We need the Gatekeeper."

"Send couriers through the woods, Sire?" Enri said.

Aret gave him a cold look. "Shadows attack at night. I'd worry more about mortal bandits if I were them."

Enri reddened at his unthinking cowardice and bowed. "Yes, Sire, of course."

Breakfast was long over, and Enri reported their food inventory. No one spoke about anything but business. With just one attack, the were-bear, if that's what it was, had struck a deep psychological blow to Aret's men.

The long gray walls of Histerland City remained unchanged. Smoke rose from its chimneys and the red flags still flew high. Two more nights like this and his men would mutiny. The siege would be over, and Hister would win.

The couriers began to return. Their messages had been delivered, but the other contingents had not seen the Gatekeeper.

Aret did all he could do. He napped. It was bound to be a long night.

CHAPTER 53

ULF'S REVENGE

Aret himself took guard duty that night. It was only fair that he take the risk he asked his men to take.

It was a long, uneventful night. Aret pulled his wool cloak tightly over his armor.

The nearby walls of Histerland City remained strong, impregnable. Would Hister and Verney simply wait Aret out?

It was almost morning when he felt himself start to doze. A scream drew him back to reality. He drew his magic sword and made his way for the sound.

One of his men, a large burly man, ran from the makeshift cemetery they had made outside camp. This was where they had buried the men who died fighting Aret's war.

There was a scratching in the dirt. Something big and black was pulling one of the bodies out of the ground, ripping it out limb by limb.

Aret's heart beat hard in his chest, and his breath came in quick gulps of frigid air. He raised his sword, surprised to find his arms shaking. Aret managed to give a meager shout to the animal.

It gave a low snarl. Its jaws still gnawed on an arm as it sized up Aret. Moonlight glinted off its one good eye, and it scratched its ear.

It *was* him. General Ulf had returned.

The shadow rose on its hind legs and bounded across the cemetery at Aret. Its nebulous feet never touched the earth.

Aret wondered if the siege would continue without him, if his men would be able to protect Valora, if Queen Gwendolyn and his son would be safe.

Aret raised his sword and poured all his energy into a primal scream, bracing himself for what would probably be his last fight. The gold gryphon of Valora blazed upon Aret's chest.

The bear jerked to a stop. Its black fur showed shades of gray in the intense light from Aret's breast. It brought a claw up over its eye before fading into the night.

The glow subsided and Aret collapsed. He tried to move, to grab his sword, but merely twitched a finger. If the bear returned, or if Hister attacked, Aret would be completely helpless. The sudden exhaustion reminded him of the weakness he felt when donning the magic armor for the first time.

His men, attracted by the light show, picked Aret up and carried him to his tent. As they lifted him, Aret caught a glimpse of the dead face Ulf had desecrated. It was Golga, who had once served as Ulf's second in command, but later died in loyal service to Aret. Golga's limbs were strewn across the cemetery.

CHAPTER 54

HELP ARRIVES

Aret had successfully rid them of the were-bear for one night, but a second effort like that could kill him, or leave him helpless while another killed him. The monster would return, and there was nothing Aret could do to stop it.

The king dozed throughout the day, exhausted by the previous night's exertion.

The sun was setting. Dinner had been served and fires had been lit in every corner of the camp. No one felt like sleeping. They would see the monster when it came for them, but they would not be able to stop it.

Aret looked upon the darkened walls of Histerland city and wondered if Hister was watching Aret's campfires, waiting for the bear to signal the final attack.

Enri rode a wave of excitement and announced that the Gatekeeper had brought a friend to their camp. Vida was a large man with long blonde hair. Aret had ever seen a mortal man with a torso as sculpted as Vida's. Vida wore a silver broadsword on his back.

They made pleasantries and introductions.

"I'm sorry for taking so long to get back to you," the young wizard said. "I only heard about your situation this morning and had to find Vida before I came."

"Vida knows how to kill were-bears?" Aret said.

Vida spoke in a thick northern accent. "I kill many monsters."

"Vida knows how to use life magic," the Gatekeeper explained. "Particularly useful against creatures of shadow."

"Life magic?" Aret said.

"The magic of life energy," Gatekeeper explained. "It is what you emitted when you feared for your life."

"I wasn't afraid."

Vida snorted. "You were scared. Blowing out your energy like that is the act of a man resigned to death, impossible to control. You need to manage your magic better. Let it out slowly, contain the creature so we can end it, not just scare it away."

Aret narrowed his eyes at the barbarous blonde. "So you *can* kill him?"

"Bring him to me," Vida said, "and I will kill him."

"Well, that's the trick then, isn't it?" Aret said. "How do we bring him to you?"

The Gatekeeper had inspected the location of the first attack. "Blood had splattered over the protective circle I drew around your camp, and my protective wards had been weakened by time. There was nothing to stop Ulf's shadow from creeping into your camp, even into your tent, and killing you while you were asleep."

Aret took a deep breath. "That doesn't make me feel any better."

"But he didn't," Vida said. "The creature is dead, a true ghost with no mortal body. He operates on instinct alone."

"Then why come after my camp," Aret asked, "and Golga specifically?"

The Gatekeeper raised a thick black eyebrow. "I believe the ghost retains what my people refer to as *the subconscious*."

Vida nodded. "We call it an echo."

"We can be thankful," the Gatekeeper said. "It has no conscious mind to plan with, and the Necromancer isn't here to direct it."

"How do we kill it if it has no mortal body?" Aret asked.

"Bring it to me," Vida said with a confidence Aret likened to arrogance.

Aret thought for a moment. "It seems drawn to Golga and myself."

CHAPTER 55

BAIT FOR A GHOST

Even through the pile of skins, Aret felt the chill of the hard, frozen ground. Next to him was the dismembered corpse of his friend, Golga, thankfully hidden from view by a sheet. The Gatekeeper sprinkled powder on the ground around Aret's prostrate body, but stopped before he had completed a circle.

"I'm no expert in magic," Aret said, "but doesn't the circle need to be complete to offer any protection from evil spirits?"

"If we wanted it to work," the Gatekeeper agreed.

"We don't want it to work?"

"No," the Gatekeeper said. "We want the monster to think he can get to you."

"He can," Aret said. "Shouldn't I have my sword, at least my shield?"

"No," the Gatekeeper said. "Rest. Try to get some sleep."

Aret sighed. He rolled himself in furs and rested his head on the pillow they had brought. "Sure, a relaxing nap while I wait to be killed."

The Gatekeeper gave Aret an amused smile before fleeing into the bushes and extinguishing his lamp. Vida, the monster slayer from the north, was already hidden.

Aret lay still and silent, listening to the sounds of the night as his eyes tried to adjust. Moonlight reflected off the snow, showing trees as gray silhouettes framed by starry skies. A twig snapped and he peered into the darkness, probing uselessly with his eyes. An owl hooted above him. He wondered why he was working so hard to remain quiet. He was the bait, after all; they wanted the were-bear to know he was there. At last he really did close his eyes, bringing the furs snuggly over his head.

Had he heard something? He peeked out of the furs. There was no sound, but cold chilled him from the inside out.

A silent shadow moved around The Gatekeeper's circle. It stopped where the Gatekeeper had left the gap and sniffed the ground.

Amid the trees, Vida was kneeling in the dark, holding his hands on the hilt of his broadsword as if in prayer. Why didn't he do something? Did he want to see Aret sweat? Or did he intend to let Aret die?

A claw broke the circle and yanked the sheet from Golga's remains. The face of Aret's dead friend was highlighted by moonlight.

Vida sprang up, his sword igniting with silver light. The bear recoiled from the swinging light, bounding in the opposite direction. The monster slid to a stop before the Gatekeeper. The young wizard had one hand on his chest, and the palm of his other hand emitted a soft light that repelled the beast.

Vida's glowing sword sliced thought the monster's shoulder. Desperate to flee the light, the shadow charged unarmed Aret.

Aret, no weapons to protect himself, closed his eyes and felt warmth at his chest.

"Not all at once!" Vida shouted.

Aret opened his eyes and crossed his arms over the glowing emblem on his chest.

The beast had turned away from him.

Vida plunged his sword directly into the shadow's chest. Glowing silver erupted from the beast's back.

The shadow monster seemed much smaller now as it clawed at Vida. Its now human hands grabbed at the sword in its chest.

Vida pushed the blackened form of General Ulf down. The point of the glowing blade staked the monster to the cold earth. Ulf grimaced and spat wisps of black smoke up at Vida. Finally, Ulf's twitching body withered and wafted away.

Vida closed his eyes and brought his sword up to his body once more, whispering silently to himself as his glow subsided. "The ghost is gone," Vida said, "but its evil will stink up this forest for years to come."

Vida and the Gatekeeper joined Aret for breakfast and then napped in the camp. Golga's body was reburied, and the Gatekeeper renewed his protective circle around the camp before he and Vida bid Aret goodbye.

CHAPTER 56

BETRAYAL

A courier brought news from Valora. Aret tore open the parchment and fell back on his feathered pillow. Flickering lantern light illuminated the words of his queen.

My Noble Lord Aret,

> *Despite rampant hunger, everyone is well here. There was a rash of burglaries, mostly people stealing food, but nothing Sheriff Morto and Garnet Woodsman couldn't handle. You were wise to leave them here.*
> *For the most part, the war in the capital has left the outer provinces untouched.*
> *Your brother is doing as well as can be expected. We have tried to supply him with comforts, but the Husk destroys whatever is left in his cell after dark. I've had a few problems with your sister, Mimi. She sometimes oversteps her authority. I think she still thinks she is queen. It is nothing I can't handle. She is a great help with our son.*
> *Little Magna Junior is developing a head of thick black hair. He eats constantly and grows stronger every day. We both want his father here to hold us.*

We will be much happier when you finally return to your place on the throne by my side. Come back to us soon.

Your loving Queen,

Gwendolyn

Aret clutched the letter to his breast and sniffed the subtle floral scent. Aret remembered their last embrace and the kiss that kept him going when the night was cold and victory a distant dream.

Enri interrupted Aret's momentary peace. "Sire! The Iberians are leaving. They're deserting us!"

Aret jumped from his cot and rubbed the disbelief out of his face. Enri must be somehow mistaken. Aret left his tent to find the Iberian cavalry riding southeast, back the way they had come.

Alonzo watched them from his horse. He turned and greeted Aret. "I was waiting for you. Hister and King Luis have worked out a deal."

"A deal?"

"It is best for everyone," Alonzo said. "Hister has agreed to surrender his western territories to Luis."

"Including Valora?"

"Especially Valora. As our ally, you will be allowed to continue to govern your hereditary lands… and more. You will be our regional governor."

Aret grabbed the reins of Alonzo's horse. "Why wasn't I told about this earlier?"

"What are you upset about? We have won! It's done. Hister will remain in his city, just another weak king. As an Iberian territory, you will be, for all intents and purposes, completely autonomous. Just a small tribute and short annual terms of service for Luis' armies, standard, but very lenient compared to your obligations to Hister."

Aret looked to the stone towers of Histerland City. "But we are so close to victory. Why should we trade one Hister for another?"

"Come back with us," Alonzo pleaded. "Come back to your people and we can start to heal this land."

Aret sighed. Arim rode towards them, and Alonzo stiffened. He must have seen the anger burning on Arim's face.

"Think it over," Alonzo said. "We will await you in Valora." He jerked the reins away from Aret and spurred his brown horse after his men. "I trust you will make the wisest decision."

"Traitors!" Arim yelled after them. "I just heard," he said to Aret. "What will you do?"

Aret shook his head. "We have to go back. The siege is over. We can't allow them to have Valora."

"But that's what Hister wants!" Arim said. "He wants us to leave him be, let him reclaim his lands here while we fight amongst ourselves. Once his enemies have killed each other, his armies rush in and reclaim his lost lands, *including* Valora."

"What do you want me to do?" Aret asked. "Without Alonzo, our army is cut by a third. We can do nothing here, and Valora is helpless."

"You left good people in Valora," Arim said.

"A small force. They are no match for trained cavalry. Even if they knew what was coming, they couldn't fight them off without help."

A horn sounded.

An army capped the horizon. Around 250 dark soldiers bore the flag of King Lyon. Aret had eloped with Lyon's daughter and had killed Lyon's son in a fight for Valora's throne.

"Hister's reinforcements!" Aret exclaimed.

Arim's voice was low. "Not now. Not when we are at our weakest."

"We can't meet them in battle," Aret conceded. "We must surrender."

Verney, high general of Histerland, leaned on the gray walls next to a weak and hungry archer. He sighed with relief as he watched the Iberians ride away.

Hister would never have agreed to give up territory, but Verney now considered Hister a lost cause. It was now obvious that the High Necromancer had been the true ruler of Histerland. If Verney followed Hister's orders, they would all be dead.

Verney raised his hand above his eyes to block the sun's glare. Another army approached. Expanding his telescope, Verney saw that they carried the flag of King Lyon. Lyon could always be counted on to support the victor. He must have heard about the Iberian's withdrawal and realized Hister wasn't beaten. Victory for Histerland was at hand, but why didn't Lyon's flag bearer carry the flag of Histerland as well as the flag of Lyon?

As long as they had come, that was all that mattered.

Aret's army formed a line at the rear of their camp, but kept men watching Histerland City for any signs of activity. They were surrounded. Aret and Arim rode out under the flag of Valora to meet King Lyon, the man whose son had died at Aret's hand. King Lyon, purple cape billowing behind him, rode to the front of his army with his flag bearer. They met in the middle of the two armies.

Lyon was a tall man with a helmet shaped like a crown. Streaks of gray were barely visible in his blonde beard. "Greetings."

Aret and Arim gave a slight bow and waited to hear the conditions for their surrender.

"How goes the siege?" Lyon asked.

Arim and Aret looked at each other. Aret was about to ask Lyon for his terms, but Arim answered before Aret had a chance to speak. "They are about to fall, Sire. It is only a matter of time."

"That's what I had heard. Although the size of your army was somewhat exaggerated, I can see the writing on the wall. Hister's days are nearing an end. Have you thought about who will replace him?"

Aret was glad that Arim had spoken before him. Lyon was not here to fight against them after all, but Aret wasn't so sure Lyon was here to help them either.

"No one will replace him," Aret said. "The barons will rule independently."

King Lyon laughed and glared at Arim. "I'm sure that's what the Golden City wants, a weak collection of baronies, no threat, easily conquered."

Arim shifted in his saddle uncomfortably.

"No," King Lyon explained. "The baronies are no longer self-sufficient units. The economy of Gaul is dependent on a central trading center. That's the way the Necromancer wanted it to be. It made us easier to control. Trade will have to be renegotiated with the individual fiefs. Alliances will be made. Little fiefdoms will spring up and grow, spawning new Histers. There is the matter of Histerland City and the surrounding lands under the direct control of Hister. Who will rule them? My son, you haven't thought of any of this, have you? It looks like I've arrived just in time. Where are your positions weakest? I will send my men to reinforce them."

"Thank you," Aret said. "That is very good of you."

Aret escorted King Lyon and his men through the camp. As soon as Aret could get away, he instructed a courier to ride at top speed to Valora and warn them about the Iberians. An army, even light cavalry like Alonzo's men, traveled slower than a lone horseman who traded horses mid journey. The courier should be able to beat Alonzo by at least a day.

CHAPTER 57

BACK IN VALORA

The young courier dug in his heels, spurring the horse to the greatest possible speed. He then pushed the animal even harder. The exertion might kill his horse, but that didn't matter now. Halfway along, he would get another. He had to arrive in Valora before the Iberians.

He was barely out of camp when the arrow came. He never suspected the Iberians would have left someone behind. The arrow must have been moving incredibly fast, but seemed to float in midair. He pulled the reins to the left, but the arrow was already in his neck. He dangled limp from the saddle while his horse galloped on past the assassin.

Queen Gwendolyn was meeting with Sheriff Morto and Garnet Woodsman when Rowen rushed into the throne room. The scarred stable boy was out of breath.

"The Iberians," Rowen began, panting. "The Iberians are back."

Queen Gwendolyn raised her hands to her mouth. "King Aret?"

Rowen shook his head. "They carry our flag, but none of our people are with them, only the Iberians."

Queen Gwendolyn had a bad intuition, but she could not jump to any conclusions. She met Alonzo on the steps of Castle Valora. Her maidens had all fawned over the charming foreigner, but Gwendolyn had never trusted him. Alonzo's men remained on their horses, lined behind him with their brimmed helmets and light chest plates. They did not appear to have lost anyone on their travels. Gwendolyn was only flanked by four Valoran guardsmen: two old veterans, much past their prime, and two barely old enough to hold their swords out in front of them.

"Where is King Aret?" the queen asked. "How goes the siege?"

Alonzo gave a slight bow and handed Gwendolyn documents sealed with the official imprints of Hister, Luis… and Aret. "The siege is over, Queen. As you can see, Hister, Aret, and noble King Luis have come to an agreement."

Queen Gwendolyn broke the seals and read the document with astonishment. "Why didn't Aret send word about this?"

"I do not know, My Queen," Alonzo answered.

The queen forced a false facade of calm, her voice a perfect monotone. "This is unexpected. My council must examine this document to make sure everything is in order."

"Of course." Alonzo nodded with confidence. His troops were already in the city. Nothing Queen Gwendolyn could do now would change that.

Once she, Morto, and Garnet were safely within chambers, Gwendolyn summoned Purvis to examine the document. "Well?"

Purvis shook his head. "This is not the true seal of Valora, and the signature is not Aret's. It is a forgery."

"That may not matter," Morto said. "They are trained soldiers and they outnumber us. If we had known before they passed the defenses, we might have stood a chance, but now… All our best men are on the front."

Gwendolyn gritted her teeth in unladylike fashion. "Then we have no choice. If we play along, maybe we can survive until Aret returns." *If* he returned. Aret would have sent word about the Iberians if he could.

Gwendolyn sat for a moment with her eyes closed, forcing her angst into a tight ball in her gut. There was no other choice, not yet. There was no point in jumping to conclusions.

They met Alonzo on the great lawn with his men. She bowed her head in submission. "What does King Luis require of his subjects?"

Alonzo flashed his perfect white smile. "The mountain passes between Iberia and Gaul are treacherous this time of year. My men must live here while we await reinforcements. We will need lodging and food."

Queen Gwendolyn had been struggling to keep the people fed since Aret left, now there were more mouths to feed. "Of course." She waved her hand, signaling the servants to bring food and drink.

CHAPTER 58

THE WALLS COME DOWN

Aret took off his boots and gloves, extinguished his lantern, and lay back on his cot. He never took off his entire armor anymore. Except during his brief imprisonment, his armor had been a second skin over the last year. He drifted into an uneasy sleep with dreams of Gwendolyn, Alonzo, and the Necromancer.

It was still dark when he awoke. Unable to return to sleep, he lit his lantern, rubbed his eyes and put a clean parchment on the table.

Dipping a quill in ink, he wrote:

My Beautiful Queen,
Please send word from Valora. I have written many times, but have yet to get any response. None of my couriers return. I can only assume the worst and am sick with worry. The state of things here has not changed since last I wrote, although I cannot know if you ever received that letter.
We camp here day after day while Hister and his men stay behind their walls. If smell is any indication, then they must fall soon. When the wind blows across the city, a horrible stink assails us.
Be brave. I will be by your side as soon as—

Enri interrupted from the curtained entrance, "Lord Aret! Are you awake?" Aret turned from his desk, and Enri needed no response to see he had not been sleeping. "The gates are open!"

It didn't sink in at first. Aret didn't even put down his pen. There had been no activity from Hister in weeks. "Open?" Aret said in a daze. "Are they sending out soldiers?"

"No!" Enri said. "A rabble of peasants took off running, but the doors are just sitting there propped open! Fires are flickering inside the walls!"

Aret jumped from his writing table. "Call the men to arms! Prepare Snow!"

Aret pulled his gold mail hood over his head and frantically strapped on loose pieces of armor with twitching fingers. He emerged, metal plates still loose, and found King Vincennes. "Help me with these buckles."

Vincennes smiled, happy to help. He had a simple gray armor that matched his bushy beard. "Do you think they are really finished?"

Aret dared not get his hopes up. There was no way to know for certain what it meant until he saw it for himself. "Hurry up with those buckles and we will find out!"

The bugle blew, and Aret rode up and down the camp. It seemed painfully long for his men to prepare. The weeks of sloth had left them slow. If they didn't attack now, they could miss their chance.

Aret charged the city alone, ignoring Arim's calls to wait. Aret smiled as he heard horses speeding behind him. He knew his men wouldn't allow him to ride into danger alone.

No arrows assailed them as they approached. The gate to the city was only halfway open, but there was no resistance as they pushed it wide. The streets of Histerland City were practically deserted. The few soldiers they saw dropped their swords and ran, or bowed in surrender to the invaders. The statue of proud Hister had been toppled.

Aret's soldiers broke open stores of food and wine. They pushed open all the doors and gates in the city. Two peasants rushed out of a burning building with overstuffed burlap sacks.

Gold and jewels from the noble families of Histerland clanged and jostled in the sacks.

A crescent moon fell from the sky behind the peasants. The moon was a curved sword shining in the night. The peasants fled from a boy skating through the air. Skylar's cape billowed behind him and he held his sword horizontally. The boy overtook the peasants, slicing through them as he passed. Aret feared the boy would crash into the ground, but Skylar made a running motion and wind blew down from his feet, spinning him back in the direction he had come. The tiny wings on his shoes were a blur of motion. Skylar saluted Aret as he skated by.

"The Hellenans are in!" Aret said to Vincennes.

"Sire!" Enri called. "Look!"

The robes had fallen loose from one of the dismembered peasants, revealing gray mail. "Search everyone," Aret ordered. These were no peasants. These men were soldiers trying to escape with Aret's new riches. This military campaign had not been cheap, and Aret needed that treasure to rebuild Valora.

There was a scream and Aret turned toward it.

Arim held Aret's shoulder. "Leave it, Aret."

Swarthy men in fur hats were swinging a young girl by her dirty-blonde hair. The girl landed flat on her stomach.

"What is the meaning of this?" Aret asked.

One of the men sneered. "Go away. You have no authority over us."

Aret pointed his sword.

The men raised daggers and knives. "She is ours."

Aret remained firm. "She is not property."

They came at him. Aret brought his sword arm back, arced it forward, and the impossible happened. A hand caught his blade mid-strike, a hand in thick leather and fur. Nothing had ever resisted his sword so completely. Aret knew this must be the infamous Hun leader.

Stavros tightened his grip on the sword and punched Aret with his other hand, bare knuckled against Aret's helmet. Aret's faceplate pounded against his nose and he staggered back, eyes watering, but he clung to his sword.

Kay and Enri stood behind Aret with raised blades.

"The woman is theirs," Stavros said. "We have as much right to booty as you, or the Hellenans, or those golden boys."

Aret narrowed his eyes. "The girl is not booty."

Stavros released Aret's sword and eyed the girl. "I beg to differ."

Stavros brought back his gloved hand, and impossibly long knives sprouted from his fingers. He wiggled them, scraping the blades together.

That glove was immune to Aret's blade. Aret had no way to know if his armor could resist those claws, but he stood firm, gripping his sword two-handed.

There was a buzzing breeze, and Skylar interrupted them. "We must move on to Hister's castle. There will be riches enough for everyone!"

Aret redirected his anger and lowered his sword. "Hister is who I'm here for, not a band of barbarians." As soon as it was out of his mouth, Aret regretted saying it, but after being punched in the face, he couldn't resist one last barb.

"Barbarians," Stavros said. "That's how you label us, dismiss us. I am here to make sure you won't forget us. There is much more at stake than one stupid girl." His claws retracted slightly as he relaxed his arm. "To the castle!"

Aret nodded and allowed them to proceed ahead of him.

Dirty fingernails on his forearm gave Aret pause. He looked down into the girl's doe eyes. Beneath the dirt, there was a face that paintings would be jealous of.

"You saved me," she said. "I'm yours now."

"You belong to no one." Aret turned away. "Be free while you have the chance."

"You don't recognize me," she said. "Do you?"

For a moment he saw the girl in a gown, with her hair and face clean.

"I was your queen's lady," she said. "You left me at Troll Keep when you took her."

Aret's mouth gaped wide. Here was another who had suffered because of Aret's rash actions.

"The Huns were right," she said. "I am property. There's nowhere for me."

Aret sighed. It wouldn't do for Stavros to see the girl with Aret's men. He would think they were stealing her for themselves, but Aret could not turn away from this beautiful maiden who had suffered because of him. Aret directed a man to take the girl back to camp. "My queen will be overjoyed to see you again."

The girl blinked away tears. "Thank you!" She repeated it again, but Aret was already far ahead, making his way for Hister.

CHAPTER 59

HISTER'S HEART

Aret and his men strolled into the unguarded castle. They ignored the Huns who were pulling artwork from the walls. Aret's men battered their way into Hister's rounded throne room. Hister slumped on his shadowy throne. Aret alone approached the High Seat, but Hister did not acknowledge him. Aret nudged him. Wooden branches released Hister's arms, allowing his body to fall to the floor.

High General Verney sat in the shadows. "He's dead."

"You killed him?" Aret inquired.

"No," Verney said. "It was his heart. His artificially preserved body couldn't take the strain of the siege. He went to the magic throne for rejuvenation, but … it was too late."

Aret eyed the gnarled chair. In the wood there was a petrified face frozen in a scream. This throne had been the secret to Hister's longevity.

Lyon raised a lantern over the high general, now the highest ranking man in the city. "It is done then. You must surrender to me."

High General Verney stood, drew his blade, and everyone tensed. Verney dropped to his knees before Aret and presented his sword in flattened palms. "I surrender my sword to you, King Aret Valora."

Lyon shook his head. "Aret is not technically king of anything anymore. You could have surrendered to any of us."

Aret accepted the sword and looked over his shoulder at his father-in-law. Before he could say anything, Arim came in laughing. Accompanying him was a broad-shouldered man in a golden chest plate. The man's arms were as large as Aret's thighs. It was General Ultor, from the Golden City.

Ultor carried two bottles of wine from Hister's stores. "At last the old boy is dead," he said.

"Wait," Aret said. "Not everyone is here yet."

King Rollo of the Normans wasn't far behind Arim and Ultor. The Gatekeeper placed lanterns around the room, chasing away the gloom. A stout man with a thickly curled beard and a rich cloak entered with Skylar and Stavros; Agamemnon, leader of the Hellenans was here.

Stavros saw Verney still on his knees and sprouted claws from his glove. "I know what to do with him."

"No," Aret said. "He surrendered to me. We can use him."

Verney nodded. A single tear fell from his eye. "I am yours to command."

Stavros sneered, but retracted his claws and took a glass. They opened a bottle of Hister's own wine and drank a toast over the dead ruler's body. The leaders embraced. Even Aret and Stavros shook hands.

Aret looked down at Hister's puffy, chalk-white corpse. This was the man he had served and feared. For longer than Aret had been alive, Hister had been in power here. "This seems... anticlimactic."

"Indeed," Arim said.

Agamemnon shook his head. "It's not over. There is chaos outside."

Lyon nodded. "We must regain control of the men, plan for the future."

Aret looked to his prisoner. "Verney, can you help us get your people under control?"

Verney nodded again. "I can try. The chain of command has collapsed, but my words may still hold some weight with the men."

Then Ultor and the young Gatekeeper did something unexpected. They brought out spades and began digging around the wooden throne.

"Is there treasure under there?" Stavros asked.

The young Gatekeeper wiped his forehead. "Nothing you would be interested in."

Nonetheless, Stavros remained, waiting to get a piece of whatever they might bring up.

They uncovered thick gnarly roots, revealing the throne to be a kind of twisted tree.

Verney stuck close to Aret when he and Arim went outside. They watched the men gleefully running through the streets, dragging bags of plunder.

Aret patted his horse. "You were as instrumental in our victory as any of the men, Snow. What boon would you have? I saw several good mares in Hister's stable."

Snow whinnied, seeming to nod his head, and Arim laughed, provoking a smile in Aret. Aret had seen one mare in particular that would be a suitable mate for his faithful horse. Whether king or thief, foolish or brave, Aret could always count on Snow.

Verney's expression relaxed. "You've changed since you were last here, King Aret."

"I've been through much since then," Aret said. "But I'm no different."

Verney shook his head. "You are more in control, more confident, less rash."

Aret shrugged. "Perhaps."

CHAPTER 60

THE MOOR

A tiny slit of sunlight crept up the wall. As it ascended, Magna's time as a man waned. Even his daytime existence wasn't really the life of a man. He lay on a slashed mattress, feathers spilling over the stone floor of his cell. A desk was overturned in the corner, its finish marred by more cuts. At least his chamber pot had been emptied, and a tray of rich food sat by the door. Magna only nibbled at the food when his body forced him to. There was no pleasure in it. He lived like livestock, but even livestock served a purpose. Magna only served a purpose at night, and that purpose was death.

The creak of a heavy door echoed off the walls, and Magna hid behind his hand, face buried against the cold stone wall. A lantern accentuated the shadows of his cell, and ringed fingers clinked against the bars. The jeweled rings briefly gave the lantern light a sparkling green hue.

"This is no place for the rightful King of Valora."

Magna did not look at the source of the staccato voice. "What would you know of it?"

"I am Raziq, the Moor, just arrived from Iberia."

"With reinforcements?" Magna said.

"I *am* the reinforcements."

Magna peeked over his hand. The Moor, Raziq, was a brown, round man in red robes and black turban, hardly threatening.

Alonzo smiled behind Raziq, a full head taller. Even in the prison gloom, His teeth glowed white. "You would be king if not for your curse."

"My brother is king," Magna said.

"What if I could remove the Husk?" Raziq asked.

Magna now met Raziq's eyes.

Raziq held his jeweled hand next to his temple and nodded. "Yes," he croaked. "I can do it."

There was a long silence before Magna asked, "What would *you* get?"

"We want what you want," Raziq said. "Peace in Valora and our new territories. Peace here means a Valora on the throne. I reiterate what Alonzo should have already told you: our deal with you is no worse than what you had with Hister."

"My brother—"

"Your brother hasn't been heard from in over a month," Alonzo said. "If Lord Aret ever returns, you may choose to abdicate your throne to him. That's up to you."

Magna stared into the corner of his cell, and Raziq motioned Alonzo to unlock the door. "Get him out of here and clean him up."

Magna struggled against Alonzo, and another man was needed to help pull Magna from the safety of his cell.

"It will be dark soon!" Magna shouted as they carried him away.

Magna stopped struggling, but was stiff as the servants tore away his rags and dropped him in a tub of warm, soapy water. They scrubbed the gray stains off his rough skin and drowned his fleas in the soapy lather. His eyes met those of a certain maid, Camille, and he remembered these people serving him in another life. Camille's eyes were lined and hard. There was no longer any love in what she did; she simply followed orders.

Magna froze when the barber scraped a sharp blade up the side of his neck. The razor shaved away tiny black hairs. Magna thought about jerking forward, letting the blade slice through his neck. But he would only awaken again the next morning. The Husk would not let him die.

At last he stood, and they dried him. It was pleasant to be clean, perfumed, and he did not resist as they dressed him in velvet.

CHAPTER 61

MAGNA'S NIGHT

The door opened onto a parlor lit by a blazing fireplace. Mimi and Gwendolyn played chess. Sheriff Morto paced in the corner.

Magna immediately turned, banging his fists on the door as it slammed shut. "Get me out of here!"

Queen Gwendolyn touched him on the shoulder.

Magna turned without meeting her gaze. "I will change," he said. "You are all in danger while I am here."

"Nightfall is still a time away," Sheriff Morto said. He held the hilt of his sheathed sword. "I will be ready."

Magna looked at the sword on Morto's hip. "It won't be enough."

A baby cried in the corner and Mimi lifted him from the crib. "You've woken little Prince Magna."

"Prince Magna?" The elder Magna looked at the tiny white bundle in his sister's arms. "You named him Magna?"

"He's probably hungry," Queen Gwendolyn said. She unlaced her blouse and took the baby into the corner. Magna's former fiancée was nursing a nephew with his name. Magna and Gwendolyn had never consummated, yet here she was with a glow like he had never seen, and here was Magna, a sickly beggar in royal clothes.

His sister, Mimi, tried to distract him. "Would you like to play chess?" She reset the board. "We always played chess when we were children."

Magna looked to her and then back to mother and child.

"You have the first move," Mimi said to him.

Magna sat across from his sister and moved one of the pawns.

Mimi immediately began winning, taking his pieces from the board. "You were a much better chess player when we were young."

This fired up Magna's competitive spirit. He narrowed his eyes and studied the board.

Again, however, Mimi stole his men from the board. Magna smiled, having lured her into position. "Checkmate!"

Mimi stared at the board in disbelief. "How did you do that?"

"Look!" Morto shouted. "Out the window!"

Mimi gasped. After a short silence, Magna laughed hysterically.

Queen Gwendolyn handed the baby to a servant and followed their gaze. Outside the tower window, darkness had fallen over the fields of Valora. "It's night." She turned to Magna, and awareness crept in. "It's night!"

She grabbed Magna in a tight embrace, and he stopped laughing, slowly putting his hands around her soft waist.

She pushed herself back and stared up into his eyes. "We should have a celebration!"

Mimi agreed. "Yes. Perhaps the queen and I should go the kitchen and wake Cook."

"I'll go too," Magna said.

"Why go to the kitchen?" Mimi said. "You can go anywhere you want now."

Magna looked at Mimi, then to Gwendolyn. He directed his gaze to Sheriff Morto. "Do you think they would let me… survey Valora's defenses?"

"Don't ask me, Lord," Morto answered. "I'm only the sheriff."

Magna straightened himself and banged on the door with authority. An Iberian soldier opened it, and Magna commanded, "Prepare a horse."

The Iberian flung the door wide and bowed. "At once, Lord."

Morto smiled. "It's good to have you back, Lord Magna."

Magna and an escort of soldiers walked the halls of Castle Valora. A few servant's and Valoran knights failed to avert their eyes when they passed. They stared at Magna as if he were a ghost, for in a way he was. Remembering themselves, they bowed to their former king. The Iberians all bowed too and opened the doors for Magna, showing him the consideration they had failed to show Queen Gwendolyn or any of the others.

The great lawn was lit by a bonfire. Few people were out, but anyone that saw them, even if they didn't recognize Magna in the dark, knew by his escort that something important was taking place.

Rowen arrived with a horse. Magna pulled the boy's face towards him and saw the long scars left by the Husk. "I'm sorry."

"For what, Milord?" Rowen asked.

Magna ignored the question. He patted the horse, put a foot in the stirrup and hoisted himself over the saddle with a grunt. It had been a long time since he'd been on a horse. He rode down the road and saw that a light was still on in Mack's Tavern. Magna dismounted and knocked on the door.

Mack stared through the open door with a gaping mouth. "Magna? Lord Magna?"

"Yes."

Mack dropped to his knees and kissed his lord's hand. "It's a miracle."

CHAPTER 62

MIMI AND GWENDOLYN

Mimi banged on the royal chef's door. Cook opened the door in a fit of rage, but stifled it and bowed when he saw who his visitors were. He had a white tuft of wavy hair on top of his bare head. Gwendolyn had never seen him without his chef's hat.

"A miracle has happened," Queen Gwendolyn said. "We need you to throw something together tomorrow."

"Tomorrow?" Cook said. "Just throw something together for tomorrow?"

"Lord Magna has returned to us!" Lady Mimi said.

Cook looked to Queen Gwendolyn. "Lord Magna? *King* Magna? I thought he died."

The queen nodded. "He is back!"

Cook grabbed his hat and waved his hands frantically. "I will not fail you, My Queen!"

Immediately he sprang from the door and rushed to the kitchen, leaving Mimi and Gwendolyn alone in the hallway.

Lady Mimi's eyes probed the queen. "I don't know what you are going through right now, but you must be careful around Magna. I know you have feelings for him, but you are still married to Aret."

"What are you saying?"

"I don't blame you for what you must be feeling, I just—"

"I am a good, true queen and wife! How dare you question your queen!"

Lady Mimi bowed. "I meant no disrespect. I just thought you might need—"

"What I need is the obedience and respect of my subjects."

Lady Mimi nodded. "Yes, My Queen."

Queen Gwendolyn turned away. She didn't want to meet Mimi's eyes anymore. Mimi was right, of course. Gwendolyn was awash in feelings she didn't understand, didn't want to understand, but she certainly didn't want to talk them over with the sister of the two men she loved.

The two men... Gwendolyn pushed it out of her mind. She had a job to do.

CHAPTER 63

MAGNA'S ADDRESS

Raziq and Alonzo sat on the castle steps, casually puffing sweet vapor from hoses on a chalice-like device. When they saw Magna and his escort, they stood and bowed.

"I trust you enjoyed your ride," Raziq said.

"I don't know how you did it," Magna said, "but thank you. I owe you a debt that I will never be able to repay."

The Moor waved away Magna's thanks with his bejeweled hand. "That is what allies do for each other."

Alonzo saw Magna staring at the smoking device. "It is called a *hookah*. Would you like to try?"

The smoke smelled sweet, but it had already been an eventful night. "Perhaps another time."

Raziq nodded. "Of course. You must be tired."

"No," Magna said. "I want to watch the sunrise."

"Very well," Alonzo said. "When you are ready to retire, the master bedroom has been prepared for you."

"The master bedroom?" Magna said. "That's Aret's room."

"We are short on bed space now, Milord," Alonzo said. "All the other rooms in the castle are occupied."

Magna nodded and left them to their smoke. He climbed to the uppermost tower and found Queen Gwendolyn gazing at the eastern horizon.

"Couldn't sleep?" he asked.

She shook her head. Ruby rays peeked over fields now scarred by trenches and mounds.

"Have you been happy?" he finally asked her.

"Your brother treats me well," she said, "but things haven't been easy."

"Do you ever wonder what might have been?" he asked.

Her eyes darted away. "Sometimes. But what's the point?"

"I don't know. These people seem intent on giving me the life I could have had. It's like I'm living a dream."

"Only your brother stands in your way."

He turned from the rising sun to the queen, who continued gazing over the land. "It's not like that," he said.

"Do you think he was killed in the siege?" she asked.

"I don't know."

"Would it be better if he was?"

Magna studied her, but could read nothing from her face. Did she secretly wish Aret dead, or was she testing him? "Don't say that."

"But if he did?"

It was his turn to look away. "He never wanted to be king."

"He's changed," she said. Magna was grateful when she switched subjects. "This Moor, How did he remove your curse?"

"Magic."

"Yes, but... Did he wave his hand over you, chant, give you a potion?"

Magna wasn't sure what she was getting at. "No. The cure took me completely by surprise. Why?"

"The Necromancer was the most powerful wizard I have ever seen, but he always had some method, some formula to his spells. Raziq seems to conjure things from the air. What is the source of his power?"

Gwendolyn was harder than she had been, but was still the same at her core, always looking for the angle, always thinking.

"The Necromancer must have known the Moor's secret," Gwendolyn continued. "King Luis never dared threaten Valora while the Necromancer was around." She noticed Magna smiling at her. "What?"

"You truly were born to be queen."

Raziq whispered into his hand and made a tossing motion over the assembled crowd. With this gesture, multicolored flower petals fell over the entire lawn.

"It can't really be him," Mack's wife whispered to him. "It's some trick of the Moor."

Mack held his round wife from behind. "It really is him. He's come back to us."

Tiny nudged his little buddy. "Is this a good thing?"

Brownie shrugged. "I don't know. This isn't the king that took us in, gave us food and money. I don't know this guy."

Magna looked down at the throng shouting accolades. "They still love me. Even after all the Husk did to them."

Queen Gwendolyn whispered, "Aret kept your curse quiet."

Magna cleared his throat, and spoke from the diaphragm. "I am Magna Valora." The crowd cheered, but Magna raised his hands to silence them. "I am not your king anymore, but I will lead you until my brother returns. I thank the Iberian's for their help protecting us until our men return. For this service, I have pledged our loyalty to King Luis."

There were a few cheers, but most stared up at Magna in silent confusion. Magna continued, "We will send word that a Valora still rules here. We must immediately reestablish trade with our neighbors, for we can no longer depend on Hister to distribute the wealth of Gaul. We will also need to scout out a reliable trade route through the mountains to Iberia. This will make it easier for King Luis to send us aid, and allow us to send the tribute noble Luis deserves."

CHAPTER 64

VICTORY

Aret's men celebrated all through the night. King Lyon assembled the nobles in Hister's throne room early the next morning. Most of them had not even been to bed.

Aret, Lyon, Vincennes, Rollo, Agamemnon, Stavros, and Arim gathered around a map of Gaul and the surrounding territories.

King Lyon began, "We must discuss the partitioning of Hister's lands. We can't put it off any longer."

Stavros said, "I have total autonomy and all territory East of Histerland City. There will be no more tribute. My men will remain in the city to protect our interests."

"We mustn't fight amongst ourselves," King Lyon said. "To remain unified is to be strong."

King Rollo raised an eyebrow. "And who will be king of this unified Gaul."

"Well," King Lyon began, "It should be one of us, the ruling nobles who defeated Hister. In all modesty, I am the oldest, and hold the most territory."

"I beg to differ," Rollo said. "I am king of all Northern Gaul and I was put in prison before you came of age."

Lyon pointed to the map. "My lands are central to what will be the new Gaul."

Agamemnon shook his head. "I'm with Stavros. My people want no part in your squabbles, and we will pay you no tribute either. Whoever controls this city will eventually try to dominate us. It is only a matter of time."

Aret sympathized with the Hellenans. For all their strength, they had been as scared of Hister as the Valorans. "We should all agree now not to let that happen," Aret said.

Lyon smiled through clenched teeth. "Let's not make any agreements yet."

"Why don't we vote," King Vincennes said though a mouthful of whiskers, "on who will control the city?"

Stavros shook his head and rolled his eyes. "You would all just vote for yourselves. I suppose I don't get any choice in the matter."

The Gatekeeper spoke from the corner of the room. No one had seen him enter. "Perhaps you should look to The United City-States of Hellena as an example. They have an innovative system."

Agamemnon bowed to the Gatekeeper.

"What about Aret," Arim said. "We haven't heard from him."

Rollo looked at Arim and the Gatekeeper. "You foreigners have no say in this!" Whatever loyalty he owed foreigners for his liberation seemed to have been spent.

Aret cleared his throat. "I must return to Valora. King Lyon, can I trust you to defend my interests here?"

Lyon smiled. "Of course. You can count on me. Gaul will be unified."

Arim pulled Aret aside. "What are you thinking? You can't just leave. You will lose everything you fought for!"

King Lyon interrupted. "The Golden City doesn't want a unified Gaul. They want us fighting amongst ourselves."

Aret was adamant. "I can't worry about the rest of Gaul when Valora isn't safe. I'm only taking a small force, 80 men. We can travel faster that way. The rest of my force will stay here with Vincennes in charge."

King Vincennes bowed in humble agreement.

Arim whispered, "That will leave Lyon with more men than any other in your contingent."

"Verney has gotten some of his men in line with us," Aret said. "I'm going."

"Don't worry," Lyon said. "When Gaul is unified, I will ensure that Valora is never troubled again."

"So will I," Rollo added, courting Aret's favor as well.

"Thank you," Aret said, bowing to them both. He hated letting the future of Gaul be written without him, but he had been away from Valora too long. The fate of his queen and his people was his top priority.

CHAPTER 65

EPILOGUE FOR WOOD NYMPH

General Ultor's other ships, laden with plunder from Histerland City, sailed to their home port. Ultor longed to be with them, but his ship kept sailing. He would miss the initial celebration, but he and the Gatekeeper had a special mission. He didn't fully understand the purpose, and he hadn't always seen eye to eye with the young wizard. In fact, he had hated the boy when they first met, but the Gatekeeper had earned Ultor's friendship. If not for him, Ultor would never have been made a general.

The two of them waded over the rocky seabed, carrying the dead tyrant's gnarled wooden throne in their arms. Once on shore, they put the throne in a small wagon and found a path amid the tall trees. The trunks were thick and the leaves above them became dense enough to block out the sun, producing an endless twilight. The breeze rustled the oak branches around them, making sounds like a hundred whispers.

At last the young wizard stopped and pulled out their shovels. After digging a hole in the midst of the Sacred Grove, they gently lowered Hister's wooden throne.

The branches above them parted in the breeze, allowing the sun to shine on them with full intensity. Once the roots of the throne were covered in a mound of dirt, the Gatekeeper dropped his spade and gazed at the gnarled chair as if in prayer.

Ultor tensed when the naked child emerged from among the trees, but the Gatekeeper seemed to expect her.

Her skin was a pale green in the sun. She caressed the knotted throne. Her voice was an ancient whisper. "Thank you for returning our poor sister. She has lived a hard life and will never emerge from her shell, but she is home. We will never be able to repay you for this, but now you must go." She gazed sadly at the knotted wood. "This is a time for family."

The young Gatekeeper nodded, and the green girl disappeared amid the shadowy trees once again. The wizard picked up their spades and marched back the way they had come. Ultor followed, turning to see the sunlit clearing one last time. A tiny green leaf had sprouted from the twisted throne.

CHAPTER 66

THE SPY

"Where is he?" Aret demanded, fully aware no one knew the answer.

"No scout has returned from Valora since the Iberians left," Enri said.

"Sire!" Kay dragged an Iberian into camp and dropped him at Aret's feet. "A spy!"

Aret looked the bruised prisoner over. "Your people are killing all my scouts. About time we caught one of you."

The spy spit blood. "We are just defending our lands!"

"*Your* lands?" Aret said.

The spy nodded. "The king of Valora has made a treaty with us."

"I did no such thing," Aret said. "What has become of Queen Gwendolyn and the rest of my court?"

"King Valora and his court are safe in their castle," the spy answered.

"*I* am King Valora."

"You are an imposter."

Aret narrowed his eyes, not sure what to make of this news. Were the Iberians trying to put some charlatan in his place, or was this spy just trying to make him angry? If it was the latter, the plan was working. "How many men do you have in Valora?"

"Enough," was his only response.

With a glance, Aret signaled his men to grab the prisoner firmly. "Do you have more men than you had at Histerland City?"

The prisoner looked away, and Aret smiled at this telling reaction. The mountain passes between Iberia and Gaul were treacherous in the winter months, almost impossible for an army to traverse. A small band might have broken through, but spring had not yet overtaken the mountains. If Aret hurried, there was still a chance to retake Valora. "Break camp," he commanded. "Get ready to ride."

"We have more men on the way," the prisoner said. "The Moor himself will secure our lands."

"*My* lands," Aret corrected him. "You fought beside us once. If you swear loyalty to me, I will let you live."

"Just kill him and be done with it," Kay said.

Aret silenced Kay with a raised hand. Had Kay forgotten that he too had once been Aret's prisoner? Now Kay was one of Aret's most valuable men. Golga had worked with Aret's enemies as well, but he ended up dying for Aret's cause.

The spy had no way to know Aret's thoughts. For the first time he showed real fear. "I can't fight my king… but I won't interfere."

Aret nodded. "Good enough. Tie him up."

"If they haven't gotten their reinforcements yet," Aret said, "then we should be about evenly matched."

"But they will be entrenched," Enri added. "They've had time to reinforce the city's defenses."

"We have allies in Valora," Aret said.

"Our friends may not be in any position to assist us," Enri countered.

Aret smiled at the young man. "You don't talk like a servant anymore."

Enri averted his eyes, but Aret put his hand on Enri's shoulder. "I like it. I don't have many advisors left in this army that I truly trust."

Enri bowed, hiding a smile. "Thank you, Lord"

Rowen tossed pebbles from the mound, finally landing one in a basket on the ground below. He nudged the armed Iberian beside him, but the foreigner was unimpressed.

Blue and gold on the road into Valora caught Rowen's attention. He stood, heart swelling at the sight of a gryphon banner in the distance. Aret and his men were returning!

Rowen prepared to greet them, but a roar of thunder brought him to his knees with his hands over his ears. A thick puff of brimstone stung his nose. When he looked up, Aret dangled from the saddle, dragging in the dirt as Snow darted erratically.

The Iberian beside Rowen once again took aim with the magic gun.

Valora had been betrayed!

Rowen pushed the gun barrel down. The gunman swung the weapon into Rowen's scarred face, loosening a tooth before the boy rolled off the mound.

Rowen lay in the musty earth with his head pounding. The gunman above commanded, "Remove the boy!"

CHAPTER 67

HOSTILE WELCOME

Aret and his men sped down old Histerland road. They slowed as they approached the arched bridge where they could only ride two by two.

A spy launched from under the bridge. One of Aret's archers took aim, but missed.

"Don't worry," Aret said. "They are bound to know we are coming. From the mill they can see the bridge clearly. There's no way to hide our approach from this point on."

Once over the bridge, they split into two groups. Aret led his contingent straight into the city.

Aret's heart swelled with longing when he saw the towers of Castle Valora rise into view above the blooming orchards and planted fields. Aret rode ahead by several yards. His armor would protect him while he cleared the way for his men. Earthen mounds and sharpened pikes were unchanged since the day they had left.

Could the Iberians be so arrogant that they did not improve the defenses?

Thunder cracked. Some unseen force knocked Aret from his saddle. His foot caught in the stirrup, and he dangled as the horses scattered. Aret looked away from Snow's hind legs, trying to keep his body from rolling beneath the pounding bronzed hooves.

Aret realized as he bounced along that there *had* been five guns after all. Alonzo must have smuggled one away.

On the mound next to the gunmen, archers let loose a rain of arrows. Fortunately, Aret's men weren't quite in range of non-magic weapons.

Snow's hooves continued to pound inches from Aret's head. Enri rode up beside Snow and grabbed the reins, struggling to slow him, but another gunshot knocked Enri from his horse.

Aret managed to bend forward and grab the stirrup, releasing some of the pressure on his foot so he could slip it out. Snow ran free, and Aret remained panting in the grass for a time.

Enri was suddenly next to him, covering them both with Aret's shield. The boy had one hand on the shield, the other on his wounded shoulder. Aret nodded at him, drawing his sword and taking up the shield. Enri was much tougher than anyone had ever thought.

Aret's ankle almost gave way beneath his weight. It had been twisted, but he was able to compensate, putting more pressure on the other foot. He charged with his shield held in front. Aret cut through the wooden pikes and ran up the mound. Arrows and gunshots fell harmlessly off his shield. Aret shoved the shield under the gun barrel, then sliced it in half.

The gunmen's life soaked into the earthen mound.

Aret leapt from mound to mound, careful to land good foot first as he killed all the Iberian archers.

Finally he limped to the side of his men. They had managed to bring the horses back under control. Young Enri had removed his mail shirt and was directing Kay to bind his wound. The former servant boy proudly displayed the hole in his shirt and pointed out the links of mail still buried in his flesh. Distance had thankfully mitigated the potency of the magic weapon.

"Can you continue?" Aret asked.

Enri rose to his feet and strapped on his weapons. "Of course, Sire."

Aret smiled and took advantage of the brief lull to remove his boot. He had trouble sliding it off and was surprised to see his ankle swelling before his eyes. It would be tragic to let a minor injury like this stop the whole campaign while Enri was ready to fight after a gunshot to the chest.

Kay wound a strip of fabric around the throbbing tissue. Aret tested the joint. It moved normally, though stiffly, bound in layers of cloth. He gently slipped his boot on and took a few timid steps. As long as he favored his good foot, he would still be able to fight.

Aret and his men marched around their fief's defenses and onto tilled and planted fields. They crept cautiously around the mounds they themselves had dug months before. Then, they had a clear path to the castle. Not an obstacle remained in view. Later in the year, men could have hidden in the fields and trees, but it would be many weeks into the season before the fields would be lush enough to hide any enemies.

Peasants and serfs, rather than shouting with joy, shrank back into their huts with fear in their eyes.

Aret's band marched up the road, over the great lawn, to the front door of the castle. Not a hand was raised against them, but none of their loved ones came to greet them either.

A giant bloke carried an enormous barrel of water from the river. Aret greeted the man with happy surprise. "Tiny!"

Tiny smiled broadly and bowed his bulbous bald head. "Hello, King! Why are you fighting?"

Brownie called the giant from the stables. "Tiny! Get in here!"

"Wait," Aret said. "What is going on here?"

Before Aret could probe further, thunder cut the air and blood splashed out of Tiny's arm. The giant's grin became a grimace. He let the barrel drop, flooding the dirt at his feet.

Brownie flew to his side and supported Tiny's good arm while leading him away.

Aret raised his shield and looked to the castle. In every window there was an Iberian pointing one of the magical metal tubes at him.

"That's not possible!" Aret said. "There were only five guns!"

The oak door creaked open, and Alonzo marched out with his perfect white smile. Beside him was a tawny man in a black turban. Red robes draped his round body. The infamous Moor had arrived.

Behind them, in the midst of their Iberian guards were the Valoran nobility. Lady Mimi and Sheriff Morto flanked Queen Gwendolyn and Magna. Aret was surprised to see his brother outside the castle walls in elaborate, kingly dress. He was even more surprised to see Magna's namesake, Aret's son, little Prince Magna, bundled in his arms. Color and fullness had returned to his brother's face. Above Aret on the castle steps, Magna and Gwendolyn were an imposing royal couple.

The sight had a powerful affect on Aret's men as well. Even Enri's sword arm wavered when he saw Magna, the man who should have been their king instead of Aret.

CHAPTER 68

SURRENDER

Aret wondered what it all meant. Was Magna the *King Valora* to whom the Iberian spy had referred? Had his own brother betrayed him?

"What is the meaning of this?" Magna asked Aret.

"What do you mean, *what is the meaning of this*?" Aret said. "This is my kingdom."

"Exactly," Magna said. "Why would you attack your own people? The thunder from your magic weapons frightened all of Valora. You should have sent word. This should be a time of celebration."

"Celebrate my kingdom being taken from me?" Aret saw how close Queen Gwendolyn stood to Magna. She would have been Magna's queen if things had turned out as planned. Aret had never lived up to Magna in her eyes. "Celebrate my own brother betraying me?"

Magna shook his head and strengthened his grip on the baby in his arms. "Your kingdom was never taken from you. I only kept it for you until you returned. With no word from you, we had almost lost hope."

"No word? We sent couriers every few days!" Aret cast a narrow glance at Alonzo. "None returned."

There was a short silence. Magna and Gwendolyn looked at each other and then back to Aret. "These are dangerous times," Magna said. "Law and order outside Valora has ceased to exist. Your couriers were probably killed by bandits. Alonzo sent his own scouts out to look for you, but we never heard anything."

"You believed him?" Aret asked.

"It is your agreement with Iberia that I honor, Aret. They have proven themselves to me."

"I made no agreements with them!"

Magna released a breath and his kingly confidence faded. "Aret, they cured me." He looked to the turbaned man who beamed proudly. "Raziq removed the Husk from me."

Aret was speechless. The Moor, *Raziq*, was rumored to be almost as powerful as the High Necromancer. If he had truly cured Magna, then they did indeed owe him. If he cured Magna, then there was no reason for his brother not to take Gwendolyn and the throne. Magna stood beside Aret's wife and held Aret's son.

Aret looked at the metal tubes pointing down from the windows. If they all had nine shots, there were enough magic bullets for each of Aret's men. "If they are our allies," Aret said, "then why did they shoot at us? Why did they shoot my men? *Our men!*"

Magna followed Aret's gaze to the metal tubes in the windows above. He then looked down at Alonzo and Raziq. "Why don't we all put down our weapons? Aren't we all friends here?"

Aret's men looked to their king, but their arms remained frozen, swords ready.

Magna looked up at the windows. "Stand down!" he commanded, but the guns remained trained on their targets. He looked to Alonzo and Raziq, waiting for them to back up his orders, but they were silent.

At last Raziq clapped his hands. "There is really no point to this debate." He annunciated the words with overly long pauses. "This is an Iberian territory. Things in Valora have not been this good since Aret lost his kingdom to King Brigham."

The Queen would not look at Aret. Even his trusted sheriff, Morto, looked away. It was true. Aret had brought hardship to his people and had never been home long enough to repair the damage. When it was needed most, the Iberians brought supplies and security.

Raziq whispered into his hand and his emerald ring sparkled in the sun. He then motioned at Aret's feet and waved upwards.

Hands erupted from the dirt in front of Aret. They gripped the soil and lifted armored Iberians from the ground. The earth all around Aret's men gave birth to men in light chest plates and brimmed helmets. Aret's men were now surrounded by twelve additional enemies. The newcomers bore identical expressions of frozen ferocity.

"Stop this," Magna said to Raziq. "This has gone too far!"

"So," Aret said, "your reinforcements did come."

Raziq and Alonzo smiled at each other.

"They just arrived," Alonzo said. "As you can see, you are outnumbered, and, thanks to Raziq's magic, we have duplicated your guns."

"Simple," Raziq croaked, "once I assembled all the elements. The Necromancer did our job for us; there are no wizards left in Histerland to protect Gaul from my power. Give up now. Be part of our future."

"Aret," Alonzo said, "I don't want to see you harmed. We need good men to rule our new territory. King Luis said that if I could not convince you or Magna to accept our rule, then *I* would be made king of Valora. Most people in my situation would have had you killed so they could take the throne, but I am not a selfish man."

Aret shook his head, eyes burning.

"What difference does it make?" Alonzo said. "Bow to Luis, or to Lyon, or to Rollo. You will bow to someone."

Magna's proud bearing was completely gone now. His royal clothes couldn't hide that he was a defeated man, as defeated as if he were still cursed. "Don't be an idealist like I was, Aret. We must live in the real world."

Gwendolyn crossed her arms, a mix of pity and disgust on her face.

Aret's men waited with swords raised. Guns pointed at them from above. They all knew what the magic weapons could do to a man at this distance. Mail or armor was little protection against the magic bullets. They awaited Aret's orders.

Alonzo also waited. "The lives of your men are in your hands, Aret."

A tear dripped from Queen Gwendolyn's eye.

Aret looked up again at the guns trained on his men. He could race up the steps, cut up however many Iberians he could, but his men would be shot to pieces. He closed his eyes tightly, sheathed his sword, and removed his helmet. Slowly, he fell to one knee. It took a moment, but his men finally started to relax their sword arms.

CHAPTER 69

THE MOOR'S SECRET

Alonzo beamed on the steps above Aret's men. "Very good. You made a wise decision. We will honor our initial offer. Tribute will be no more than it was under Hister."

Still on one knee before the castle steps, Aret considered their fate. It might not be so bad, if Alonzo was telling the truth. Valora had prospered for sixty years under the thumb of Hister. Perhaps it could prosper again under someone else.

Snapping thunder was heard from the opposite side of the castle. Aret's second contingent was being shot at, and they couldn't know about Aret's surrender. In the time it would take to communicate it to them, they would suffer heavy losses, and for nothing.

His men would never stop fighting until they heard the order from Aret himself. Every crack of gunfire caused Aret to jerk, imagining his men cut down.

Alonzo and Raziq turned away, distracted.

Aret drew his blade. He hacked the sword arm off the Iberian blocking his path up the steps. Thunder and smoke fell behind him, ending in screams from his men, but Aret didn't look back. It was too late for that now.

"Cling to the walls," he shouted to his men, "where they can't get a clear shot!"

Smoking bullets fell harmlessly from his shield.

The barrage paused, coming in spurts as the shooters pumped their guns, aimed, and fired. Clouds of brimstone hung before the castle windows.

Aret made his way up the castle steps, but was pulled back, almost twisting his ankle again. The Iberian that Aret had sliced apart was still standing, still pulling at him with his remaining arm, and his grip nearly crushed Aret's shoulder. A bullet meant for Aret exploded with a dry cloud of dust in the Iberian's chest. The Iberian lost his grip on Aret, stumbled back, but remained standing and continued reaching for Aret.

Aret stared into the frozen face, and with one wide arc of his ivory sword, sliced off the man's head. The neck was bloodless, and the headless Iberian still came up the steps at Aret.

At last Aret struck low, cutting off the undying man's ankles. The man's remaining hand curled around the steps and continued to pull him toward Aret. Was there no way to stop these men? More fingers sprouted from the earth and gripped the stone steps. Two more invincible men pulled themselves from the dirt.

"Aret!" Gwendolyn's voice called his attention up the steps. Gwendolyn motioned her head toward Raziq, who was whispering into his folded hands.

While bullets spat from above, Aret's men fought an impossible battle with men who did not die. Alonzo and Raziq were the keys to all this. Aret found their guards human, easily killed with a single stroke each.

Alonzo jumped in front of Raziq, who still whispered into his hand. Aret's former ally fell back when his sword was sliced in two, leaving Raziq defenseless and his utterance interrupted.

The Moor raised his arm against the sight of Aret's sweeping sword. Raziq howled, trying to catch his severed hand as it plummeted to the ground and landed in a splash of blood.

Raziq shrank back as though in fear of his own dismembered limb.

The emerald ring on his lost hand flickered and emitted a puff of red smoke. The crimson cloud grew and coalesced, assuming human shape.

The smoke became a lean, black man. He wore a turban and red robes nearly identical to his jailer. The newcomer was a full head taller than Aret. He had thin strips of beard and pointed ears.

Aret had never seen a jinn. He had never even known someone who had encountered one. Elemental beings, jinni could be even more dangerous than a human wizard.

The jinn from the ring stretched with a deep, echoing yawn. The gunshots and clanging swords stopped. Raziq made one last lunge for his severed hand and the magic ring, but his former slave had already lifted it from the steps.

The jinn's voice was deep and resonant. "Looking for this?" The jinn, with some trouble, removed the emerald ring from a pudgy finger. He placed it on his own slender digit and admired the jewel. "Free at last."

Raziq held the sleeve of his robe tight against his bleeding forearm and backed down the steps. The jinn extended his fingers at Raziq.

Raziq turned into a full sprint.

The shadows on Raziq's terrified face disappeared. He dissolved into an ethereal being of smoke. The echo of his scream faded as his body was sucked into the ring.

The jinn gazed ecstatically into the jewel. "Ah, the sweet tortures awaiting you."

Aret hid behind his shield and studied the newcomer. He kept his sword arm down, but tense. Despite their great power, jinni were vulnerable to simple magics and certain charms. Aret didn't have any of that at his disposal. It was no wonder the Moor had never set foot in Histerland. The Necromancer could have bound the jinn, or even turned him back on his master.

The jinn looked at the men around him until his gaze settled on Aret. "I am Azazil," the jinn said. "You are the one who freed me. I owe you some small debt." With a snap of his fingers, something shattered against the stone steps and made Aret jump.

One of the gun barrels had fallen from a window and crumbled as rust against the stone steps. All the guns in the windows had rusted apart. Their stocks were now unhewn blocks of wood.

The jinn then put his palm to his lips and blew down the steps. The men from the ground froze. Their glamour of armor and flesh blew away as a film of dust. They collapsed into piles of the Valoran earth from which they had been made.

Aret ran his boot through a trail of dirt on the castle steps, a trail shaped like a severed arm reaching for his foot.

The jinn whipped off his outer robe, revealing an identical robe underneath. The outer robe fell to the ground as a large rug.

"I've undone all magic I worked here for my jailer," the jinn said. He stepped onto the center of the rug, and Aret glimpsed one of the jinn's furry feet. He had two oversized, blunt toes, resembling a goat's hoof.

Wind whipped along the edges of the carpet, and the jinn cast a mischievous glance at Alonzo. "I believe the odds are a bit more even now."

The rug rose into the air and Azazil's gaze fell briefly on Aret once more. "Until we meet again."

The carpet lifted Azazail as high as the castle's tallest tower. It blurred over the southeastern orchards, disappearing in the distance.

Aret stared awestruck after the jinn for a moment, but then narrowed his eyes and pointed his sword at Alonzo. Alonzo found his few remaining supporters, the real men who had originally accompanied him to Histerland City, spread thin and none close enough to help him. His reinforcements had largely been figments of the jinn's magic.

"Magna!" Alonzo called. "Magna, you owe me!"

Aret stood straight and gave a crooked smile. "I've been gone quite some time, but we still have a prison, right?"

Morto nodded his head and smiled. "Indeed, Lord, we do. Good to have you back, King Aret."

Queen Gwendolyn let out a long breath and closed her eyes. Alonzo dropped his broken weapon, and Morto pulled him away.

Many of the men who had entered town with Aret were wounded, but they had heeded his advice, managing to cling close to the castle walls or keep enemies between them and windows.

Most, including Enri, continued to hold their swords at their enemies.

They were evenly matched again. The Iberians found the allies at their sides replaced by piles of Valoran dirt. Both their masters were gone, and they had no contingency plan. They dropped their weapons and allowed themselves to be taken by Morto's guardsmen.

"Our prison is going to be overcrowded." Aret sheathed his sword and dropped to his knees before his queen. She smiled, leaned down and kissed his head. He rose, but being four steps above, she still towered over him. They held each other with Aret's face buried in her soft bosom. He had almost forgotten the subtle scent of her skin.

Magna cradled the baby's head as he bowed in shame and submission to his younger brother, his king.

Aret cooed at the sight of his son's black head of hair and took the baby from his brother. The infant seemed to struggle against Aret at first, making a pained face before looking up at his father with big blue eyes. Aret had made this being, this person. This new being would play in the castle as Aret and Magna had played in the castle. He would fight. He would learn. He would quest. He would love. One day, he might even rule. Aret and Gwendolyn had made him. *This* was magic.

Joy and relief sounded from reunited loved ones. The heroes who could walk went back to the homes they had left months before.

"My husband?" A woman circulated among the returned heroes. "Have you seen my husband? Does anyone know what happened to him?"

Aret was reminded that he still had men at Histerland City.

"Sire!" Garnet Woodman bowed deeply.

"Garnet!" Aret exclaimed.

"Where have you been?" Gwendolyn asked.

"Prison," Garnet answered. "Alonzo thought I could get a message to Aret if I was left free." A slight smile crossed his face. "He was probably right."

The healer man climbed the castle steps. Aret directed the healer to attend his men. Aret's ankle was trivial compared to their wounds. The healer called on almost all the returning heroes. All had injuries. Some were minor. Others, even magic couldn't fully repair. Remarkably, no Valorans died that day.

CHAPTER 70

HOME

As the men returned to their homes, the royal family also returned to their chambers within Castle Valora. King Aret and Queen Gwendolyn walked arm in arm. Magna remained a few steps behind, alone and quiet.

They were all tired. A public celebration could wait until the next morning. This was a time for family and a simple meal.

After so many months, Aret was finally able to remove his magic armor. He peeled off his second skin. He felt naked and vulnerable without it, even among family. The armor had become part of him. Scattered white hairs now mixed with the brown hair at Aret's temples.

Once shaved and dressed for dinner, Aret found Magna alone in the master bedroom.

"I'm sorry, Aret," Magna said. "I was using this room while you were gone."

"They treated you like the king," Aret said.

Magna wouldn't look him in the eyes. "Yes."

"And you liked it?"

A faint smile crossed Magna's lips. "You know I did, but it was an illusion. I was never in charge."

There was a short silence before Magna said, "You are a good king, Aret. I'm proud of you."

Aret shook his head. "I brought trouble to Valora."

Magna nodded. "For a higher purpose. Queen Gwendolyn told me how you have grown while I was away. You started out as a conformist, a boy who avoided all responsibility, a sheep to be led, but you took the idealism I lost and became a better king than I ever could have been."

"Gwendolyn said that?"

"In different words, but yes, your queen said that."

"But I thought—"

Magna shook his head and raised his finger. "She is your queen, and has never been otherwise. Even when we were both certain you were never coming back, she was always yours."

Aret let out a sigh of relief and put his arm around his brother. "I should have never doubted you. Either of you."

"Come on," Magna said. "Let's see what Cook has prepared for us."

The family's eyes were on Aret as they ate their freshly caught fish; already Garnet Woodsman was taking care of them.

Aret lapped up their attention. "So, there I was," he continued, "Lying alone in the freezing cold forest. The middle of the night. No weapons. I had no idea when Ulf's ghost would pop out of the shadows, but I knew he would come. My companions were hidden away. I couldn't even be sure—"

Sheriff Morto interrupted the family's simple meal. "My apologies. An envoy of King Lyon has entered Valora with an escort of four armed men."

Magna reacted immediately. "Keep his guards outside. Escort the messenger into the throne room."

Morto looked from Aret to Magna and back again. Magna realized his mistake, adding, "If it is King Aret's will."

Aret's expression was cold now. He nodded consent, then left the dining room without another word. It would be more difficult than Aret had expected to have both he and Magna living in Valora. Even with things settled between them, there would always be a conflict of authority, two roosters in the henhouse. It was fine when they were kids, they were brothers after all, but now Aret was king. The one and only king of Valora.

The main halls were being decorated for tomorrow's ceremonies: a memorial for fallen heroes, and a celebration of victory.

Lyon's messenger was a short young man. He bowed to King Aret, and Aret nodded.

"I am happy to see you back on your throne," the herald said. "We had instructions to help you retake Valora if needed."

Aret studied the short man and remembered that there were only four armed guards with him. "I don't think you would have been much assistance, but thank you just the same."

The herald then said, "Your presence is urgently requested at Histerland City. A vote is to be taken. All the nobles are coming to elect a new high king.

The herald handed Aret a copy of the ballot. *A new high king.* It was true, of course; there would always be someone to bow to. This was perfect timing, however. Aret could not afford to leave Valora again, not after being away for so long, but he could send Magna as his representative. Magna was smart, capable, and most importantly, Aret trusted him. Perhaps Magna would find a position in the new high court.

"Perfect!" Aret said. "When is the vote to be taken?"

"Three days."

It didn't give Aret much time. After making arrangements for the envoy's lodging, he raced up the stairs to tell Magna.

He found Magna cooing over his namesake's cradle. "Magna, I have great news! I'm sending you to Histerland City to vote on the next high king."

"I see," Magna said.

"You don't seem happy."

"You want me gone."

"Think about it," Aret said. "We can't have two kings in Valora. I am going to make sure you have a position worthy of you."

Magna nodded. "Is that the ballot?"

Aret handed it to him, and Magna perused the names. A sudden smile crept across Magna's face. "You may want to go yourself."

"I can't leave now," Aret said. "I must take measure of Valora, stabilize my lands."

"You haven't read the names, have you?"

Aret took the ballot back. There between the name of King Lyon and King Rollo, was the name KING ARET OF VALORA. "No."

"My little brother," Magna said. "High king of Gaul."

"I don't have the support Lyon or Rollo has. How did my name end up on the ballot?"

Magna laughed, but then grimaced and clutched his chest.

"Are you alright?" Aret asked.

Magna nodded. "Perhaps when you are high king, you would see fit to bestow a kingdom on your elder brother." Magna raised a finger, to say, "Wait," while he made for a pitcher of water on a nearby table. He stumbled and fell.

"Magna?"

Magna tried to stand and mouthed the words, "I'm fine," but no sound emerged from his lips.

"Magna!" Aret called. He kneeled down to his brother. Magna's skin was so cold. "Call the healer!" Aret shouted.

Magna looked up at his brother and grabbed Aret's arm for stability. His fingernails sliced through Aret's heavy sleeve.

Aret gasped and looked behind him at his son's cradle. When the jinn removed all Raziq's spells, it must have included Magna's cure. Magna was becoming the Husk, and Aret was unarmed.

"Guards!" Aret shouted, shoving his brother away. He grabbed the junior Magna from his crib and made for the door. Aret looked back once more at his brother. Magna's skin was tight and gray around his bones. His glowing eyes matched the setting sun in the window behind him, and he lumbered for the doorway. Aret swung the door shut and held it tight. A passing servant took the baby and ran from the scratching and scraping at the other side of the wood. The door only locked from the inside. Luckily, as dangerous as the Husk was, he was no stronger than his mortal host, and Aret was able to hold the door.

A draft blew through the corridor, causing the torches to flicker with erratic shadows. The breeze was followed by childish giggling. Decorative armor fell with a clang. Two guards leapt over it as they climbed the stairs.

Aret shivered with a sudden chill that struck him from the inside out. The scratching at the door suddenly stopped.

Aret pressed his ear to the door, straining to hear. The Husk's clawed feet swished against the floor, and the cradle toppled over. Then the mirror on the opposite side of the room crashed with another burst of childish giggling. Someone was in there with the Husk.

Aret thought of Skylar, the invisible boy with the magic hat and shoes, but Skylar did not pass through walls, and did not giggle like a girl.

All sound ceased from the room. Aret took a sword from one of the guards. He waited for a moment, listening.

His brother was his responsibility.

Still hearing nothing, he slowly pushed the door, scanning the interior of the room as it opened wider. He stabbed behind the door, making sure nothing was hiding in its shadow, then flung the door wide.

The room was empty.

He ran to the window and scanned the horizon in all directions. A fluttering shadow directed his eye to the graveyard where his brother had once been entombed. A black silhouette flapped in a circle. The Husk was chasing something into the mountains beyond the kingdom. Part of Aret's heart flew after it.

Something had lured the Husk away from Valora. In doing so, it had saved Valoran lives and spared Magna embarrassment, but Aret doubted its motives where benign. Aret was balanced on a fine edge. He loved his brother and ached to leap onto Snow and chase after him, but the Husk was already far outside Valora. Aret would not be able to pick up his trail tonight. His people were exhausted. They needed to rest, and they needed their king. All

Aret could do was send couriers northwest in the morning, try to find out where the Husk had struck, where Magna had ended up. Aret had a horrible feeling that he would never see his brother again, and he dreaded delivering the news to Gwendolyn.

Was this an oversight, or had Azazil known *all* his spells included Magna's cure? Everything had almost been perfect, but a shadow now tainted Aret's happiness.

His first duty was to his people. Their suffering was finally bearing fruit, and it was time he finally treated his Gwendolyn like the queen she was.

Aret's couriers would never stop searching for his brother. If they found traces of him, only then could Aret act.

The scarred fields and orchards of Valora were dark. The people were safely in their homes, huddled next to loved ones, or awaiting word of loved ones still in Histerland City.

Lyon and Rollo would not allow Aret to be high king. Aret had no desire for the honor. He was not cut out for the conniving machinations of high court. He would call the rest of his men back in the morning.

Aret was King Valora. No matter who wore the high crown, if they sought to abuse their power in Aret's lands, the people would be ready.

ABOUT THE AUTHOR

Matthew Barron spends his days mixing and analyzing human blood as a medical technologist in Indianapolis Indiana. His diverse stories have appeared in *House of Horror, Roboterotica,* and the *Welcome to Indiana* Comic anthology. His dystopian book *Secular City Limits* and his children's book *The Lonely Princess* are available now. He is currently working on a play and an urban fantasy graphic novel called *Temple of Secrets.*

For more information,
visit submatterpress.com